A Whore's Conscience

U. E. Wynn

A Whore's Conscience

ISBN-13: 978-1-7320325-4-5
ISBN-10: 1-7320325-4-5

ABOUT THE AUTHOR

U.E. Wynn

A self-educated, business savvy, humble entrepreneur was counted out at a young age by his peers, teachers, and family members. After enduring life altering events that would destroy and/or diminish any individual, he chose to overcome and excel. He turned what would be deemed a negative into a positive. He reevaluated himself and reclaimed a positive position within society.

U.E. Wynn is the founder of 501C nonprofit, Save a H.O.M.I.E. Inc. and an active activist within the community. He continues to assist disenfranchised youth, feed and clothe the homeless and bring forth literacy to the illiterate. Wynn also helps in providing a positive, productive and social atmosphere for the youth to unwind and enjoy themselves throughout the Carolinas via events, concerts and parties.

This is Wynn's second novel presenting you with a page turning, nail biting, exotic read.

DEDICATION

First and foremost, I would like to thank Allah, the most high, for any and everything that is any good. A super salute goes out to the Aye twins, Apple Berry Susan and my business partner, Amina!

Chapter One

"Ohh shit!!" moaned Money, as the morning sun rushed through the blinds, and his body tensed up instinctively. But the rays of light weren't the cause for his body tensing or sudden curses. No, the cause of these responses came from a source much closer, but just as hot as the sun.

Her name was Andrea a.k.a. Blu. And just like clockwork, every second Friday, she would wake Money up with the most insane blow job known to man. Today was no different. Money had yet to open his eyes, knowing this would inspire Blu to plunge deeper and suck harder on his morning wood.

Damn, she ain't playing no games, thought Money, as he took a peep and saw Blu slowly freaking his dick with her mouth like it was a rare treat meant to be savored. On her worst days she was more than capable of bringing him to an orgasm that left his balls twitching. But the work she was putting in now was bound to leave his balls looking like nuked prunes.

"Mmm..." Andrea hummed as she felt Money's dick spasm, signaling he was nearing his climax. She took her tongue and slid it under his dick head and closed her lips over the remainder of his penis and began milking her man with a rhythm beyond hypnotic.

"Aww...Oooh shhitt!! Ooh... FUUUCKK!!" screamed Money as his whole body shook and his eye's began to twitch and roll uncontrollably.

"Good morning, baby," Andrea said after swallowing every trace of sperm that her mouth could find. "Give me a minute to freshen up and I'll start breakfast."

Before he could respond, she leaned over, kissed the head of his dick, then hopped off the bed heading towards the bathroom.

Damn, life just don't get much better, Money thought, as he covered himself and reflected over the state of his affairs. *I got more money than I can ever spend. Three cars fully loaded. My right hand man is my only neighbor. I own my home and I got shit on smash. But the sweetest part, is Andrea. She down for whatever and handles herself like a true thoroughbred. Shit don't get no better,* he thought relaxing.

"Money! Yo Money!! You gonna help me cook, right?!" Andrea yelled, cutting into his thoughts.

After a quick shower, and getting dressed, Money went over to the adjoining bedroom where Andrea's daughter Alana was still resting.

"Alana. Alanaaaaa!!" Money called out her name in a long drawn out song while teasing her nose with the sleeve of his shirt. Alana wasn't his daughter, but his love for her was that of a father.

"Uhhh... Stop!!" Alana whined as she squirmed trying to avoid Money's shirt sleeve.

"Get up and get clean girl. Breakfast will be done soon. Hurry up because Uncle Shawn and Aunt Ree-Ree will be here soon," Money said, as he kept shaking Alana insuring she wouldn't fall back asleep.

Bam. Bam. Bam.

"That's probably them at the door," Money stated as he rose and left the room.

"I got it baby. Go stir them grits, please," Andrea said to Money as he walked up the hall.

"Morning girl. Everybody up?" Ree-Ree asked as soon as the door was opened.

"Yeah! Come on in. Breakfast is ready," Andrea replied, as she closed the door behind them.

Shawn and Ree-Ree were engaged and the closest two people in the world to Money. Shawn, a.k.a. Splash, was his business partner and lifelong friend, which was a true rarity in this era's drug game.

It was time to re-up again, and every two weeks the same routine was observed. The five of them would get together, have breakfast, then the ladies would watch the men head off to one of heir four different re-up states. This weekend was going much like all the other's over the past two years. Small talk, laughs, then sudden silence.

During this time, Andrea figured everyone at the table was thinking about the pending journey. Everyone except for Alana. During these periods of silence, while Ree-Ree worried for Splash, and Splash and Money pondered over what lay ahead, she was usually thinking about *him*. Not Money, but *him*. Him represented whatever dick or dicks she chose to fuck for the next two days while Money was doing his re-up thang.

Every two weeks she would cut up like a fool fucking and sucking all the dick and pussy she could get a hold of. Money was clueless of this much, she was sure. Being that she only fucked with people three or more counties over eliminated most chances of fucking a dude her man might know. Her only loose ends were Ree-Ree and Splash due to the fact that both of their town homes were adjoined. Andrea was sure, shit was more than certain, that Ree-Ree knew she was fucking around on the regular.

At first she had called the dude's her cousins. That is until the night she'd gotten Ree-Ree drunk on Moscato. Andrea worked her magic and ate her pussy coaxing her to over four hours worth of orgasms. Ree-Ree had been in near tears, fearing Splash's reaction to her lesbo experience. Of course, Andrea swore silence, and the next chance that arose, and each one after that, she took full advantage of her only leverage. Since she now had the upper hand over Ree-Ree, she didn't even hide her fuck sessions and had been fucking insanely ever since. Whenever Ree-Ree's eyes got too inquisitive, she gave her a stare that simply said, '*My secret, for yours.*'

"You about ready?" Money asked Splash, breaking Andrea's lustful thoughts and bringing her back to reality.

"Give me about twenty minutes," Splash replied, as he stood and ushered Ree-Ree towards the front door to leave.

"I'll meet you out front," Money responded as he closed the door behind them.

"Alana, wash the dishes and get dressed, alright?" Andrea ordered as she grabbed Money and led him to the bedroom by his Robin jeans. "We got twenty minutes come on," she stated as she shut and locked the bedroom door.

Moments later, sweat covered his bald head, and Andrea was drenched all over, as Money pumped "10" inches of thick dick deep into her guts. With her ankles on his shoulders, and her legs pent to her own chest, all she could do was take every lovely, soul thumping inch of his dick. She enjoyed the pleasure that came from having a man who knows how and where to lay his pipe.

Honk! Honk!

"Oooohh…Shhit!!" Andrea moaned as she came at the exact moment Splash honked the horn, notifying Money that it was time to bounce.

"Fuck!!" Money barked, upset that he would have to stop.

"Baby, I'm good. I got one," she stated, trying to calm him.

"I know, it's just…"

"Baby, go handle your business. I'll be here when you get home. And I'll make sure its nice and wet for you," she said, cutting him off as she pushed off his dick and began to stroke her pussy.

"Damn love, you know you ain't right," he scorned as he crammed his love muscle back into his jeans.

"Until I get some dick, this gone have to do…mmm!" Andrea replied suductively as she rolled her eyes upward and slid three fingers, nuckled deep into her coochie.

***

"You sure you not mad at me?" Ree-Ree asked Splash, as she stood outside beside the car waiting for Money to come down from his crib.

"Baby, be easy. What's done is done. Just relax and stick to the script. Alright?" Splash responded, as he popped the trunk for Money who was now descending the steps and approaching the custom camero they used solely for their re-up trips.

"My bad, fam. The wifey had something she just couldn't wait to share," Money sated, as he climbed into the passenger side and shut the door.

Splash smiled knowingly and turned to Ree-Ree. "I love you, boo. Don't forget to handle that," he stated, after kissing his lady softly on the lips.

"I won't. Y'all be safe, Ok?" she replied, as Splash threw the Camaro in gear and cruised off.

Ree-Ree watched the car fade into the distance and only when her eyes lost sight of the Camaro, did her heart begin to thump viciously. For over a year and a half, Andrea had dangled their sexual encounter over her head, but not anymore. All that was about to cease. Her man knew and loved her honesty. But what Splash had cherished even more was the reason for her confession. She told him everything about her and Andrea, and about all the dudes she had been screwing for the past year and half.

Ree-Ree loved Money like a brother, and knew how deep Splash's love and loyalty for him ran. Money was more than the boss to them. He was blood. He was family plain and simple. And if telling the truth, in order to protect Money meant losing Splash, then it was a risk she would have to take. But instead of anger, she got understanding.

Splash had loved her more for not being able to continue doing nothing, while his partner in crime was was being done wrong. Ree-Ree had been prepared to beg for Splash's forgiveness, not because of his baller status, but due to him being a rare jewel in today's day and time. He was an all around good man. And except for Money, she couldn't think of a man that could come close to equaling his characteristics.

After shedding some tears, she and splash had come up with a plan to get all of their questions answered. They had also sorted out ways to respond once all efforts to salvage Andrea were rendered hopeless; which every female instinct in Ree-Ree body believed the case to be — hopeless. But regardless of how she felt personally, she had made a promise to her man. A promise she fully intended to keep.

Her task was simple. She had 48 hours to figure out why Andrea was so damn trifling. Then she had to discover if she could and would do right by Money. Ree-Ree took a deep breath, and said a silent prayer as she turned and looked up at the ceiling to floor windows of Money's upstairs town home. There staring back at her was Andrea, wearing a devilish smile. She looked Ree-Ree over from head to toe, as if thinking about which part of her she'd most like to ravage.

Ree-Ree was barely 5' feet tall, with skin that was flawless and creamy, yet extremely dark. Her lips were luscious and always looked like they longed to be kissed. Her eyes slightly chinked, but she couldn't tell you why. She wasn't half Jap or nothing. She was full blooded Trinidadian and proud of it. Splash loved the way her body was built. No stomach, plenty of hips, and an ass plump enough for a man to lose at least two fingers in the cuff of her lower butt cheek. Her breast was her best asset. They were full, yet perky and no matter how hard gravity tried, her boob's just refused to sag.

Look at this silly ass bitch. Straight sucker for love, dumb ass trick, Andrea thought, as she caressed her breast through her robe and singled Kameron to come on up.

With another sigh, Ree-Ree plastered a beaming fake smile on her face and repeated the prayer she had first offered only moments before.

Dear God, please give me the strength I need to keep from dragging this whore. PLEASE!!! And with the prayer completed, she began climbing the stairs and prepared herself for the mission at hand.

Chapter Two

I wish I could take a journey through your mind
And find emotions that you always try to hide

Joe's ghetto throw back of love resonated throughout the convertible Camaro, as Splash and Money made their way across the interstate.

"Ever since you got engaged, you've been filling my eardrums with these sappy ass love songs. What's wit you bruh?" Money asked as he shifted in his seat to mockingly grill Splash.

"It keeps me focused, but you can change it if you want to," Splash replied almost roboticly.

All morning long Money had been feeling something wasn't right with his partner. He noticed the unusual silence at breakfast and the weird stares Splash and Ree-Ree kept giving each other. At first he dismissed it as just an issue between the two of them. Not his business, he had concluded, and let the moment pass. But once they got alone, the same gloomy spirit was lingering over Splash, but much stronger than earlier. Something was up and Money was gonna find out what.

****

After riding with Andrea to drop Alana off at her Aunt Netta's, Ree-Ree and Andrea went and got their nails and hair done at *Hair Estates*, then headed back to the town house where Ree-Ree insisted on cooking a late lunch.

"Let's see... something good, simple, and sweet. Hmmm. How about spaghetti?" Ree-Ree asked Andrea. She took out a package of ground beef from the fridge, placed it in the microwave, and pressed the setting for defrost.

"Sounds good to me," Andrea replied, as she sat in Splash and Ree-Ree's living room texting her new lover. "Got anything to drink? Something with some kick to it?"

"Yeah, I got something for you," Ree-Ree answered grabbing a champagne glass. She reached into the cabinet to pluck a few choice bottles they could sip on. Moments later she had three glasses of her special mixed drink made for Andrea. One glass was for now and the other two were placed into the fridge to chill until they were needed. After setting the drinks in the fridge, Ree-Ree grabbed a bottle of Patron for herself and took the first of the three drinks to Andrea. As an ex bartender, Ree-Ree knew her liquors and how to mix which one's for the desired effect.

It's time we talked, Ree-Ree thought to herself as she sat next to Andrea on the couch and handed over her drink.

****

"Enough is Enough. You got something you wanna get off your chest, partner? Money asked Splash as the two of them exited the McDonalds and stood at the hood of the Camaro.

During the course of the trip, Splash had said very little and no matter how hard Money tried he couldn't coax a rise out of him. Something was eating at Splash, and the two of them weren't going any further down the road until the shit was settled.

Splash had known Money for years. Hell, since they were nine years old they'd been a two man team. Unbreakable. You name it, they went through it, unphased. But this was different. This drama was of the most personal kind. A situation Splash hated like hell that he was gonna have to be a part of.

Gotta keep him clueless 'til Sunday, Splash reminded himself mentally as he took a seat on the front corner of the Camaro. "Take a seat, cuz. We gotta talk."

"What's up? You and Ree-Ree got a problem?" Money asked, as he took his seat on the hood next to Splash.

"Naw cuz, we good. I just been thinking over some things. That's all." After a short pause, he asked, "You trust me... Right?"

"Yeah, why you ask?" Money answered, as he pulled out a

strawberry blunt and began rolling the cigar between both hands to loosen up the tobacco inside.

"Because I made a couple decisions without consulting you. Nothing risky though."

"Let's hear it."

"We're not going to Florida. I worked it out so that the exchange goes down in Norcross, Georgia instead. I took care of all the details. I left no stones unturned."

"OK! OK! I trust you fam. What's the second decision?" Money asked impatiently.

"That one involves Ree-Ree and your girl. She gone call me tomorrow sometime and let me know how to prep you," Splash loosely explained.

"Prep me? Prep me for what? Yo, you my man an all, but we ain't flipping chicks cuz. Last time we pulled that stunt the chick you had got scared when I walked up to her with my dick swinging."

"That wasn't my fault. I told you to sneak up on her," replied Splash, laughing.

"Whatever man. But all jokes aside, prep me for what?" Money asked again between laughs.

"There's really not a whole lot I can say right now. I'll know more come tomorrow. But what I can say is this. Whatever does go down, was unavoidable. And no matter how it may look, know that your best interests are being met. Basically, you gone have to trust me on this!" Splash answered as he rose up off the hood and hopped back behind the wheel.

He noticed Money had yet to move. No doubt he was racing through his mind in search of clues as to what Splash could be referring to.

"Yo, Money!! No matter the outcome, good or bad, you still come out good. That's word on Allah!" Splash stated, knowing this proclamation would ease his friend's mind some.

"I come out good, regardless?" Money asked as he hopped into the Camaro.

"Yep," Splash answered, as he turned the key, kick starting the ignition.

"Then there's no sense stressing. Let's get this show on the road. I got a surprise to get home to," Money stated, as he turned up the sound system listening to *Keisha Cole* belt out the chorus of her song

'I Might As Well Have Cheated.'

Splash drove the car out the parking lot and back towards the interstate as Money horribly sung along with Keisha Cole. *Damn, I hope this works and I pray he understands,*" Splash pondered to himself as he found the exit leading them back to the interstate.

****

Meanwhile, things were going according to plan for Ree-Ree. Andrea had already knocked back two of the three glasses of the special drink she was slyly pumping her with.

"Thank you, girl. You know, if I didn't know better, I'd swear you were trying to get me drunk. Ooh-shit!! You want me to suck that pussy again, don't ya?" Andrea commented as she slowly and sensually ate her spaghetti.

"Trick please! Here!" Ree-Ree jokingly responded as she passed the last of the mixed drinks over to Andrea. "I just don't want to be alone tonight, that's all!"

"I feel you girl. Me neither. So what's on your mind?" Andrea asked after taking a deep swallow of her drink.

"I was just thinking over some of my past experiences. You know, my first love, first crush, my first..."

"Fuck!!" Andrea interjected, causing them both to laugh.

"Do you ever find yourself reminiscing over past times? Or is it just me?" Ree-Ree asked, between sips of her drink.

"Trust me, you are not alone. Sometimes I wish like hell I could forget though," Andrea stated, after taking another deep swallow of her drink.

"Let me guess, a lost love?" asked Ree-Ree, as she slid closer awaiting the answer.

"Hmm...nah! Lost innocence, maybe. But not love. Definitely not love. His name was Anthony. He was my eldest brothers best friend." Andrea paused between sentences to finish off her drink.

"Go ahead, I'll fix you another while you talk."

Ree-Ree grabbed the glass and headed towards the counter as Andrea took the cue, and resumed her tale.

"I was eleven and he stayed home from school because of my first ever period. I spent much of my time lying in bed or in the bathroom. I let my brother know whenever someone called or warned him when mom or dad came home. He always kept a girl down stairs. He called these moments freak sessions. Whatever they were, all I knew was they always caused the bed to squeak, and was always accompanied by lots of yelling."

"Now at eleven, I was built more like a sixteen year old. Quite a few times I had caught Anthony staring at my ass. He never said nothing though. So I never thought much about it. Well, anyway, hours had past since I'd last checked my pad for blood, so off to the bathroom I went."

"When I dropped my panties, blood was everywhere. Girl I freaked. I cut the water on, stripped butt naked, and thrust my pussy directly under the water spiket. The sensations from the water pressure and its warmth made me yelp out loud with joy. Never had I felt such pleasure. I quickly lodged myself under the water until the feeling began to settle down. Somewhere along the lines I must have closed my eyes. Cause next thing I know, the room got dark and Anthony was wrapping me in his arms and snatching me out from under the water. He pent my back against the sink and began to look at me slowly as I stood before him naked and dripping wet. I still remember every word he said to me that day."

"Your brother just got into the shower downstairs. He said he'll be a while. He told me to check on you," Anthony said as he stepped between her legs. With just his left thigh, he spread her thighs as wide as they would go.

"Ant, what are you doing?" Andrea asked as her heartbeat quickened and her virgin clit throbbed uncontrollably.

"How this feel?" he asked as she took his right index and began to rub her clit.

Before she could respond, he placed the middle finger alongside the index and rubbed a bit harder, causing her breath to catch and making her legs violently tense up. With his left arm, he reached around her back and lifted her, placing her butt on the edge of the sink. Before she could question he took his right index finger and slid it knuckle deep into her pussy. This time her breath damn near choked her.

Damn this must be what a freak session is, Andrea thought as a jolt of pain brought her back to reality. Anthony now was unsuccessfully trying to cram three fingers up inside her, but without much luck. Her pleas for him to quit when unanswered for a moment before he eventually withdrew his hand.

Before Andrea could muster a sigh of relief, Anthony slung her towards the toilet and bent her over fast. She barely had time to protect her face before it grazed the back of the toilet. With nothing more than instinct, she reached behind her back attempting to remove his arm from the center of her back. Without success, she found the arm she was using to free herself was now being used to further entrap her. He took her arm and lifted it as high as it would go behind her back. Andrea let out a screeching loud yell, but to no avail. Her brother was downstairs having a freak session and would not hear her plea for help.

"Sshhh! It won't hurt long unless you scream again," Anthony warned.

The next sound she heard was the clanging of his belt buckle as his jeans crashed to the floor. Then suddenly, shit got really real. Pain ripped through her threatening to tear her in two. Her legs instantly became jelly. The pain was unreal. *What the fuck was he pushing in me now,* she wondered. It seemed as if whatever he was pushing inside was trying to break through her pussy and out her mouth. Her brain screamed for her to yell, but she couldn't. With each never ending stroke and vicious thrust, he drained her.

Anthony's arms were locked firmly on each of her hips and the force of each thrust left her cursing her brother in ways that even now aren't describable. Just when she thought she couldn't take another lunge, something strange happened. The pain subsided, and although it wasn't exactly comfortable, there suddenly was somewhat of a pleasant sensation beginning to grow. Apparently Anthony felt it too, for he thrust what seemed even deeper inside her, more savage than before.

He was beating her pussy so hard that it forced out the first moan her mouth ever uttered for any man during sex. No sooner than she started to moan, Anthony's legs suddenly tensed. He jerked his dick out of her, simultaneously releasing her hips in the process. Her legs instantly buckled underneath her, having her mouth only inches from what was the first dick her eyes had ever seen.

His dick was as thick as a zucchini and as long as the width between her wrist and elbow. From the slick head dripped a milky reddish fluid. Noticing that Andrea sat only inches away from his dick with her mouth gaped wide trying to breath, Anthony sprang forward and thrust his dick down her throat. The fit was beyond tight and her teeth were painfully grazing his manhood. So with two nicely measured slaps across her jaws, Andrea slacked her mouth and was forced to taste her own blood. No sooner had the taste of blood faded, it was replaced by a thick gooey substance. The stuff coated her jaws and hung all around the back of her mouth. Anthony had her head locked in place and was pumping her mouth as he had her pussy. Then suddenly his body went limp and he pulled his dick from my mouth.

Andrea took a sip from her drink and stared at the corner of the of wall.

"Did you tell your parents? Your brother? Please tell me you told somebody?" Ree-Ree protested.

"Tell?! There wasn't anyone to tell. My mom took far worse from my dad and my brother wasn't exactly my idea of a Knight in Shining Armor," Andrea replied, regaining her sense of humor.

"So what happened then?" Ree-Ree asked.

"Anthony fucked me about three or four times a week, for almost a year. That is until I met Scar. Scar and his boys ran up on Anthony one day and beat his ass real good. After that, he left me alone," she replied as she began to play over the remains of her spaghetti.

"So what happened with you and Scar?" Ree-Ree asked as she was intently listening to the story.

"Oh, how quickly we jump from the former to the later," Andrea spoke in a solemn yet mocking tone.

"My bad girl, it's just... Well, I thought you might have wanted to move on to a better topic. Scar was better, wasn't he?" Ree-Ree asked hesitantly before grabbing her plate and heading to the kitchen.

"When it came to sex, frankly, I preferred Anthony. But for all other issues, I'd take Scar, hands down," Andrea said as she rose with her plate and glass in hand, and followed the now fuming Ree-Ree into the kitchen. "Girl, you acting like he took *your* pussy or something. Hell the way I see it, I took the lemon and made some tang."

"It's lemonade. Oh, never mind. Can we please get back to Scar?" Ree-Ree retorted.

"Well, since you asked so nicely. Scar was my first crush. He was about 17 years old. Just a year under Anthony. We kicked it from the time I was twelve right up to about a month or so shy of my fourteenth birthday. He was fun all the way to the time before we split."

"What he do?" Ree-Ree asked half hoping and praying this story would be better than the last. She braced herself for a tale her gut was telling her wouldn't at all be nice.

☐

Chapter Three

Money and Splash had arrived in Norcross, Georgia a little over two hours ago ahead of schedule. They made contact with their connect and made sure everything was still a go. With no foreseeable problems, all involved agreed to move forward as planned. Both guys had showered and tried to call their ladies to let them know they had arrived safely, but neither of their attempts were successful.

"Andrea not answering her cell either," Money commented as he replaced the receiver of the hotel's phone back up on its jack. "You think something's wrong?"

"Doubt it. Ree-Ree good for leaving her cell in the car. Ain't no telling what they into," Splash answered as he crossed the room to grab his all black waist length chinchilla. "You ready to eat? I think I saw a Ruby Tuesday about a block from the hotel."

"I'm with it," Money replied as he grabbed his chinchilla and led the way out the room towards the car. Even though he hid it extremely well, Splash was more than a little worried about the girls not answering the phone. But there was no need to overreact prematurely. However, tomorrow at this time would be the time to worry. Especially if no contact at all had been received. But then again, there was no need to stress. At least he hoped it wasn't.

"Either I was more hungry than I thought, or the Ruby Tuesday's back in North Cack ain't hitting on shit," Money stated as he pushed away his emptied plate forty minutes later.

"True, true. Yo Money, can I ask you something?" Splash asked from across the table of the booth they were lounging in.

"What's up?"

"Remember back when we were freshmen in high school?" Splash questioned.

"Yeah, I was going through my little poetry phase," Money answered, causing them both to erupt into laughter.

"Little my ass. You thought you were the black Don Juan. I remember you use to have this poem about your dream girl. What you call that shit again?" Splash teased.

"Blackmoon!" they both said at the same time.

"Sometimes I sit down and just stare at my girl, and without her, I wonder can I make it through this world. Cause each shared day is another magnificent dream, and truthfully life's not worth living without my queen." Splash quoted an excerpt of the poem.

"You remembered it?" Money asked, sounding both shocked and touched at the recitation of his poem.

"Remember it? Hell, because of Ree-Ree, I'm living it. Do you recall how we all first met?" Splash asked going back down memory lane.

"How could I forget? We were both seniors in high school and Ree-Ree was the hot new transfer student. When she walked into our homeroom that morning, you damn near spit drool on my black and silver Bo Jacksons," Money reflected humorously.

"Whatever cuz. All jokes aside tho, when she walked in that morning, I heard that poem. And that's real talk cuz. And I've been hearing it ever since," said Splash as he sipped on his bottle of Ciroc.

"Damn cuz, I'm touched. No jokes, really."

"Do you hear it?" Splash question was swift and came without warning, just as he intended it to be.

"Hear what? The poem?" Money stalled, trying to maneuver around the question.

"When you're with Andrea, do you hear it? Is she your Blackmoon?" Splash words were delivered in a casual way, but also in a way to demean an answer.

The eyes were the first to betray Money, for the realization of the negative pending response hit him instantaneously. The silence went on for a moment, then a few seconds, to an almost full minute before Money finally answered. The word he uttered was unemotional and barely perceptible.

"No."

Chapter Four

"Unless you skipped something it sounds to me like Scar was that nigga," Ree-Ree said as she and Andrea hovered around the counter preparing to have themselves two of the Keese & Keyshia's Homemade Red Velvet Cupcakes.

"Girl bye! Showing off doesn't come close to describing how that nigga flipped."

Before Ree-Ree could ask for more details, Andrea began relaying the story as she walked from the counter towards the living room with her cupcake in hand.

"Shit hit the fan for us about a month after I'd healed up from a case of the claps. I knew Scar had given me that shit, but since I was still occasionally fucking Anthony, I couldn't afford to black all the way out. Not with there being a chance that I gave the shit to him, you feel me? Mmm!! This cupcake is banging," Andrea stated between bites, as she licked some cherry cream from the side of her fork.

"But anyway, I was just getting over the claps when the annual *'Keep It Popping'* post New Year's party was going down. This was a party Scar threw at his home each year about two days after New Year's. It's how and where we first met."

"As usual, the house was jumping and people were all over the place getting their freak on. The scene was mostly high schoolers mixed with the occasional college kid. I had been left in charge of things while Scar had left with Yosh to go handle something. After about twenty minutes, some nigga puked all over the living room couch. So off I go looking all over the house for cleaning spray to fix this mess before Scar got back and flipped."

"As I'm searching the upstairs closets I hear a thumping sound coming out of Scar's room. So naturally, I go see what the fuck is up. When I opened the door, I saw Toya, the town hoe, sandwiched between my man and Yosh. Now, remember, that's my first love in there fucking the town hoe. A bitch he knew I hated!" Andrea spat out the words with a tone that made one believe this matter was more recent than it was.

"So what you do?" Ree-Ree asked.

"I closed the door and went downstairs and grabbed the first dude I saw looking at me like he wanted to fuck. His name was L.A. and girl, he was all legs. I'd heard tall dudes were, you know, bigger. So off we went up to Scar's parents' room, which was only across the hall from where he was fucking Tonya."

"I fell back on the bed and let L.A. have his way with me. I made him take it slow. Luckily he wanted to screw me so bad that he did everything I told him. He kissed me, then licked me from head to toe. I made him massage my whole body, then he fingered me and ate my coochie before I let his dick anywhere near my pussy. I did all this to make sure Scar had enough time to finish fucking, then come look for me and catch me fucking L.A."

"Right after L.A. stuck his rod inside me, which by the way was the smallest dick I'd ever seen or felt, Scar and Yosh were in the room, snatching him off me and beating him with anything they could put their hands on. I hopped up, grabbed my clothes, got dressed as fast as I could, and began to walk home. I figured out later that it wasn't the smartest move to make being that my crib was all the way across town. But maybe an hour later, Yosh came riding up in his Chevy Tahoe. Took him some time to get me to get in, but he eventually I did. He took me to the ice cream parlor, then to the Green Top Inn."

"The Green Top Inn?" Ree-Ree stated more than questioned.

"You know, the back seat of the car. When you on your back in the back seat all you can see is the top of trees and shit. Get it? Green Top Inn!" Andrea joked.

"Don't tell me you fucked him too?" Ree-Ree asked, but before she could get an answer, there was a knock at the door. She hurried over and peeped out the window. She saw a guy she didn't know but had seen around the area more than she liked. It was Andrea's newest friend.

"Girl, who is it?" Andrea asked as she finished off the last of her cupcake.

"It's for you," Ree-Ree said sarcastically.

Andrea noticed the change in Ree-Ree's voice and went to the door to see who the mystery guest was.

"Ooh, its Reek," she said in a very frank manner.

She quickly opened the door with a sexy smile planted on her lips. From her pocket, she pulled out the keys to her place and handed them to him. "Go on up. I'll be there shortly," she said before closing Ree-Ree's door. She turned and headed for her purse and coat on the arm of the couch.

"You fucking him, ain't you?" Ree-Ree spat out, not attempting to conceal her disgust.

"Let's just say that once we finish doing what we do, I won't have that urge anymore. And unlike Scar, he won't make me clap," she said smiling at her joke.

"Huh?!" Ree-Ree blurted out, clearly showing her apparent confusion.

"Oh, my bad. After the party, when I fucked Yosh, I found myself back at the clinic a week later, for the claps. Apparently, the hoe at the party wasn't the first hoe they ran a train on. Yosh set my ass ablaze. But it was worth it. Hell, he gave me my first orgasm. Speaking of which, I gotta go. Thanks for the food and drinks," Andrea added as she hurried to the front door to make her exit.

"Anytime," Ree-Ree said more from instinct than sincerity.

"Tomorrow morning at ten o'clock, breakfast at my place. What do you say?" Andrea asked as she paused at the half opened door.

"That's cool," was all Ree-Ree could muster up to say.

"Alright, see you then." And without another word uttered, the door slammed. The faint sound of heels clicking quickly up the stairs was all that could be heard.

***

"I miss you too. Alright boo, see you Sunday. I love you too. Be safe Boo. Bye-bye." Andrea did all this while she slowly rode her lover's dick, cowgirl style. *Damn, I'm good. I'm breaking off one nigga, while stringing along the next,* she thought to herself as she hung up her cell and gave her full attention to the sexual needs of Reek gritting his teeth beneath her.

Chapter Five

Meanwhile, down in Georgia, Money lay on his back across the bed staring at his cell phone. Why did it take Splash's question to make him see that his feelings for Andrea weren't as deep as they should be? They had been together for almost two years, but except for the strong desire to see her taken care of, he knew the emotions he had for her were a far cry from love. It wasn't like he hadn't tried. But something deep inside him just failed to allow her to become endeared to his heart. Their union was more of a mutual convenience than love.

"Fuck! How did I not know?" Money pondered as his cell erupted. "What's up?"

"Money? Is that you?" the voice asked.

"Yeah, who this?" he asked, trying to catch the voice on the other end.

"It's me, Mookie. Baby, what's wrong?" Tracey asked, calling Money by his childhood nickname.

Tracey had known Money even longer than Splash. They had been neighbors during their childhood and as far as he could remember, she had always seemed to pop up during the times he needed her most.

"What you want?!" Money barked, trying to sound mad.

"Don't disrespect me, Mook. Just because you out of town, don't mean you can't still get your shit split. Now, what's wrong?"

"I just realized— Hold up. Who shit you talking about splitting?" Money asked, between chuckles.

"Yours boy!" she said smiling.

"Yeah, whatever. Look, I'm sorry bout snapping at you. It's just..." He was cut off before he could finish.

"I know. Love can drive you crazy when you try to fight it," Tracey said in a playfully seductive voice.

"Every time I go out of town, you call me with that same crazy shit," Money replied light-heartedly.

"It's only crazy if it's true. Am I lying? Tell me you don't love me. Tell me you don't think about me when you fucking her. Better yet, tell me you don't wish you could make love to me one more time. Hello? Money!!!" Tracey knew he'd hung up. He always did.

The two of them had shared something wonderful over two and a half years ago. She was about to leave for an internship in Paris when they had hooked up. That night removed all the doubts about Money's exact place in her heart. Not to mention, it also put the fear of God in her about how she should handle dealing with her new discovery. So, like most love struck fool's, she kicked dust and took off for Paris without a word being spoken to Money.

Within a years' time, her mind, body, and soul were taking turns driving her crazy. That is until she eventually got fed up with her cowardice and moved back to the states only to discover that her shared night of passion with Money had made him put aside his playa ways and had inspired him to try his hand at love. She found this to be a great thing, except for the fact that he was making this step with a chick other than herself. So for almost two years she had maintained a constant communication with him and kept her ears to the street, praying for his bitch to slip.

Something about Andrea never sat well with Tracey. And since her instincts about women were rarely wrong, she played the role of friend to perfection, all the while praying for the chance to swoop in and reclaim what was rightfully hers. Tracey had almost begun to lose hope when Ree-Ree had called three days ago and gave her the scoop on ole' girl. If not for her and Splash's airtight plan and endless begging, she would have left that day to find and fuck that hoe up. But instead, she chilled. She hung up her cell and sighed with great relief.

Just another day, Money. Hold on baby. I promise I'll make this right, Tracey thought as she unpaused her SWV cd, allowing the beginnings of the song *'Weak'* to resonate throughout her bedroom.

***

"O.K. so she's been through some serious shit. I get that. But that doesn't give her the right to clown my man," Splash said after hearing Ree-Ree's recounts of how her day had gone.

"I didn't say it did. I was just letting you know what I learned."

"I know, baby. It's just that we're running out of the time," Splash said.

"I know, but things went better than I thought they would. By tomorrow night, I'll know if there's any chance to avoid hurting Money," Ree-Ree stately confidently.

"I'm doing my part to prepare him for the worse," he told her as he thought about the fucked up outcome of the situation.

"You think he knows what's up?" she asked.

"I doubt it. But if I'm not careful, he will," he confessed.

"I'll be so glad when this crap is over. The sooner she's gone the better," Ree-Ree said, sighing loudly into the receiver.

"Sounds like you've already given up hope." Splash could hear the sound of sorrow for Money.

"Let's just say, from the way things are looking, I don't see her making any changes in her lifestyle."

"Then tomorrow call Tracey and tell her to round up Money's sisters and tell them all to crash at our place until me and Money arrive Sunday morning. Oh. And don't forget to rig the bedroom and..."

"Baby, chill. I got this. Now enough about them, let's discuss us," Ree-Ree interjected as she and Splash changed topics and began chatting about their forthcoming wedding.

Chapter Six

Saturday started extremely early for Money and Splash. They needed to case the meeting area to ensure no surveillance was being done on the spot. After discovering nothing odd they mapped all areas for an ambush or hiding spots for a federal sting. They isolated their findings, then drew up the route and position they would take during the exchange. With this completed, the two made their way to Just's for a much-needed breakfast.

While this was taking place, Splash couldn't help but notice that Money wasn't all there. He noticed how his distant behavior persisted during their breakfast making him wonder if Money had caught on to what he and Kameron were up to. He doubted Money had, but the longer the silence lasted, the more he questioned that possibility.

Money's mind was occupied with Andrea, but not in the way Splash was thinking. Instead of thinking about what they had schemed up for him and Andrea, Money was trying to figure out why he was even with her. Last night between Splash's questions, and Diznee's persistence, something within him had opened. All he knew was every time he thought of Andrea, 'IT' - whatever it was, tried to close. When he thought of Diznee 'IT' would expand, leaving him with a sense of peace.

'How can this be?' thought Money, as he realized more and more what his emotions were screaming for him to hear. If what he was feeling was true, then he had a tough task awaiting him once he got home. But how could he? She had been the perfect wifey in almost every way. 'How can I choose Diznee?' Money thought to himself, as he allowed the peace that now accompanied her name to consume him whole. As the sensation consumed, it also purged in one blissful emotional swoop. Andrea was no more, leaving Diznee with complete ownership of Money's heart.

Chapter Seven

"You need some help?" Ree-Ree asked Andrea, as she approached the stove to see where she could lend a hand.

"Yeah, stir those grits for me," Andrea replied as she turned the turkey bacon over.

After the cooking was done, and their plates were made, they each sat down at the kitchen table and dug in.

"Andrea, can I ask you something?" Ree-Ree asked.

"Go ahead," she answered.

"Last night I was thinking about our talk and was wondering to myself…" Ree-Ree hesitantly eased out her word.

"Girl, just say it," Andrea interjected.

"Have you ever had any good men in your life?" Ree-Ree questioned.

"Of course! There's Rell, and before him, it was Boo-Boo Dollars. Then Hysheem and White," she said as she placed a fork full of food in her mouth.

"White? That sound like a white boy name," Ree-Ree said humorously.

"He was white," Andrea confirmed.

"Oh, hell no!! A white dude?!" Ree-Ree was shocked at the revelation.

"I was almost fifteen when we met. Oh, did I mention Lindsey?" Andrea responded.

Ree-Ree shook her head as she chewed on her cheesy scrambled eggs.

"Lindsey was my best friend. She was white too. I met White through her. His heart was so sweet, but I wasn't trying to be in love. I was more focused on how to run game. See, after that incident at Scar's, I realized I had a certain amount of power previously unknown to me. If perfected and used it right, I could give dudes the same crap they had given me.

I took my time with White and studied the nature of men. When I was through with White, I took everything I learned and gave back what I'd been receiving to any and all men who came across my path." Andrea stated, pausing between sentences to sip on her coffee. "I guess you could say, that after White I sorta came into my own."

Ree-Ree's stomach was churning with disgust at the shameless, ignorance of the woman sitting across from her. But without revealing her true opinions, she kept focused and continued to let Andrea dig her own grave.

According to Andrea, White looked like a Jon B. wannabe. Sideburns and all. White swore that her coochie juice was the reason why his facial hair was so thick and plentiful. Together the two had taken every position known to man and practiced every hip movement possible. Once Andrea was certain she could make a dude cum in less than ten minutes in any position, she went off to test her theory. Now mind you, she kept White more than happy, all the while seducing and fucking others. After going through seventeen dudes of varying races and nationalities, she found herself looking for a true challenge. An adult man. None of her dudes had been older than eighteen during this time.

Maybe a step up was what she truly needed. With her new agenda set, she wasted no time locating and plotting on her new targets. Yes, targets. For she had located two men she felt more than comfortable in her ability to seduce and fuck. See, women fuck men. Men don't fuck women. If a woman doesn't first, in her own mind, decide to fuck you, then a man's only hope at fucking her is to rape her. Point blank, any consensual sexual experience ever had by any man with any woman, was initially approved or allowed by the woman before the guy ever had a clue. So with this logic in place, Andrea set off to fuck Coach Todd her track instructor and Mr. Hall her night-time manager at Bo'Jangles.

A Whore's Conscience

Her plan took almost a month to accomplish. But by the third Friday after the start of her mission, she was found in Coach Todd's office, standing in front of him with nothing on but her towel wrapped around her. At fifteen, Andrea's body rivaled many of those possessed by adult women. Her breast was swollen full C-cups and her lower body was a perfect mirror image of Trina, the rapper. Her face was best of all, for it was the portrait of innocence. The devil within her was masterfully hidden behind the Angelic mask. This blessed image, for which she effortlessly portrayed, would be the undoing of many men. And Coach Todd unknowingly was about to become her first target.

"What's wrong?" Coach Todd asked as he rose from behind his desk, rounded it, and sat on its front corner. With the coach only a few feet away and the adrenaline of the moment overcoming her, Andrea felt her body begin to respond in a most blissful way. Her nipples shot hard, threatening to rip holes through the front of her towel. While beneath her navel, her poo-nany, as White called it, was soaking wet.

"It's Lindsey... she's—" she started, then drifted off.

"Is she hurt?" Coach asked, half rising from the desk.

"No!" Andrea blurted out, as she quickly closed the distance between them, placing her hand on his hard chest as she pushed him back onto the desk, and stood between his thighs.

"Lindsey is fine. She's our lookout," she replied as she allowed her hands to cup her breast through the towel.

"What are you talking about?" he asked, as his breath half choked him as she dropped the towel from her body during the middle of his question and stood before him completely nude.

'Damn, she's incredible!' thought coach Todd, as he marveled at how large yet extremely perky her breast where, and how wet the hairs covering her coochie was. When he silently ogled her, his rod had shot to full erection. A discovery Andrea was apparently already aware of.

"Lindsey's watching out for us," Andrea stated, as she gripped his dick through the fabric of his windbreakers as firmly as possible. His teeth gritted at the force she used to hold his manhood.

"Andrea... I'm... I'm..."

"Yes?" Andrea, toyed with her victim, enjoying the rush the moment was fueling insider her.

"I'm gay," Coach Todd had scrambled to come up with the lie. But between his hormones and her age, one, if not both, were about to get him thrown under the jail.

With a movement that was blisteringly fast, she snatched down the front of his windbreaker, and locked her lips firmly around the throbbing head of Coach's cock. Andrea began to take more and more of the his dick into her mouth until she had all nine inches of his rod surrounded by her mouth.

'Gay, huh? Not today,' she thought to herself, as she began to suck harder on his dick seeking to make him cum in under ten minutes.

Exactly seven minutes later, she had reached her goal. Without a word spoken, she reached down, grabbed her towel and left the office. After dressing and meeting Lindsey in the courtyard of the school, the two discussed what had gone down with the coach and laughed about how he would look and act come Monday's practice.

Lindsey was the yin to Andrea's yang. They complemented each other well. Lindsey was innocent and she was also loyal. She was 75% White and 25% Brazilian. This was due to her mom being all white and her dad being half Brazilian and half white. Whatever she was, she was certainly, unquestionably well endowed. At least for a white girl's standard. Her hips and ass looked like she'd been taking the dick just as long as Andrea had. Easily, Lindsey's butt was one of the top five plumpest in their entire school and this was not as easy as some may think.

Lindsey's breast were firm B-cups, but very few could have told you this with any certainty because if one looked at her upper body, her breast would be the furthest thought from their mind. Lindsey was gifted with lips that were wide, full, and thick. Many dudes would choose her mouth over her pussy without a further thought, due to their screamingly blatant sex appeal. Her eyes were a piercing creamy jade green. Between her lips and eyes, Lindsey was more than a handful for any man who entered her life.

The two made their way through the courtyard to the school's senior parking lot where White sat waiting for them.

"You didn't?! Girl, tell me you didn't!" Ree-Ree stated.

"What?" Andrea questioned confused.

"Tell me you didn't kiss that boy after just swallowing the coach's sperm?" Ree-Ree clarified.

"And? It wasn't like that was the first time. Hell, that day he tasted two niggas nuts," she responded as she sipped on her coffee.

"Two?" Ree-Ree asked, befuddled.

"Yeah. After catching a quick bite to eat, me and Linsey had White drop us off at work."

She went off into the corners of her mind and began recounting the day she gave true service with a smile.

After clocking in, she spent much of the day working the drive-thru, while Lindsey worked the front counter taking orders. The day flew by as it normally did. The manager, Mr. Hall, was up to his usual antics. Trying his best to sing the pants off Andrea or Lindsey. Mr. Hall, or Greg to those he flirted with, was taking the till from Lindsey's register when he nudged her butt with his hip and started singing the opening lines to *R-Kelly's, 12-Play*.

"Would you mind... If I gave you some of my... Twelve Play," Greg sang loudly with a smile on his face. He spun away from Lindsey as they both began to laugh.

"Greg! You got a minute?" Andrea asked, snatching out the drive thru's till and following him to his office before he had time to respond.

"What's up, heartbreaker?" he asked by calling her by one of a hundred varying names he had for her and Lindsey.

"Nothing serious. I just wanted to hear my song," Andrea stated as she handed Greg her till. "Hold on, okay?" she asked as she sprinted from the office and then returned in less than ten seconds. "Now I'm ready." she replied, as she shut the office door and pulled her work shirt out of her pants.

Greg looked beyond stunned. He was in his mid-twenties at least, or so he appeared. He was about 5'10 and weighed about 220lbs. He was solid, with a teddy bear build. He had very little facial hair, which made him seem cute. The various expensive spectacles he wore simply made him all the more delicious. Andrea couldn't wait to see if she could steam up his Gucci framed glasses.

"Girl, don't play! If I whip it out, it's on," he stated as he half turned away from her to sit her till down on the counter behind him. When he turned back to face her, she had kicked off her shoes and was stepping out the last leg of her pants. Greg's king cobra stood at attention instantly, ready to spit.

"My song please, Greg." Before she could finish her sentence, he went into one of his original songs. One he knew she liked.

"Let me look into your eyes. Let me reach into your soul—"

As he sang she raised her shirt bottom and lifted it over her head. She wore no bra because she didn't need to. Her breasts were like missiles. So with the shirt removed, all she had left on was her socks and her beaming smile.

"Don't stop singing," she instructed him as she leaned over at the hips, and unzipped his slacks. No sooner than she had finished unzipping his pants, out plopped the most beastly dick she had ever seen since Anthony's. Greg wasn't as long, but he was much wider than any of her previous lovers. His girth alone was 5 inches in circumference. She looked at it as if he was gonna hurt.

"I can make you feel so good... The way no other could..." he continued to sing as she took him by the shirt, coaxing him to rise from his seat to stand behind her as she placed both of her forearms flat against the counter. She then shifted her hips enough to easily lift her left knee onto the counter exposing her swollen and extremely hot pussy for easy access and maximum penetration.

As Greg gripped her hips and stepped closer, she reached back and halted his movement. "Fuck me, Greg. Beat this pussy up, baby." She gave him a look that said she meant every word. The statement clearly shocked Greg and caused him to stop singing.

With a nod of the head showing her he understood, she removed her hand from his dick, arched her back and said, "Keep singing."

She bit her lip hard preparing for a sensation that promised pain and most certainly pleasure. Greg smacked her ass with enough force to bring tears to her eyes, then instantaneously, rammed, crammed, and forcefully stuffed his cock into her too tight cunt. He gripped her left hip with one hand and pent her face to the wall with the other, all the while fucking the natural born shit out of her.

Meanwhile, peeping in the office was Lindsey. She stood eating on a cinnamon biscuit and mentally taking notes.

'So this is how you serve a black man,' Lindsey thought as she watched Greg fuck Andrea so hard she swore her girl's pussy would be blistered.

VREEN!! VREEN!!

Ree-Ree answered her phone on the second ring. "Hello?!"

"Ah, yeah! Give me thirty minutes," she replied, then hung up.

A Whore's Conscience

"What was that about?" Andrea asked as she placed their dishes into the dishwasher and pressed start.

"Some people Shawn knows. They supposed to meet me at the Innkeeper Hotel off highway 55 and follow me back home in their U-Haul truck," she answered as she rose from the table.

"I'll see you when you get back then," Andrea said, as she escorted her to the door.

"Actually, I was, uh... Well, I don't know these guys and well..." Ree-Ree was laying it on thick.

The guys in the U-Haul were part of an investigation team hired by her and Splash. While she met with them and let them trail her back home, the other members of the investigator's team would be placing hidden mics and cameras all over Rell's townhome. All she had to do was get Andrea to come on the ride with her, but the bitch wasn't taking her bait.

"Look, if you want me to beg, I will," Ree-Ree blurted out.

"Girl, please! Give me a few minutes and I'll meet you downstairs," Andrea replied as Ree-Ree exited the crib and headed down the stairs towards her Porsche, Panamera. When she cleared the last step, she exhaled deeply.

'So far, so good,' she thought, as she pulled out her cell and dialed up Steph.

***

Meanwhile, upstairs Andrea was scrambling, rushing to find the right coat to match what she was wearing. In the process, her mind couldn't help but question why her past all of a sudden became so important to Ree-Ree. If not for her confidence in the fact that Ree-Ree feared she'd lose Shawn behind their Lesbo experience, Andrea would have long ag cut off the trip into her past.

But knowing Ree-Ree wasn't going to risk her relationship by snitching on her, made Andrea feel bolder and even somewhat untouchable. Not to mention she had felt a sense of relief as she revisited what she reflected to as her past demons. Even though she hated to admit it, she had more than once found herself cursing herself for the way she was treating Rell. But, momentary regrets were never strong enough alone to replace a lifetime of bad habits and poor choices.

"Ungh! Oh shit!!"

Andrea grabbed her stomach and ran to the bathroom arriving

just in time to lift the toilet cover as vomit spewed from her mouth. Nausea and slight dizziness followed. What the hell was going on? That was the third time in five days she had thrown up. At first, she dismissed it as something bad she ate. Then she thought she might have caught some type of stomach virus. But now, as she gurgled her mouth with Scope, trying to rid it of the vile taste that accompanies vomit, she had to admit there was possibly a more logical reason for the occurrence. One she hated to consider, but knew it made sense than her other previous thoughts.

"Fuck! I must be pregnant!" Andrea stated, shaking her head in disbelief as she headed out the bathroom to leave.

Chapter Eight

"We'll be there. Just make sure she don't catch on," Steph stated.

"I got my end covered. Look, I gotta go. Don't worry. I gotcha," Ree-Ree said, then hit the end button cutting the connection.

"You ready?" Andrea asked as she approached the passenger side of Ree-Ree's Porsche.

"Yeah. You alright? Cause you look like shit."

"I'm good. When you get the chance though, stop by a store. I need something to snack on," she replied, rubbing her stomach.

"Alright. Oh, before I forget. Steph and Money's sisters are coming over. You might wanna call your *'FRIEND'* and tell him not tonight," Ree-Ree warned, not to help cover for Andrea, but to sell the image of her looking out.

"Good looking girl. Let me take care of that now," she responded as she pressed a single button that instantly dialed up her lover's number.

The trip to and from the hotel went without any problems. The U-Haul now sat parked in front of their house, as Ree-Ree drove Andrea to the corner store.

"I won't be long. You want something?" Andrea asked as she rose out of the car.

"Naw, I'm good!"

Moments later, Andrea, was back with a bag full of assorted snacks.

"So where we off to now?" Ree-Ree asked.

"Let's hit the mall," Andrea stated as she busted open a bag of Fun Yuns and dug in.

***

Meanwhile, back at Shawn and Ree-Ree's townhome, Steph was making sure the cameras were properly placed and that the transmitters were sending clear, recordable pictures. All was a go. From Spash's plasma flat screen TV, Steph could see anything and everything that took place in Rell's home. The hidden mics were finally up and running and with the task officially completed, she watched the investigator crew leave the townhome.

'Everything is set,' Steph thought as she picked up her cell and called KiKi, Rell's sister.

☐

Chapter Nine

Down in Georgia, all was going as planned. At least according to the guy's usual routine when they came to Norcross to re-up. As always, the two made a stop at Money's grandparents' house. The Gainey's were a lively couple. Mr. Gainey was a fan of Western films and spoke in a mild drawn out tone. His words were far and few, but once spoken, you could tell they were well thought over.

Mrs. Gainey was more of a soap opera and college sports fan. She was an extremely well dressed woman and talked a great deal more than her husband. However, her constant words didn't annoy. They more often than not soothed you.

Mr. Gainey was about 6'2 and around 190lbs, while Mrs. Gainey was about 5'1 and weighed about 140lbs. The two were proof that opposites could maintain a successful marriage. Rell was their eldest grandchild, yet, he was still without a wife or child. To say his family, especially his grandparents, were dogging him about settling down would be the understatement of the year.

After the hugs, and greetings, Shawn found himself enjoying lunch with Rell and his grandparents. The food, as usual, was great. Mrs. Gainey had cooked some homemade beef and vegetable stew that was sinfully good. As the four of them were eating Shawn couldn't help but notice that the cloud that had circled Rell most of the day was still very much present. Luckily, he wasn't the only one to notice.

"Rell, is something wrong Sugah?" Mrs. Gainey asked, after taking a long sip of her ice tea.

"Nah, nothings wrong. Just trying to figure out something. Nothing major," he said, answering her question just enough to hopefully make his grandma move on to another subject.

All this, however, was of no avail. His grandma seemingly had caught a scent, and like a bloodhound, was on the hunt.

"Is it that hot tail girl? I bet that's what it is. Who she done screwed now. Little skank! I never liked her in the first place. I knew she was a fast one," Grandma Gainey stated rapidly, and with an considerable amount of emotion.

The blatant statement shocked Shawn so badly, he half spat out his half swallowed tea. Apparently, Shawn wasn't the only one speechless. When he looked across the table, he saw Rell sitting there shaking his head as if in disbelief. The smirk on his face was the only sign he gave to show he wasn't upset at the current direction of the conversation.

"She ain't screwed nobody, grandma," Rell replied comically.

"Boy, is you blind or just downright dumb," she damn near shouted at him.

"My monies on blind," Grandpa Gainey chided, as he cut his wife off mid-sentence. His words were unexpected, hence the reason its meaning gained the maximum effect, causing all to double over in tears from laughing so hard.

The rest of the meal went much the same with comments of playful ridicule made about Rell's Aunt Pam, Kay, and Sam. Then there were comments about his mom Ce-Ce and his two jailbird Uncle's, Buster and Wayne. Grandma Gainey single handedly removed the cloud that had been floating over Rell and every ounce of Splash knew that she had performed this miracle not by accident, but on purpose.

Grandma Gainey was no fool, she knew from the moment Rell entered her home that her grandbaby needed to be spiritually lifted. And lifting his spirits she had done, along with everyone else's.

Once everyone was through eating, Rell pulled out a cherry blunt of loud and headed outside in the midday chill to smoke.

"Shawn, help Viv, will you?" Grandpa Gainey remarked as he handed Shawn the dish towel and started walking behind Rell.

"Only a fool would say no," Shawn responded, heading towards the kitchen.

Rell had just lit the blunt when his grandfather came up beside him and stood gazing out across the backyard. They stood their quietly for a moment sucking in the peaceful sounds of silence. But Rell knew it would only be a matter of time before he started kicking some profound knowledge his way.

"Some people say the devil hisses. Don't believe that my boy. That's a lie. How many people ever been face to face with the devil? I mean really FACE-TO-FACE," Grandpa Gainey stated, as he turned and stood only mere inches from Rell's face.

"None that I know," Rell answered.

"Exactly. Now listen, son, and listen good. I have been having those visions, dreams or what not, about you doing some bad things."

"Grandpa... I'm not." Rell was only saying as much in an effort to convince himself more than his grandfather.

"Shh... son. In my dreams you killing folks. At least two. A guy and a girl. They did something awful to you, cause you in lots of pain. Deep pain. Deep enough to make me wake up in tears," Grandpa Gainey stated, placing both hands on Rell's shoulders.

"Gramps, I'm fine. Really!" Rell interjected, trying to ease his Grandpa's soul.

"I got three things for you to think over. Promise me you'll think about the words I'm about to say."

"Yeah! Of course!" Rell affirmed.

"First, I need you to be mindful of that snake. It don't hiss, my boy, it whispers. It whispers God-Awful things, son. Some call his words devilish thoughts of the mind. Hogwash! When your mind is attacked by such thoughts, that's the snake whispering. Some say if you listen closely after the snake stops whispering, you'll actually hear him hiss. It's how you know which of your thoughts come from him and which come from God. I want you to think before you act. No matter how upset or hurt you may become, always think first. Ok?" These were the words of true wisdom that were spoken from Mr. Gainey lips.

"Okay."

"Secondly, beware of the Temple. When one has no temple fire one has no..."

"Soul!!" Rell finished the sentence.

"Exactly. This should help you see the snake coming before he has time to whisper. And lastly... here!"

"What's this?" Rell asked, taking the CD his Gramps handed him.

"Listen to the words closely. Listen to the words over and over until you're certain you know what they're trying to say to you. This came from your Grandma. If you catch the message in time, the snake won't stand a chance."

BAM!

"Sorry, Mr. Gainey. Rell, we gotta go!" Shawn said as he came out the house letting the screen door slam. "Good to see you again, Mr. Gainey."

"You too Shawn. Go on. I'll give your grandma your love. Just remember all I said," he stated as he hugged Rell and watched him hop into the Camaro.

As Rell and Shawn pulled out the yard, Mrs. Gainey came out just in time to wave bye.

"So, how'd it go?" she asked, watching the Camaro vanish down the street.

"We did our part. Now let's pray to God he can do HIS," said Mr. Gainey as he pulled his wife close, and held her tight.

No sooner had he pulled out the driveway, Rell popped in the CD and the music filled the car.

There was an old lady sittin' under a tree
She called me over and she said to me
My days left here may not be long
I wouldn't waste my time tellin' you nothin' wrong
But love is a flower that needs the sun and the rain
A little bit of pleasure's worth a whole lot of pain
If you learn this secret, how to forgive
A longer and better life you'll live
No pain (no pain), no pain (no pain)
No gain (no gain), mmm
No pain (no pain), no pain (no pain)
No gain (no gain)

The CD played only this verse from the song made famous by *Betty Wright*. There was a message in her words that his grandparents wanted him to hear. A message that they felt would be needed. He pressed repeat and let the song play again.

"Bruh, you alright?" Shawn asked as he leaned over turning down the volume.

"Shh..." Rell replied, turning the volume back up. This was important to his grandparents and until he got the song's message, he would play and replay it until he received what he needed... understanding.

Chapter Ten

"Girl, what's taking you so long? You got bitches thinking I'm some kinda stalker dike," Ree-Ree complained jokingly, as she pretended to check her face for blemishes in the mirror of the mall's bathroom.

"Just a minute!" Andrea stated as she sat on the toilet sweating the results of the pregnancy test she'd taken.

"I told your ass Fun Yuns and sardines, don't mix," Ree-Ree jested.

Damn. What's taking so long?' Andrea thought to herself. No sooner had the thought passed through her mind, the results of the test began to emerge. Andrea shook the test strip, hoping the results she'd viewed would change.

"Damn!!! Fuck!!!" Andrea blurted loudly.

"Girl, what the hell is wrong with you!" Ree-Ree asked frowning.

"Nothing. It's nothing."

Andrea stared at the positive results of the pregnancy test in dread. She was pregnant and with no exact date on how far along she was, not that it would help. She was absolutely clueless as to which of the three men, four if she counted Rell, could possibly be the father.

Damn, here I go again.' She stood and flushed the toilet, leaving the test strip on the floor. She left the stall and joined Ree-Ree at the sink.

***

A Whore's Conscience

"I ain't with all this cloak and dagger shit. I say we beat this trick ass, then tell her to get out of town before we really open her ass up," Kiki stated, growing more intense with each word. She was heated about this bitch cheating on her brother.

"Girl, ain't nothing I'd enjoy more. But with no proof, it's our word against hers. With proof, ain't shit she can say or do but take her ass whooping and keep it moving," Steph replied, trying to convince Rell sister to be easy.

"I'm gonna get the rest of the girls and..."

"No! It's just gonna be you, me and Olivia. Us, plus Ree-Ree should be more than enough," Steph interjected in order to stress the importance of only involving those that were absolutely necessary.

She and Ree-Ree both felt, in regards to Rell, that only a chosen few should be told about the situation. The one's that already knew were people that would want to know what side of the problem they stood on. So they had both agreed to tell only Kiki and Olivia. Other than being Rell's sisters, they both have a helluva fight game and were not afraid to use it. To let this go down without them involved would have been unforgivable in their eyes.

"Alright, let me call Liv, then we'll be over about nine tonight," Kiki stated.

"Alright," Steph responded, before ending the call. With all the loose ends now taken care of, Steph exhaled loudly and began cheesing as thoughts of what was to come filled her mind.

Chapter Eleven

"So whatever happened to Lindsey?" Ree-Ree asked Andrea, as the two stood in line at the mall's Baskin Robbins waiting to order themselves a frozen treat.

"Huh!?!" Andrea replied. She was caught between thoughts when the question was sprung on her.

"You made it seem like ya'll were real close," said Ree-Ree.

"Who!?!" Andrea asked confused.

"You and Lindsey. Girl, you sure you alright?" Ree-Ree asked as she turned to face Andrea.

"I'm good. I just wandered off a bit. But yeah, Lindsey was my girl. A bit slow, but she was my girl," She finally answered.

"So why doesn't she ever come down to see you?" Ree-Ree asked, prying deeper.

"Because she "WAS" my girl. Was, not IS, is the keyword," Andrea replied with a slight attitude.

"Oh, damn girl! What you do?" Ree-Ree stated, fronting like she was upset at what she might hear.

"I ain't do shit. She's the one who broke the code!!"

"The code?" Ree-Ree said, looking for clarification.

"Yeah, check it! Me and Lindsey got really close. We started doing everything together. And when I say everything, I do mean everything." Andrea's face took on the look one gets when discussing something very personal and extremely sacred. The look one has when they're deep in love.

From the age of fifteen to seventeen the two girls had fucked and sucked some of the best around their age that Durham had to offer. They would often spend the nights sharing sexual conquests or plotting out future ones. The two had made a game out of sex. Each girl planned from the beginning of each month, to fuck as many guys or as many times as possible, before the month ended. The one who took the least dick had to spend at least two hundred dollars on a gift for that month's winner. For the past two months, Lindsey had won, and with much confidence, had promised to win a record setting three months in a row. A feat, neither of them had yet accomplished.

Not one to bow out from a challenge, Andrea swore she'd win the next month. The bet was whoever lost, would have to eat the winner's pussy out for a whole weekend while waiting on them hand and foot. The two girls shook hands sealing the bet and set off to get shit popping.

Andrea wild out. By the end of the month, she had fucked or sucked forty-three guys. She was more than confident she had enough to win. Hell, she had topped her previous best by three. But Lindsey had straight went crazy. When she finished counting her tally, she had screwed or milked over fifty-seven guys.

"Ain't no mother fucking way!" Andrea protested. After an hour later, and most of the guys on Lindsey list had been verified, she conceded defeat.

"How in the hell did you pull off fifty-seven?" Andrea asked, clearly mind blown by the number.

"Being that it was February and Black History month, it was a plus for me. The twenty-eight days, however, wasn't. So I came up with a scheme. It was one I knew that would work. For every guy, black, white, or whatever, I gave blowjobs and quickies in honor of the month. Shit, it worked out so good that I hit the number fifty-seven on the eighteenth of February. I spent the rest of the month watching you trying to catch up," Lindsey stated with a chuckle.

Andrea shook her head in an *'I can't believe this shit'* type of way. "What's so funny?" Andrea questioned.

"Nothing! Just picturing you eating this pussy," Lindsey said, making a 'V' with her fingers and licking between them, seductively.

"So it's like that?" Andrea asked, trying to back out of her commitment after losing the bet.

"Mm... Hmm!" Lindsey replied smiling.

"Damn!!" Andrea, cursed, then gave a smirk. "Fuck it," she said sending both girls into a laughing frenzy.

***

Weeks passed and nothing had taken place. Either their schedules conflicted, or fear of being caught in the wet, loomed around them. It wasn't until a week after Andrea's seventeenth birthday when the best chance came about. Lindsey's parents had gone out of town to a business convention, leaving her and Andrea all alone. With a week's advance notice, Andrea knew what was up. It was time to pay the piper. Figuring, she was going to have to eat some coochie, she might as well enjoy it. With this thought in mind, Andrea went to the mall, then to a novelty store across town, and picked out a few things.

'Yep! Might as well have me some fun too.' Andrea thought as she packed her purchases into her suitcase and got ready to stay with Lindsey.

After dinner and some small talk, the two wasted no time in getting busy. Andrea gave Lindsey the bag of goodies she'd purchased and told her to go get ready. Once in her room, Lindsey discovered the bag she carried had lingerie and a few exotic toys and goodies.

'Damn, she really gonna do it!' Lindsey thought as her heart thumped rapidly with each thread of clothing she removed.

Moments later she was all set. "I'm ready!" Lindsey yelled as she stood in the middle of the floor of her room wearing the powder blue and white crotchless teddy, white fishnet stockings and garter, Andrea had given her earlier. Her knees threatened to buckle as she heard music coming from the living room. Andrea had cut on the surround system full blast allowing the music to engulf the entire home.

Let me lick you up and down, 'til you say stop.
Let me play with your body baby, make you real hot
Let me do all the things you want me to do
Cause tonight baby
I wanna get freaky with you

'Damn! That's my song!' Lindsey thought. Her breath hung in her throat when she saw Andrea enter her room with a look in her eye she'd never seen before. She stood inside the threshold of the room completely naked except for the huge strap-on dildo she wore around her waist. The plastic dick strapped to her waist was so huge Lindsey nearly overlooked the other one she held in her left hand.

Lindsey had only been joking about the bet. She had no real intentions to make her friend eat her pussy, but at that exact moment, her pussy was hotter than it had ever been. The feeling was obviously mutual, for Lindsey noticed a long glistening line of wetness running from her Andrea's coochie all the way down her thigh past her knee. When she looked up from Andrea's legs, she found her friend devouring her with her eyes. Never in all her previous experiences had she felt as desired or longed for as she did now.

"Tonight, I'm gonna make your toes curl," Andrea stated sensually, as she scooped the oils out the bag on the floor and laid on her back across the bed. "Turn around, real slow." After Andrea gave Lindsey the order, she took her right hand and began to squeeze the oil over the full length of the strap on she wore. "My God!"

"What!" Lindsey asked nervously.

"Your ass looks absolutely stunning in that teddy. And your legs... their incredible," Andrea stated as she rose up and rested on her elbows. She curled her left index finger indicating she wanted Lindsey to come closer. "Put your pussy on my stomach," Andrea ordered tenderly.

Lindsey did what she was told and straddled Andrea's hips, dripping coochie juice all over her stomach in the process.

"Damn, baby! You wet as hell!" Andrea stated as she took her oil laced right hand and slid three fingers deep into Lindsey's pussy before she could protest.

"Oh... Oh... Oh my GAWD!!" Lindsey shuddered spasmodically as she moaned from having her G-spot stroked for the first time. Andrea had been studying for over a week by watching self-help films and reading manuals on female oral sex techniques. What she was doing now was called finger popping.

'Damn, this shit really works!' Andrea thought as Lindsey's cunt set her fingers on fire. Her coochie went from hot, to inferno, as Andrea's fingers suddenly became coated in something really gooey. Pulling out her fingers caused Lindsey to whine in protest, but Andrea had to see if she had made her cum. If so, she wanted to let

her see her swallow each drop.

'Tonight, I'm gone turn her ass out', Andrea thought, as she locked eyes with Lindsey and began to suck and lick away each drop of her friend's cum. When this was completed, she rolled Lindsey onto her back and began to expose her breasts.

"Relax," Andrea whispered softly, sensing her uneasiness. The dildo she wore was every bit 15 or 16 inches long, hence the reason behind Lindsey's tense body. "You're gonna be begging me before I hit you with this dick," she said as she lowered her head and began to gently kiss her neck, slowly working her way down to Lindsey's breasts. Andrea took her time savoring each breast. She kissed, licked, and sucked every square inch of her breasts, all the while tenderly squirming with mind numbing pleasure.

Andrea was glad the music was blasting, cause the way Lindsey was yelling, the neighbors would swear someone was trying to kill her. That's when it hit Andrea. It hit hard and fast. She was in the middle of having sex and wasn't focused on getting through with the act. She was actually yearning for the experience to never end. Her heart was beating rapidly. She wasn't sure when it had begun, but the feelings it brought along with its chest numbing thumps, had her spinning out of control.

'What's happening to me?' Andrea thought as a seemingly uncontrollable force was guiding her mouth down Lindsey's body, closer and closer to her vagina.

As Andrea's lips kissed Lindsey's navel, she heard her breathing quicken. When her lips kissed just below her navel, the first scent of her pussy reached Andrea's nose. The smell was like blood to a tiger. Instantly, she was clawing at Lindsey's thighs, fighting to spread them as wide as possible. Then came the first lick. It was made just behind the hood of Lindsey swollen clit. The lick was soft and wet. She was slowly making upside down U's with her tongue all over the top of Lindsey's clit. The taste was indescribable and addictive. It was tangy, but not tart. The flavor to Andrea was just right.

Andrea kept right on her, licking and kissing her cunt. She even began to play with her G-spot again, coaxing her to a near orgasm only to stop and lower her mouth to literally tongue kiss her whole pussy. It was during one of these moments when Lindsey's leg spazzed apart. A thick liquidly substance shot across her mouth and down Andrea's throat, and she accepted it without protest. She lowered her mouth and reached as deep into Lindsey's cunt with her tongue as she could and began to suck that pussy like it was a Wendy's milkshake.

The sensation caused every muscle in Lindsey's body to lock up. Then when the last drop of cum was sucked out her coochie, Lindsey's legs lifelessly fell limp to the bed. She was utterly drained. Her chest heaved, her heart jumped violently, and she was flushing red from head to toe.

Andrea was on her knees, between Lindsey's legs admiring her work. Looking at her dripping pussy she knew she wouldn't have any problem getting the strap-on dick in her now. Slowly, Andrea leaned over and grabbed the vibrator she entered the room earlier with. Turning the bottom slightly, she activated the motor.

"Remember, I said you would beg," Andrea said tenderly, touching the tip of Lindsey's clit with the humming vibrator, ever so lightly.

"Please!! Oh… Oh!!"

Lindsey's pleasure was becoming unbearable. Then, without warning, Andrea slid almost every bit of the 16-inch strap-on into Lindsey violently. The force of the thrust alone brought tears to her eyes. The sensation that followed overloaded Lindsey's senses, causing her body to twitch and shudder, as tears began flowing freely from her eyes.

Andrea knew this was the effects of not pain, but extreme pleasure. So she kept her stride, and continued to slowly make love to her. The two were locked in a storm of conflicting emotions that neither cared to explain. All Andrea knew was that she had given at least two orgasms to Lindsey and had experienced three of her own in the process.

'Was this what love felt like?' Andrea wondered, as her thoughts were broken up.

Lindsey took her luscious lips and locked them around Andrea's. She moaned deeply into Andrea's mouth as the two shared the most exquisitely erotic kiss of their lives. During all this, Andrea never broke stride, keeping it hot on Lindsey cunt. Lindsey, in the grips of yet another, even stronger orgasm, jerked her mouth from Andrea's and wailed like nothing Andrea ever heard.

'Yeah, baby. Feel my love!' Andrea thought to herself, shocking her heart with the confession her soul had just made. Her personal

revelation was interrupted by the cries of Lindsey.

"Lindsey!! What's wrong? Did I hurt you?" Andrea asked as she lowered her body next to her and pulled her close.

"Andrea..." Lindsey muttered.

"Yes?"

"I think... I think I love you," Lindsey stated then burst into tears again.

"Shh... Love doesn't make you cry. If it did, I'd be in tears too," Andrea said, rubbing her back.

"No Andrea. I'm not talking about home girl love. I mean…"

"I Know!" Andrea said, cutting Lindsey off. She looked into Lindsey's eyes and split her soul with four words. "I love you too." By this time tears were streaming down Andrea's eyes as well.

Finally, Ree-Ree and Andrea found themselves at the front of the line.

"Girl, you know what, I'm good. You go ahead and get something for yourself," Andrea stated as she headed for a nearby table to sit and wait for Ree-Ree.

'Damn, this bitch got issues!' Ree-Ree thought, as she turned back towards the counter and placed her order.

Chapter Twelve

"Yo, Ma. You think they coming?" Lorna asked as she sat behind the wheel of her pink pearl colored Navigator, sweating the shopping complex's main entry points.

"When have you ever known them to stand us up?" Alexi replied.

"I'm tripping right?" Lorna stated, as she pulled out a tube of lip gloss and placed another coat upon her lips.

"Be easy, Ma! We gone get these cats," Alexi said, giving her girl dap.

Lorna and Alexi were from LA Perla, Puerto Rico. Born and bred, and true thoroughbreds in every way. The two had made their names back home from murder, robbery, extortion, and moving weight. Their backings back home was solid, which was how they still were able to obtain product without hassle or delay.

For almost four years the two of them had been dealing with Rell and Shawn. Business was always straight amongst them. Lorna knew Rell and his man was about their cash and never once had Rell or his man tried to snake them. The girls had even given the duo an extra brick of Yay once, only to have the duo come through with the street value in cash at the next meeting for that brick in hand. Lorna found it funny that Rell had given her the money made from the extra brick and cautioned her about being more careful before he slowly looked her over from head to toe.

"Is that them?" Alexi asked as she sat up in her seat to get a better look.

"I think so," Lorna answered, resting her hand on her 9mm Berretta. "I can't believe we doing this," Lorna thought as she glanced over at Alexi with doubt written all over her face.

"Chill, Ma! I might be wrong," Alexi said as she too grabbed her own 9 milli and opened the door, ready to set things off. Lorna stayed sitting behind the wheel as Alexi stood against the passenger's side of the hood, dangling the gun she held in her right hand behind her back as Rell and Shawn approached.

"Ladies!" Rell greeted the two, handing the knapsack of cash across the hood to Lexi. "One of these days they gonna trust us," he jokingly said to Shawn.

"Let's just keep playing dumb," Shawn smirked, as he responded.

"Lexi, you hear this?" Lorna asked retrieving the bag of cash from her girl.

"I don't know what they talking about," Alexi said, still playing her position beside the hood.

"Go head, Shawn," Money said, cueing the man.

"Well, Lorna's got something no smaller than a nine milli resting on her, but aimed at us. And Alexi, well from the lack of any serious strain on her right shoulder muscles, she can't be packing anything bigger than a 45," Shawn stated as he shot Alexi a look that dared her to call him a lie.

"Cute! Real cute," Lorna stated as she slung the cash into the back and pressed the button to release the trunk.

Alexi strolled towards the back of the Navi to finish business with Shawn as Rell while Lorna kept them busy up front.

Alexi sat in the back of the Navi and spread her legs as wide as she could and placed the bag full of kilos between them. This was a first to Shawn. Between the milli in her right hand, and the silky thigh she caressed with her left, Shawn froze. He was uncertain as to what move he should make. Alexi was gorgeous with long wavy black hair and a face that was a masterpiece in its own right. She had perky B-cup breasts and a firm shapely ass to go along with her richly golden tanned complexion. She was all that and then some.

"Don't be scared. I don't bite, Papi," Alexi said as she pulled open the bag exposing the dope inside.

"ALexi, all jokes aside, what's going on?" Shawn asked.

"Nothing. Me and my girl thought since this was you and Rell's last time coming together, we should make tonight special. That's all."

"Our last time? Who told you that?" he asked.

"Come on, Shawn. All the signs are there. You arrange the entire meeting by yourself, no Rell involved. And now we meeting at a shopping complex instead of the usual spot. Both changes are a first. How slow do you think we are?"

"We just thought it was time to change the routine, that's all. Honestly. But wait, what did you mean by make tonight special?" Shawn asked, not hiding the curiosity from her earlier statement.

"Well, my girl Lorna been wanting to get at your boy for a minute now, and tonight we were gonna break ya'll off real proper. But since this ain't gone be…"

"Hold that thought," Shawn said, cutting her off. Fucking round was something Shawn had long stopped doing. But he had failed to figure out how Rell truly felt about Andrea, and time had all but ran out. But this little development presented some interesting possibilities. If Rell fucked Lorna, then maybe Shawn and Ree-Ree could convince him to let Andrea go with minimal drama.

"Yeah! Let's do that. Unless you scared," Shawn baited him.

"Scared! Bull shit! This pussy muy fuego, papi," Alexi stated as she grabbed and pulled Shawns' shirt, drawing him close. She then leaned in and laid a kiss on the brother to show him she meant business.

Chapter Thirteen

"You sure you alright?" Ree-Ree asked Andrea, as she sat down to eat her ice cream.

"Yeah! It's just... sometimes I miss that hoe," Andrea replied with a half smile on her face.

"I ain't trying to press you, but I ain't gonna front like I don't want to know, either. But, what happened after that night?" Ree-Ree asked in a blunt, yet round about fashion.

"Well, since you asked so nicely," Andrea responded, shifting in her chair to get closer to Ree-Ree.

For about a year after that night, Andrea and Lindsey were in love. The fall was sudden and extremely mind-blowing. However, like all things previously in her life, nothing for Andrea stayed peachy for long. Her love for Lindsey was no different. From the very beginning of their lesbian affair, they had agreed to still fuck guys, but promised that they would never share their pussy with another girl.

Both agreed, and all was good until about three months shy of a year. That's when Lindsey met Juan. From day one he had her mind blown. Juan was Cuban and physically flawless and his talk game was tight. Too tight. From day one Andrea smelt trouble, but before she could warn Lindsey, Juan had got her girl's digits and given her his in return.

A Whore's Conscience

That very moment marked the beginning of the end of Andrea and Lindsey.

Juan was twenty-three at the time, and from the moment he got the green light from Lindsey, he had her ass going in circles. Andrea went from making love with Lindsey at least four times a week, to barely even once a week. The lovemaking went from mind-blowing to just downright disappointing. Every free moment was spent with Lindsey praising Juan. To hear her tell it, he was Superman with a dick made of gold. Just when Andrea thought it could get no worse, word on the street was that Juan had Lindsey at some frat house party, blindfolded, sucking him off while his whole crew watched.

Andrea was upset how the girl was letting some limp dick have the power she had taught Lindsey to never let go of. But she knew that she was helpless in being able to convince Lindsey to wake up before it was too late. Some lessons must be learned the hard way. When three weeks before prom, she heard Juan had Lindsey tossing some tricks salad on camera, Andrea flipped. After giving up some pussy for a copy of the tape, Andrea was shocked when she viewed the contents of the video.

Lindsey went down a line of three couples, licking each guy's ass then pulling their dicks out of their girls, and tossing them up too, all the while being fucked in the ass by Juan, who coached her the entire way. Andrea's heart shattered. How could Lindsey break their promise? Andrea was consumed by anger. She wanted Juan's blood, but knew it wouldn't do any good. He wasn't the problem. Lindsey let him exploit and play her. Hell, she was basically allowing herself to be pimped. No. The problem wasn't Juan... it was Lindsey.

"Bitch wanna play games, huh!? Okay! Alright! Don't nothing beat the cross, but a double cross!" Andrea concluded as she formulated how she would enact her revenge on the trick she once loved.

It didn't take long for her to realize how to pay Lindsey back. Realizing that through Juan Lindsey had hurt her. She decided that through Juan, she too would hurt Lindsey. Once Andrea knew the method of revenge, she focused on the perfect place to orchestrate it.

Bing!! Bing!! The Prom!

It was the perfect occasion. Their senior prom was all the two had spoken of for weeks. The prom would be the place where Andrea would serve her brutally cruel dish of bone cuttingly painful 'get back'. This would be a prom night Lindsey would never forget.

Prom night arrived and everything was going as planned. Andrea and Lindsey had Juan and White rent a stretch limo for the occasion. When Lindsey wasn't looking, she passed Juan a note telling him how Lindsey told me he was fucking her in the ass, and how she said he knew how to open a girl up without too much pain. She then told him to meet her at the limo so he could take her ass virginity. After awhile, she pretended to head to the restroom, then bee-lined out to the limo.

Before getting in she told the driver to roll up the partition window, but to lower it if my her friend came out. With that said, Andrea opened the moon roof and laid back on the seat with my legs wide. She began to masturbate slowly while she waited for Juan come. He didn't keep her waiting long. She was in mid stroke when the limo door flung open. Juan looked a little paranoid at first, but the sight of her knuckle deep in her pussy chased away all his fear. He tried to rush into things, but this notion was killed when she unzipped his pants, pulled out his already hard dick, and began milking him.

Softly, she licked and bit the head of his dick. Lindsey had blabbed about how this drove him crazy and she now saw for herself that it was. Occasionally, between sucks and licks, she would ask him if he liked it. Whenever he got close to nutting, she would squeeze his balls as hard as she could, then resume milking his rod. Andrea pushed him back, then slid to the floor of the limo, and arched her ass into the air.

"You want some of this pussy?" she asked as she swayed her hips seductively.

"Hell yeah!" he answered.

"Fuck me then, daddy!" Andrea moaned, as she threw her left knee up on the seat, and thrust her pussy out further.

Trying to hurry up and slide in Andrea's pussy, Juan banged his head hard against the window. He sucked air in loudly through his teeth as he sunk deeply inside her.

"You like this pussy?" she moaned.

"Oh, shit!" he yelped, shoving in deeper.

"Damn Papi, you too big," she lied, trying to gas his head.

"Oh... fuck!" he moaned loudly when she squeezed her cunt muscles as hard as she could around his dick.

"Oh... Oh... Fuck! Oh... Juan! It's too big! It's too... BIG!" she screamed as he crammed his 9 inches completely into her.

Juan was in a zone. He never heard the partition window slide down. Nor did he hear Andrea lock the doors.

"Stop!!" Andrea moaned, as she reached back and gripped the base of Juan's dick.

"What's up?" he protested.

"I want you in my ass," she said as she pulled apart her cheeks for him. Just as he was about to enter she let go of her cheeks.

"Wait! What you gonna tell Lindsey?"

"Huh? Fuck Lindsey! I ain't got to explain shit to her," he barked.

"But don't you love her?" she asked as she reopened her cheeks.

"Who, Lindsey? Fuck no!! She ain't nothing but a trick!" he barked, as he eased his head into her ass.

"Is that what I am too... a trick?" she asked, reaching back stopping his progression.

"Naw, Mami!! You the shit. You know dat" Juan said, trying to ease forward.

"Oh, so it's like that, huh? I'm a trick, now!" Lindsey screamed from above, as she looked into the limo from the moon roof.

"Lindsey! Mami! I can explain," Juan stuttered as he fumbled to pull up his pants.

"Fuck you, nigga!! And you... bitch you ain't shit," Lindsey yelled as she spat twice through the moon roof, both times hitting Andrea.

"Oh fuck no!! I know you didn't let that hoe spit on you?" Ree-Ree asked, cutting the story off.

"Oh, she got that off. But I rocked off once I got out the car and caught that ass," Andrea replied, demonstrating the beat down she gave Lindsey that night. "And that's why we don't kick it no more," she stated as she rose from her seat and grabbed her purse.

"Come on, girl. Let's go do some shopping. All this Lindsey talk is making me sad," Andrea, said grabbing her cell to send out a text message.

Chapter Fourteen

Ding-dong!!

"Its about damn time. I thought ya'll hoes left me hanging!" Steph said excitedly as she opened the door to Shawn and Ree-Ree's town home.

"Hoe you tripping!" Olivia jokingly replied, when she and Kiki entered the crib.

"Where she at?" Kiki asked Steph.

"Who Ree-Ree?" Steph asked, somewhat confused by the question.

"Yeah, her too," Kiki replied.

"They still at the mall. I thought we settled this already. Until Rell gets back..."

"I know. I know! Nobody can touch Andrea," Kiki spat out between clenched teeth.

Oliva felt the tension in the room and decided to change the subject. "Why don't we go over to Pam's tonight. Something's always popping off over there and..."

"Bet! Let me grab my stuff," Steph blurted out, cutting Olivia's sentence short.

"I don't care what we do, as long as we back over here tonight,"

Kiki said, adding her two cents to the convo.

"Chill, girl, damn. We gonna bust her fucking shit! Just chill," Olivia said to Kiki, trying for the um-teenth time to calm her.

Kiki and Olivia were Rell's sisters. He and Kiki shared the same mother, while he and Liv had the same dad. Kiki and Liv were the same age, and both extremely short tempered. This trait, paired with their natural ability to whoop ass, gave the two girls the skills to terrorize damn near every broad that crossed their paths. The older they got, the more thirsty they got to show hoe's they still could thump with the best of them.

Kiki stood around 5'8" and weighed in around 90 to 100lbs. She had a tight petite frame and looked years younger than her true age of twenty-seven. Liv was a little taller. She stood about 5'10" and weighed around 130lbs. She wasn't as petite as Kiki, but damn close. Though she didn't look quite as young as Kiki, she also didn't look any where near her true age of twenty-seven either. No one would ever think that two cuties such as them, were trained to go. But they were.

The sisters and Steph had always been close. Steph's dad, Mr. Shives, owned the only boxing gym in Durham and made sure his only child learned how to box. As he taught her, he also trained Rell, Kiki, Live and Shawn. By the time they each had reached the age of twelve, they were fierce with the hands. Mr. Shives had taught them well.

"Alright, let's roll," Steph said, as she left a handwritten note for Ree-Ree, telling her where they would be.

***

After putting together a plan on how things would go down, Shawn and Alexi parted from the back of the truck to tell their comrade what was going down.

"Yo Rell, yes or no. I need to know if you would fuck Lorna if she was with it?"

As Shawn was filling in Rell, Alexi was informing Lorna that everything was on and popping.

"Cuz, stop playing. You know how we do," Rell answered.

"Well, you and Alexi gonna go to our spot and stash the Yay. Then it's on, fam!" Steph explained.

"Be easy cuz. I'm down and all, but I'd be a fool not to ask where all this came from. I mean, one minute you don't fuck around, then BAM! Now you do. What's really good, cuz? You got something you wanna tell me?" Rell's curiosity was beyond peeked and each point he listed was extremely valid. From where Rell stood shit sure smelled funny. Real funny. Shawn had to let him know all was good, without revealing his true motives.

"Yo, I'm gonna act like I didn't ever hear that. Cause I know you don't think I'll snake you. Bottom line, Lorna wants to fuck. She wants to wine and dine us, then get broke the fuck off. Now me, I been wanting to knock down Alexi, but ain't nothing popping unless you down. So what's up?" Shawn responded as Alexi crossed the lot and slid under his arm.

"We ready. Is something wrong?" Alexi asked, as she noticed the silence that surrounded her.

"Naw, Ma! Everything's good," Rell answered.

"Cool. Me and Shawn gonna follow y'all. Just tell Lorna how to get to the spot alright?" She gripped Shawns' hand and began walking towards the Camaro.

' *Damn! What's really going on? Am I slipping? Why do I feel like I'm out the loop?*' Rell thought, as he walked semi-consciously towards the Navigator.

"Rell... baby, you alright?" Lorna asked, as she crunk up the Navi.

"Yeah! Just a little shocked, I guess."

"Don't be papi! I played with you too long. Tonight, no more games. You want this pussy, papi!?!" she asked.

Knowing that many Puerto Rican chicks go crazy over aggressive men, Rell gently, but firmly grabbed the back of Lorna's head and pulled her close. As she attempted to object, he placed a hard, deep tonguing on the sexy Rilan.

'*Oh, shit!! Ain't no way!*' Lorna thought, while kissing Money and stroking the full length of his shaft through his Robin denims. When she finally reached the head, she couldn't help but grab for his dick extended damn near to his knee.

'Oh, yeah, papi. Tonights gonna be very interesting,' Lorna thought, as she broke away from the kiss and threw the Navi into gear.

Chapter Fifteen

"Hold up girl. Let me fill one of these out," Ree-Ree said as she stopped at a booth to fill out a participant information sheet.

"Girl, are you crazy!?!" Andrea mocked her.

"What? A trip for four to the Bahamas for free. How is that crazy?"

"That shit ain't nothing but a scam. You fill out that sheet today, next week you're the victim of identity theft. Trust me!" Andrea spat, pulling Ree-Ree from the booth. "The Bahamas ain't all that anyway," she added.

"When did you go?" Ree-Ree asked.

"It was one of my special perks. One of the many, at the time."

"Special perks? What you talking about?" Ree-Ree inquired.

"I was about nineteen and had been in the army for bout a year..."

Andrea began recounting the tale. After graduation, with no college option and no real ties to Norfolk, Virginia, Andrea enlisted in the armed forces. Looking for new challenges had been her initial reason for joining, but once enlisted, she found herself thrown into the biggest sexual cauldron she'd ever seen. Everybody was fucking everybody. For an establishment founded on loyalty and brotherhood, they sure had a weird way of upholding these principals.

During basic training, sex was not supposed to be going on

amongst the soldiers in training. Yet, Andrea had slept with four of the six drills Sargents and two of the seven presiding commissioned officers. During this time, while her platoon ate whatever the drill sergeants told them to eat, she ate delicious takeout damn near every night. When her platoon alternated between doing fire guard and head quarter radio watches, Andrea was licking pussy and fucking her way out of such remedial chores. She fucked for extra rest. She fucked for special privileges. She even fucked for rank. In the service she realied, if it could be obtained, it could be secured even faster through her pussy.

During this time, things were going well. She was fucking the supply sergeant, a captain, and a female Lt. Colonel. Life was good. Then BAM! She gets pregnant.

However, unlike the stories she'd heard told, she didn't vomit or feel nauseated. That's the only way the baby she carried made it to four months without her aborting it. Damn the army and their physical conditioning. Her body had been too toned for her to notice any discernable changes. So without any way to avoid the situation, Andrea found herself left with a million dollar question. Who was the father of this baby? As she began to show, which seemed almost like over night once she found out, the doors that once so forcely opend for her, were now closed or closing.

Enraged by the sudden turns of events, Andrea began subpoenaing every lover she'd laid down with. This step turned out to be her future undoing. She was brought up on charges, U.C.M.J. as the army would call it. This resulted in her being dishonorably discharged for conduct unbecoming of a soldier. *You got to be kidding.*

With only a month before her due date, she was forced by humility to seek shelter with her older sister Netta. From the moment she arrived at Netta's doorstep, she was treated with complete open arms. Netta loved her sister deeply and for more years than she could remember, had tried to get Andrea to come stay with her. For the first time in a long time, Andrea was clueless about how to handle the current developments taking shape in her life.

She was about to be a mother. Instead of worrying about diapers and Similac as most women in her position no doubt would, Andrea was more concerned with how to flip the situation to best fit her needs. The game had shot her a serious curve ball, but she was still going strong, and still very much in control.

A Whore's Conscience

***

"After tonight, this spot's dead to us," Rell stated as he loaded the last of the kilos into one of the XLR's sliding hard top compartments that had been hollowed out for this exact purpose.

The spot was a local car wash, nothing fancy. The two would come here and load up the shipment. While one would pretend to wash the hood of the Camaro, the other would load the convertibles hollowed panel. Tonight, however, the girls had blocked off the slot the guys had parked in. Completely shielding them from the road or any car that may happen to pass by.

"Hey Lexi! You see that?" Lorna asked.

"Yeah, that hollow panel shit is real tight."

"Naw, girl! I was talking about that El Dorado that just past," Lorna said, sounding a bit concerned.

"Was it the same one?" Alexi asked, securing her 9 milli.

"I think so," Lorna replied.

"You really think it's Raul and them?" Alexi asked, a little nervously.

"I don't know. But I do know ain't nothing gonna stop me from getting my freak on."

"So what's the plan?" Alexi asked.

"We gone swing back tot he hotel room and scoop up Chino and Vita. They'll hold us down while we get our fuck on," Lorna answered.

"Sorry about that. Y'all ready?" Rell asked, as he leaned into the window of the Navi.

"Yep! Alexi, fill Shawn in on what's going on. I got Rell," Lorna stated. Alexi nodded in compliance and hopped out the Navi to rejoin Shawn.

"Something come up?" Rell asked, as he hopped into the Navi.

"No, papi! Be easy. I just need to go by my hotel room to get something. Nothing major," Lorna calmed him as she threw the car into gear and pulled off.

***

Damn! Is that Sergio?' Andrea wondered, as she doubled back and swung into Nordstroms to clarify.

"What's up girl?" Ree-Ree asked.

"There was something I wanted to see in here. Come on, girl. It won't take long... I promise," Andrea swore as she locked eyes with

63

Sergio.

Quickly, and as subtlety as she could, she motioned for him to enter the dressing room in the far back. Gabbing everything she passed along the way to the dressing room that was in her size, Andrea wasted no time getting from point A to B. Before Ree-Ree could blink good she had an arm full of clothes to try on and was ducking into the dressing room.

VREEN! VREEN!

"Yeah!" Ree-Ree said, as she answered her phone sounding a bit annoyed.

"Hey, girl! It's me. You still at the mall?" asked Steph.

"Yeah! What's all that noise in the background? You at Pams?"

"Yep! Me and the girls gonna hang around here, and see what we can get into," Steph answered.

"Y'all still crashing at my place tonight, right?"

"Ain't shit changed. We just gonna come in a little later than first planned," she confirmed.

"Look, keep your phone on for me. When I get home, I'm gonna hit you up."

"What she done did now?"

"Nothing girl. We just gotta talk before I call Shawn, that's all."

"Alright. I'll talk to you then," said Steph right before she thumbed her screen, ending their call.

***

Meanwhile, back in the dressing room, Andrea was getting broke off real proper.

"Oh YEAH, Baby! Umm mmm!" Andrea moaned, as Sergio slid every inch of his dick into her. He had the biggest dick she had come across since her move to the Carolinas. Money was a better lover by far, but there was just something about his size alone that she couldn't get enough of.

"Umm… Oh yessss. Right there, baby." Andrea continued to quietly moan and groan as low as possible.

"Andrea! How much longer you gone be?" Ree-Ree asked as her sensation to pee grew stronger.

"Not long... ummm."

"Huh!! What you say?" Ree-Ree questioned, as a loud bumping sound came from inside the dressing room.

"Andrea, I'm gonna go to the restroom real quick. I'll be back."

A Whore's Conscience

"Ok!" Andrea replied before she bit her lip to keep from moaning out loud.

'Damn, he rocking my ass,' Andrea thought, as she tried to climb the wall with the pleasure she was receiving from him. Sergio was her older sister's ex-lover. Though Netta didn't know her little sister was fucking him, the fact alone would bring Andrea instant drama. But fuck it. Good dick was like a drug and for good dick, Andrea would cross her own mother.

Sergio was from up North and the idea of fucking her was one he first opposed, but grew to love. The two didn't meet much, mostly whenever he'd come through to see how things with Netta and their kids were. That's when he'd slide through and skin Andrea. While she was dropping off her daughter at Netta's yesterday, she had learned he would be in town all weekend. She took a chance at texting him earlier, while Ree-Ree ordered ice-cream. That chance had paid off.

Sergio had texted her back, agreeing to meet. She named the meeting spot, then kept herself busy until he arrived. Ree-Ree never had a clue. All these thoughts crossed through Andrea's mind as she had Sergio continued their exotic tango.

Tap!! Tap!! Tap!!

"Andrea, it's me. You still trying on clothes?" Ree-Ree asked, as she returned from the restroom. "Andrea?"

"Yeah!" Andrea, replied, after freeing Sergio's fingers from her mouth long enough to respond. "Just a few more seconds. I'm almost there," Andrea said, as Sergio long stroked her fiercely.

Moments later, Andrea was seeing little sparkling dots and the room was spinning the way it does when god sex has just taken place.

"Ree-Ree, you ready?" Andrea yelled out from inside the dressing room, as she continued to fix herself back up.

"Girl, I been ready!" Ree-Ree replied, sounding a bit annoyed.

"Text me tonight," Andrea whispered to Sergio, as she grabbed up the clothes she never tried on, and headed out the dressing room.

'Now if Rell trip about this pregnancy, I can always use this little event to my advantage,' Andrea thought, as she mentally plotted on how to place fatherhood on whomever was most convenient.

"Anything you like?"

"Nah let's go," Andrea answered as she flung the clothes over a nearby rack and guided Ree-Ree out of Nordstroms as fast as possible.

Chapter Sixteen

"What kind of dog's are those again?" Rell asked Lorna, as the four of them entered a Spanish themed restaurant the ladies had selected.

"Chino and Vita are Kitas. Them my babies. You sure y'all okay with this?" Lorna asked again.

"It don't matter. Food is food!" Shawn interjected.

"Hello, my name is Laura and your table is ready. Please follow me," said the hostess.

"That's true, Splash! But by tonight, we gonna be face deep in some Spanish cuisine anyway," Rell stated, as he licked his lips at Lorna who was beaming from ear to ear.

"The food was great. Although Rell wasn't sure what he was eating, it tasted wonderful. The ladies had a couple of drinks to get them open, while the guys headed out back to spark an 'L.' About midway through, Shawn put Money down on why the girls had went to scoop the dogs.

"So that's what's up?" Rell said, passing Shawn the blunt.

"Since I was tailing you and Lorna, you probably didn't peep, but I noticed someone following us."

"Cops?" asked Rell, as he scanned the lot.

"Naw. Lexi caught me peeping my tail and that's when I learned our tail might be some kid named Raul." Shawn passed the blunt back to Rell.

"So what, he some stick up kid or something?" Rell asked.

"Naw, not really. Alexi seems to think he wants to take over their business. She thinks he's on some scarface shit. You feel me?"

"When we get back to the cars, let's suit up. I can't risk getting caught up," said Rell as he nodded his head toward the approaching women.

"What? No tree's for us?" Alexi playfully commented, as she and Lorna slid under the arms of the guys.

"So what's next?" Rell asked, as he placed a kiss on Lornas' forehead.

"Me and Lexi been talking," Lorna said, as the four of them walked over towards their cars. "We think that it's only right that you know that we might have some trouble popping off tonight."

Shawn popped the trunk on the Camaro and slid out the way for Rell to bend over inside.

"I know. I heard," Rell said, motioning his head towards Shawn. "If any shit do pop off, we got your back. But this offer works both ways," he added, as he pulled out two Heckler's and loaded them.

"Damn, Papi!" Lorna stated, obviously liking how prepared the two brothers were.

"You think we should use the silencers?" Shawn asked, as he checked the clips of two 45's.

"That depends on where these ladies plan on taking us," Rell answered.

"If what I'm thinking is true, we gone need to go to a secluded wooded area. A place that Raul wouldn't suspect was a trap set for him," Lorna stated, as she kept her eyes on the movements of the parking lot.

"The back side of Ft. Benning, the training site. It worked for Carlos and them," Alexi suggested.

"Training site?" Rell questioned, as he pulled off his coat and slipped on his two gun shoulder holster.

"Yeah. It's a little used training site. Isolated. Very isolated. Gun play out there would go unnoticed easily. It's perfect. Just let us go grab some blankets and shit from the hotel, then we'll be set," said

Lorna as she and Rell hopped back into the Navi.

***

"Come on Raul! Let's just do this shit now, primo!" Roja, Raul's right hand man protested as the two watched the girls mingle with the guys standing next to the Camero.

"Tranquilo, primo! Tranquilo!" Raul replied, as he signaled for Roja to follow him back to the car.

"As soon as they slip, we gonna rock these bitches," Raul snapped, as he hopped into his whip and crunk it up.

Chapter Seventeen

"So what happened after you had Alana?" Ree-Ree asked Andrea as the two of them stood in the Pavilion's food court of the mall, waiting in line to order food from the Chic-fil-a.

"Revenge. I began looking for ways to hurt the mother fuckers who'd crossed me and had me discharged," Andrea replied.

"You mean, after all you've been through, the good and the bad, you still ain't learn?"

"Learn what? How to depend on a man? Oh, my bad. Maybe I should have learned how to kiss one's ass. Then maybe if I kiss it long enough and good enough, he may just loosen his leash on me a lil bit," Andrea spat out the overly sarcastic words.

"Are you serious? Is that really how you view men?"

"Am I serious!? Let me school you on something. Better yet, let me tell you a little story," Andrea spat irritated. She stepped close enough to kiss Ree-Ree and began to talk in a quiet voice.

"After having Alana, it took me about two months to get my shape back. By then, the money I had stacked while in the army was running low. I needed a job and fast. After being turned down by Arby's, one of the workers, a chick named FiFi, pulled me to the side. She schooled me on the type of money girls made stripping. I must have looked really desperate to her, because she didn't give me a chance to object. She just gave me the number to her cell and told me to call around eight that night.

After calling her and sharing some small talk, we both decided to meet up and go to this spot called *'Planet Beach.'* It was a club on this Navy base, not far from Norfolk State University. It was a Wednesday night and the place was packed like it was Super Bowl weekend or something. That's when Blaine walked over. He stood about 6'2" and weighed about 240lbs. All muscle. Blaine was a new age pimp, with a tongue that was smoother than whip cream. He had this face that puts you in the mind of Usher, but his physique was more like The Rock Dwayne Johnson.

"If I knew then, what I know now, I would have cut his balls off on the spot and gutted him like a pig," she spat before reverting back to her story. "FiFi told Blaine about my situation and before I could catch on to what was happening, I had been offered a deal from the devil himself. Before I left that night, Blaine threw me a wad of cash and told me it was an advance for tomorrow.

"What was happening tomorrow?" asked Andrea as she stared down at the wad of cash.

"Tomorrow you go to work. Come on, let's get something to drink," FiFi said and led Andrea away from Blaine, towards the bar in the corner.

"The next day I met FiFi and she drove me out to this house by the beach. The place was laced. I mean, really hooked up. When we got there some tiny Oriental chick showed us out to the balcony where Blaine was… I guess you could say hard at work."

"Have a seat ladies," Blaine said. He froze stiff, allowing me to fully take in what was going on.

Handcuffed to his own ankle's was the biggest country looking white boy I'd ever seen. Except for the cuffs he was stark naked. His body was bruised all over and his penis looked like it had been stomped viciously with metal cleats. But the worst sight of all was the white boys ass. Blaine was balls deep in the cracker and had a dildo just as large crammed into the same spot. Blood was leaking like water from the cracker's ass.

"Don't look like that baby. This is just business," Blaine said as he winked at Andrea and ripped the white guy's anus even wider.

"Business! What type of business is this?" Andrea asked, cringing at the sight of a new flow of blood.

"This, baby doll is what's called a 'CRACK' deal gone bad. Get it? CRACK!" Blaine answered, as he whipped out his dick and smacked the white guy's ass with it, leaving a blood stained impression of his dick on the cracker's ass in the process.

Andrea dawn near wanted to rape Blaine when she saw the size of his package. His dick was the biggest she'd ever seen and no matter what it took, she knew she was gonna get her some of that dick.

"I'm a new age pimp," Blaine said, as he walked the ladies into the house. When he closed the balcony door and faced them, the little Oriental chick fell to her knees. With the wet cloth in hand, she began to cleanse Blaine's dick. "He came up short with my money, one too many times," he said, as he eyed Andrea admiring his dick.

"So to get some of that dick a girl gotta fuck with your money?" Andrea asked.

"Naw, baby girl. You can get it... in due time. But first, let's discuss business." He wrapped himself in a beach towel and turned to her. "You ever stripped before?" he asked.

"No!"

"Think you can do it?" he asked.

"I guess."

"I had a girl move on to better things, leaving me with a spot open on my team. The thing is you'll be more of a pussy slinger than a stripper. That's if you're down?" he stated, looking Andrea over, seeking to read her thoughts.

"You want me to sell pussy? Are you serious? Look, I ain't nobodies trick," Andrea stated as she rose to leave.

"Here's the facts. Three days a week, five thousand a month, plus whatever you can make stripping. It's all yours. Unless you know somewhere you can do better?" Blaine asked. He gripped his dick and shook it playfully.

"Is he serious?" Andrea asked FiFi.

"As a heart attack," she replied as she hopped off the couch and knelt at Blaine's feet to suck his dick.

"Welcome to the family," Blaine said as he motioned for Andrea to sit on the couch next to him.

'Money, plus good dick. A bitch could get used to this,' Andrea thought, as Blaine stroked her pussy with two fingers.

After enjoying the longest quickie she'd ever experienced, the three got more in depth concerning the details of their business arrangements. Andrea discovered Blaine was a bi-sexual pimp with his hands in everything worth while. From strip clubs, massage parlors,and gun running. To top it all off, he even owned 35% of all drugs flowing through the Virginia and West Virginia borders. The homo-thug was raping the game.

For the next two years Andrea did whoever and whatever Blaine told her to do. Before she knew it, she became very close to him. Even though he had a way of crippling peoples built up defenses, he had never been that way with her. Finally, she had found peace. A peace gained not out of love, but out of respect.

"Whatever he promised always came to be. And as long as my duties were upheld, he ensured that my every need was constantly met. Then out of the blue he started booking me to do jobs with people who were employed by the government and military. Some of these men and women were from the same branch I had once served. Others were the Navy, Marines and the Air Force."

"But these men I service weren't mere lower level grunts. These service men held rank. They were real big boys. I'm talking about two star Generals, Colenels, Admirals, and so forth."

"From day one I knew these weren't viewed as just paying Johns to Blaine. Occasionally, he would have me entertain congressmen, commerce members or local government officials at his beach condo near his home. The place was expensively decorated, but also very hi-tech."

"Blaine had explained to me the importance of why I should do certain sexual favors at certain angles when I did business at this particular local. The condo was outfitted with mics and cameras. Any person serviced here would immediately afterwards find themselves indebted to Blaine. It was blackmail, plain and simple. Even with all this known, I still couldn't figure out why he was entrapping so many high ranking military personnel. It wasn't until my last trick that I found out why he was suddenly so interested in the armed services."

"It was about ten or so that night when I hit the spot. My instincts were going nuts that night. Something in the pit of my stomach said something wasn't right about this job. However, being that it was my twelfth and last trick of the month, I overlooked my anxieties and went inside to handle my business."

"The entire condo was pitch black and as far as I could see, no one appeared to be there. I knew someone had to be here. Blaine always let the clients arrive first. This way they could set the mood for whatever he or she had in mind. Not to mention, someone was playing what sounded like animal noises from some type of forest. The place was creeping me the hell out."

Andrea recounted the beginning of that night, as her eyes tightened and she drifted back to the moment. Not being too fond of the darkness, she made her way in the direction of the nearest known light source. In mid stride, someone had pulled her feet right from under her. She caught herself enough to take the real sting of the impact of the fall. No sooner had she hit the floor, the sounds of feet moving frantically, and purposely, caught her attention. Her army training kicked in instinctively.

Andrea crouched low next to the back of the living room chair and slid her butterfly knife out from her handbag. Whoever was in here had chosen the wrong way to say hello and she wasn't going to stand idly by doing nothing while some military nut got off from stalking her in the dark. Minutes passed, and Andrea had stayed crouched in her same spot motionless. Growing impatient with the cat and mouse game, she rose to go back towards the front door. As soon as she stood, something stung her in the arm. Moments later, the already dark room got darker. Andrea had been drugged.

Chapter Eighteen

After grabbing a few comforter's and towels from their hotel room, Lorna made a pit stop at a convenient store to get the last and missing elements to the scheme she and the other three were brewing. Raul, or whoever it was that was tailing them, was still trying to discretely keep tags on them. As they turned off the main road and onto government property, their pursuers dared not to follow.

'Good! They kept straight,' Lorna thought as she increased her speed and quickly turned up into a wooded path.

"Is this the place?" Rell asked, as Lorna continued navigating her Navi through the poorly lit terrain.

"Almost! Just a little ways beyond that building up ahead."

Minutes later, the cars were parked, and the four of them were grabbing various items to carry to the flat sandy open area with a cluster of trees and bushes just near enough for cover if needed. Lorna had placed the dog Chino to the North, and Vita to the South of where they would be. The Akita's were professionally trained killers that responded to her Spanish commands without waver. To view the dogs as they now sat, one would think they were life like statues. That's how silent and still the two canines were as they guarded their master and her friends.

"Come on Rell, help me warm up papi!" Lorna said as she

motioned him to join her on the cloth palette she'd made for them.

"You awfully calm for a lady with a crazed stalker on her ass!" Rell said with a smirk, as he knelt at her feet at the foot of the palette.

"If you knew just how dangerous Chino and Vita are, you'd be relaxed too!" Alexi said, from the palette to the right of the one Rell and Lorna were on.

"But are they bullet proof?" Rell asked in a tone that killed all previous humor and put the subject back in its proper prospective.

"They don't have to be…" Lorna cut in. "My babies are here to draw first blood. If they die in the process, fuck it. It's what I got them for."

"If anyone comes, they will make sure we know," Alexi added as she pulled the cover over her and Shawn and thus showed Rell how certain she really was in the dog's abilities.

"We can just cuddle for now if that will make you feel better," Lorna stated, sliding under Rell's right arm next to the holstered .45 he still wore.

"I'm not trying to be noid. It's just… you don't understand," Rell ranted.

"I do. More than you know. I'm in charge of everything just like you. I can't ever be caught slipping. Nor can I let Alexi or my other workers slip beyond reason. Now someone wants to play hide-N-seek with us. They're threatening to pose a problem for us with their stalking ass behavior. But, you must have forgotten, I run shit down here, like you run shit back home. So relax papi. Let my babies do what they do. If something pops off, then we pop back. You feel me?" Lorna asked, as she slowly parted her legs angling them towards Rell. She eased her hand between her thighs and began to open and close her pussy lips, hoping to encourage Rell to let go.

***

Ree-Ree sat staring at Andrea waiting to hear what happened after she blacked out.

"So you passed out? What happened when you woke up?"

"Up and down my body was moving, but without me making it do so. Then something turned my face, causing me to open my eyes," Andrea stated as she told Ree-Ree about the first recollections she had once the drug initially began to wear off.

She knew her body was moving, not because she could feel it move though. Only because she could see herself rise up, then back down. Someone was below her. She knew this only because the person was forcing her head to stay at a weird angle. They were treating her head and neck the same way a puppeteer does his dummies. Some time passed, then came a grunt as someone's breath blew hot against her cheek. Her puppet master steered her head forward and that's when she saw that he wore camouflage paint all over his face. His eyes were wide and crazy looking and he kept ranting about not leaving well enough alone.

Out of nowhere someone came and crammed their penis between her lips, abusing her mouth with the force of their strokes. Yet, through all of this, she felt no pain. She wasn't dreaming. She was really awake. Her entire body, from the neck down, was completely limp. She was numb of all feeling. Helpless. She was unable to resist in any way. No matter how hard she commanded her body to move, it wouldn't. With each passing second, Andrea's fears increased.

"I remember asking myself if I was gonna die? Were they gone kill me? Why does he keep saying I should've left well enough alone? I thought this frantically as my attackers continued their sexual assault on me."

"This continued on for what seemed like forever. Each of the three camouflaged men would continuously rotate from my ass, mouth and pussy, having their way with me. Occasionally, they would take water or snack breaks, then resume their assault. Then, without warning, came the pain. My entire body was begging for some form of relief. Next, my voice came back, but all I could muster out were barely audible screams."

"It's about fucking time. Now we can really let this bitch feel it," said the camouflaged man with the crazy eye's.

And feel it she did. These guy's not only continued their sexual assault, but they also pinched, bit, gripped, yanked, pulled, smacked, elbowed, head butted, kneed and kicked her. They were enjoying the agony the torture caused her. The pain was threatening to render her unconscious. Between bouts of consciousness, the beatings, and beast fucking she was enduring, she found out two things. First she learned that her marathon sexual assault was courtesy of Viagra. Secondly, she had been sacrificed to these mutha fuckers by Blaine in exchange for certain military equipment. Her loyalty to him had been rewarded by treachery. Blaine was the proverbial straw that broke Andrea's back.

A Whore's Conscience

'If I ever got out of this room alive, shit gone be very different,' Andrea swore, as the pain fussed with hollowing spiritual sorrow, overwhelmed her senses, causing her to completely black-out.

"What happened? How'd you get away?" Ree-Ree asked.

"Honestly, I don't know. When I finally woke up I had tube's and a bunch of weird gadgets hooked up to me. I woke up in a hospital almost six months later and I was told I'd been in a coma," Andrea answered as she bit into her fry. She dipped the remainder into a glob of ketchup.

"A coma!?! Uh-uh girl!"

"Yep!" Andrea answered, pushing away her food.

"So, whatever happened to Blaine? Did you turn him in?"

"Nope! I didn't have to. Apparently one of the service men didn't take too well to being blackmailed. His ass got popped," Andrea stated as she emotionlessly recounted the events of her ordeal's after effects.

"How do you know it was one of the servicemen who killed him?"

"Because one day during my first week of rehab I got this lovely bouquet of flowers with a tiny sealed envelope attached. Inside it read:

Don't be like Blaine. Leave well enough alone.

Andrea sipped her Cola and gave Ree-Ree a look that was void of any emotion.

"And that was that."

Chapter Nineteen

"Oh fuck!!"

"Oh.. Ahhhh shit!"

It was like a moaning competition was taking place out in the middle of the woods. The louder Lorna got, the louder Alexi got. The more Lorna moaned, the more Alexi moaned. Rell and Shawn had been licking pussy for about twenty minutes and the yelling exhibition had been going on since the first lick.

Lorna had Rell's arms and back pent to the ground by her knee's as she straddled his face and fucked his mouth. Alexi had Shawn's face pulled damn near into her pussy as she rotated her coochie in tight slow circles against his tongue. On her back, with her legs wrapped tightly around his neck, she had him locked in. She allowed him just enough air to breath.

The girls were putting on Oscar worthy performances, making it appear as if they were completely caught up in the pleasure of the moment. But actually the girl's were baiting their pursuer's with their over the top erotic moans. Lorna never lost sight of Chino, and Alexi kept her eyes on Vita. Both dogs sat perfectly still. The moment they moved would be the sign the ladies needed to see to know their trap had been set.

Slowly treading through the empty training site, Raul and his men found it harder than they thought to locate the girls. Just as they'd begun to second guess their current course, the first faint sounds of the ladies moaning reached their ears.

"Miguel, Victor, Roman... go around that way. Roja, come with me. We gonna cover the rear." Raul spit out his orders as he signaled his henchmen to approach the girls from the right.

Miguel, Victor and Ramon each carried AK-47's with extended clips, as they crept close to the sounds of sex.

It seemed like only a split second, but Lorna nor Alexi, could explain how each of them had momentarily lost focus, allowing both guard dogs to take off in pursuit of whatever had peaked their curiosity. Both women spun from their lovers face's and grabbed their 9 milli's.

"Where they at?" Shawn asked, as he rolled off his back and simultaneously pulled his left holster's latch and drew the .45 from its sleeve.

"Alexi, Shawn... lay back down. Keep there focus. We got this," Lorna said, motioning for Rell to follow her.

Alexi and Shawn used each others bodies to conceal their drawn weapons, then proceeded to re-sale the image of sexual contentment. Vita had found, and now was stalking the three intruders she had located. Her sense of smell told her Chino wasn't far and if her nose was right, Chino had two intruder's of his own to handle. Neither of the three intruder's Vita tailed knew what hit them until it was too late.

Vita lunged forward swiftly and precisely gripped the crotch of the intruder in the middle of the pack. The dog's teeth locked around a majority of Miguel's balls sending pain to every inch of the man's body. Vita, pulled and ripped with all her might as Miguel screamed in pain.

"Aww... Ooohhh... Ooohhh shitttt!!" Miguel cried out, as he unintentionally let a number of rounds spray out of his AK. Four of the rounds found homes in Romans' chest, sending him to the ground in a howling mass of flesh. Victor jumped behind a tree for cover from Miguel's sporadic shooting occasionally peeping to see the direction Migel's AK was pointing.

Vita no longer ripped at the man's crotch, but was now clamping down on his neck. The moment he hit the ground, Vita switched her attack from injure to kill, and locked her teeth around the neck and windpipe of Miguel. With jaws that lock almost as tightly as a Pit, Miguel's death was imminent.

Hearing the first shots fired over from where Miguel and his crew should be sent Raul and Roja rushing to rejoin them. Three or four steps into their sprint Raul fell, and when he did, Chino jumped dead into his ass. He dogs teeth locked onto the upper bicep of Raul's gun hand, causing him to drop his Mac-11.

"Agh!! Roja!! Get this muthafucking dog off me!!" Raul screamed as Chino tore deeper into his arm.

As Roja turned and aimed his Mac-10 at the humungous dog, he let loose a few rounds. He was thrown on his ass forever as a sudden force tore through his chest. It left him with two holes the size of golf balls that robbed him of his essence before his brain could even register he'd been shot.

Chino lay on his side simpering in pain. The dog took two in the hind legs on his right side and was losing blood fast. Raul, though in pain, sensed the urgency of the situation and was crawling frantically towards his dropped Mac-11. Before any serious headway was made, a pair of shapely legs stepped in between him and his gun. It didn't take Raul long to realize whose legs stood between him and his possible salvation. Before he could shift his body to attempt to face his foe, Lorna emptied the clip into the head of Raul.

"The gun's empty," Rell stated, as he took the 9 milli from Lorna, who was quickly regaining her senses. She turned and faced Rell realizing they were both alright.

"How's Chino?" Lorna asked, as she and Rell headed over to where the dog lay.

BOOM!! BOOM!!

The two gunshots came from the location near the camp spot.

"Can you handle this?" Rell asked Lorna as he handed her his spare .45 and dipped behind a bush, pulling her alongside him. "Shh... someone's coming," he whispered.

He saw the moonlight reflect off the white fur of Vita who was followed closely by Shawn and Lexi.

"Damn, it's good to see you fam!" Rell said as he swung from behind the tree and dapped Shawn.

"Everything good?" Shawn asked while looking Rell and Lorna over from head to toe.

"Yeah! And you?" Rell questioned.

"I think we got them all," Shawn replied.

"Alexi, can you take care of Chino? Me and Rell gone go load up the stuff from the camp. We'll meet you back at the cars, alright?" Lorna said as she pulled Rell along.

"I got him," Alexi responded.

"How you wanna do this?" Shawn asked as he knelt by the dog's rear looking for a way to harmlessly pick him up.

"Pop!! Pop!!"

"That won't be necessary," Alexi stated as she shot Chino in the dome twice, putting the dog out of its misery. "Let's go papi," she added as she dashed back towards the area of the camp to rejoin the others.

Chapter Twenty

Ree-Ree and Andrea were making their way through the front door of her and Splash's town home after spending the entire day at the mall.

"Girl, my feet is killing me," Ree-Ree stated as she kicked off her U-neak heels and checked her home phone for voicemail.

"Mine too! Hey, you got a note from... Oh, Steph," Andrea said in a repulsed, mocking way. Just because she was trifling didn't rob Andrea of her woman's intuition. She could tell when a bitch was up to no good and each time she and Steph met, the vibe only got worse. Steph wanted Rell and the fucked up part of it was that Andrea was certain that the hoe knew she knew. Andrea wasn't letting go of her sweet thing without a fight.

"Looks like they done switched plans for tonight. I guess I'll go start the Jacuzzi while you go upstairs and grab a bikini," Ree-Ree said as she crumpled the message from Steph and tossed it in the trash.

"Naw, girl. I'm good," Andrea objected.

"Uh uh! You got to finish telling me what happened when you got out of rehab. How you gonna start telling me a story then try to leave me hanging. Fuck that. Go upstairs, get a bikini, and hop your scandalous ass in the hot tub with me. I'm giving you five minutes, then I'm coming to get your ass myself," Ree-Ree said, as she pushed Andrea out her front door to hurry her along.

"Bitch, you tripping!"

"Oh, you think so? In five minutes someone gonna be proven wrong," Ree-Ree responded, as she smirked devilishly and shut the door in Andrea's face.

'Fuck it!' thought Andrea. *'A little more girl time won't hurt,'* she reasoned, as she pulled out her cell and began to text Skinno.

***

After clearing the camp site of all traceable evidence, Rell convinced Lorna and Alexi to join him and Shawn back at their suite's to wrap things up properly.

"I still can't believe you did that shit," Rell stated watching Lorna move around the room. He sat on the edge of the bed, kicking off his chestnut colored Tims.

"What? Oh, you mean Raul and them." She lit another of the many candles scattered around the suite.

"That was some real live made for the movies shit," Rell recounted the events with a hint of awe and slight exuberance.

"I gotta let these puto's know, so I left that as a message," Lorna said, striking another match to light yet another candle.

"You poured lighter fluid, eight bottles mind you, over five dead bodies, then set them on fire."

"Yep," she replied, through a devilish grin.

"So what exactly is the message?"

"Your funeral is closed casket style if you fuck with LA Perla!" she answered as she pushed Rell back on the bed and straddled his waist.

"You sure you wanna do this?" Rell asked, knowing the answer before the question was even asked.

"You only live once, papi. Understand?"

Before he could answer, Lorna was licking and sucking on his neck. Her hands massaged his chest and arms, loving the strength she felt under her fingers.

'Damn, that feels good!' Rell thought, as he fought to keep his body from jerking uncontrollably from the pleasure her mouth and hands were administering.

***

"Mmm… Oh, yeah!" Andrea moaned.

83

"Un-uh! I know you ain't moaning?" Ree-Ree said toyingly, as she and Andrea lay beneath the pulsating water sprays of the Jacuzzi, soothing their bodies from the neck down.

"I ain't gone front, girl. This shit got a girl fucked up," Andrea stated, opening her eyes just slightly enough to prove to Ree-Ree she wasn't asleep.

"Me too. Now enough small talk. What happened after you finished rehab?"

"Damn! To hell with being subtle, huh?!" said Andrea, through a half smile.

"Fuck the games. I'm trying to see what's up."

"Well, I spent a lot of time watching movies and stuff. I had a real nice nest egg saved up from my dealings with Blaine, so working wasn't a priority. Everything was going well for me for the most part, except when I went anywhere outside like malls, fast food joints, salons and what not."

"Where was your family during this time?"

"Doing what they always did. My dad was drinking and screwing everything that wasn't tied down. My mom was getting her ass kicked all over the house, street, or any public place my dad dared to beat her at. We never got along. We just managed somehow to co-exist. As for my brother, he started smoking crack. So basically, outside of Netta, I had no one."

"What about Alana, your daughter?"

"Umph! Her too!" Andrea said with a depressed tone.

After months of looking over her shoulder whenever she went out, Andrea decided it was best to pack up and move someplace where few people would know her name. She found out about North Carolina when she was stripping for Blaine. She and a few other of his girls moonlighted at a Club Called '14K' in Durham a few times. The club was a hole in the wall, but the cash was good, and the city was always popping. So with plenty of cash, and a scheme planned, she packed up her and her daughter's belonging's and moved to Durham to find herself a country baller.

"So that's all Rell is to you, huh? Just a meal ticket?" Ree-Ree asked, with an unmasked edge.

"Girl stop tripping. He's more than just a meal ticket. He's good dick too," Andrea replied jokingly, still playing the subject as lightly as possible.

A Whore's Conscience

"Andrea, can you quit playing around and get serious, just once."

"Niggas ain't worth the effort," Andrea responded, rising up when she noticed the change in the mood inside the Jacuzzi.

"So there's no way you'll ever do right by Rell? Is that what you saying?" Ree-Ree asked, seeking to keep a remnant of control over her erupting emotions.

"Are you serious?!"

"Does it look like I'm playing. Rell is a good brother. He doesn't deserve the shit you pulling on him. What you need to do is move on and let someone who gonna hold him down get with him, before you fuck him up for all women!" Ree-Ree blacked, knowing that there was no way Andrea could honor or do right by Rell.

"Maybe I should let Steph have him. Is that it? That's what you wanna hear?"

"Maybe you should. Lord knows Rell deserve's better," Ree-Ree retorted, snappishly.

"Bitch, are you slow, or just plain dumb. What the fuck I been doing all weekend, wasting my breath? Don't you get it? You gotta get these motherfuckers before they get you? You think Rell and Shawn ain't fucking around? Bitch you dumber than you look if you believe that."

"You ungrateful, bitter little bitch. You skeezing over what you think a guy gone do?! That's dumb! How can you live your life mad at all the wrong people and being too ignorant to know who you should be mad at. Then you have the audacity to call someone dumb!" Ree-Ree blacked out before being interrupted.

"Bitch you 'ARE' dumb. Dick dumb, to keep it gangsta. You think Rell's some fucking knight in shinning armor. Some prince charming with the house and picket fence, right?! Hoe, you ain't dumb. Nah, you plum retarded," Andrea snapped, pissed all the way off.

"Hoe? Bitch you got some nerve," Ree-Ree yelled, trying to get out the Jacuzzi and away from Andrea, who was fast on her heels and refusing to let the topic die.

"Look at you. What you gonna do, huh? You gonna tell Rell? You gonna go tell Shawn? Shit! Bitch, unless you want that ass kicked," Andrea said as she walked up on Ree-Ree threateningly. "You better act like you know."

"BAP!! BAP!!"

Ree-Ree caught Andrea with a two piece that sent her stumbling back. Before she could respond to the attack, Ree-Ree jumped dead into Andrea's grill, catching her with a series of slaps. Ree-Ree was doing good for someone who really couldn't fight. Give her a knife, and a bitch was in trouble. But going toe-to-toe, fist-to-fist, was never her thang. She had always thought herself too fine to be getting her face cut or bruised.

Maybe her own amazement at how well she was scrapping got the best of her. Maybe Andrea read her thoughts. Or maybe Andrea just caught her second wind because one moment Ree-Ree was doing her damn thang, and the next she was being tossed. When she finally landed, she was sprawled inside the Jacuzzi. Her head had hit the shoulder of the Jacuzzi causing the room to spin.

"Bitch! You put your hands on me?" Andrea raged, as she rained blow upon blow down onto the left side of Ree-Ree's face. "Next time you bring it hoe, bring it right. Oh, and this ain't shit compared to how it'll be if you even think of telling my business." Andrea spat in Ree-Ree's face, then rose and headed back into the main part of the townhome to leave.

When the echoes of the front door being slammed reached Ree-Ree, she allowed her sprawled body to go limp. The left side of her face felt like she had been smacked by a hornets nest. The throbbing was her first clue that she was messed up pretty good. That, plus the fact every time she tried to climb out the Jacuzzi, her body flat out refused.

'Calm down girl. Just relax. Lay still and compose yourself,' Ree-Ree silently told herself, as she shut her eye's and quickly drifted off into unconsciousness.

Chapter Twenty One

Back in Georgia, Rell and Shawn were putting in work fucking the shit out of the two Spanish chicks. Round one consisted of thirty to forty-five minutes of straight animalistic, down right primitive fucking. Each of the four had allowed the adverse events of the night to create an unspoken understanding amongst one another. Common ground, so to speak. No sooner than the door to Rell and Shawn's suite had closed, the four of them attacked each other, seeking to obtain relief from the sexual tension created at the camp site.

Fuck the small talk. Fuck the formalities that usually accompany first time fucks. This was four adults, allowing themselves to enjoy consensual sex without the drama of 'what happens next.' The shattered barrier's left them completely exposed to their lovers. But for one in particular, the destruction of these barrier's left them vulnerable. Too vulnerable.

As the four caught their breath, they mingled around the suite's kitchenette, buck-ass-naked, drinking every cold drink they could put their hands on. After regaining some sense of control over her breathing, Lorna pulled Alexi out of listening range of the guys.

"You about ready?" Lorna asked, as she led Alexi over to the couch and sat alongside her.

"Sorry girl, but my legs are still shaking. I came three times off what he calls his bullshit dick. Anyway, how was... Lorna what's wrong?" Alexi asked, as she finally came out of her dick trance long enough to see Lorna was wearing the strangest look on her face.

"Nothing."

"Bullshit, Mami! What he do?" Alexi asked, sliding over closer to her girl as a means of comfort.

"Alexi, chill. He did nothing. I'm just... We gotta go."

Alexi was confused at Lorna's choice of words and the tone in which she spoke to them. It clearly indicated something was wrong with her. But she was clueless to the source of her discomfort. Before Alexi could put more thought into the matter, both guys walked over, dicks swinging. The sight alone of what Shawn had dangling between his legs was more than enough to distract any woman. But Alexi's mind was blown when she saw the size of the salami Rell was swinging.

'Dawn! Now I know why my girl was ready to go,' Alexi thought, as she pulled Lorna close so she could whisper into her ear.

"Look, we can switch if Rell's too big for you. Shawn or Rell don't matter to me. I'm just trying to get my fuck on."

"Say what?!" Lorna asked in a terse and shocked tone, sharply leaning away from Alexi and looking angrily into her homegirl's eye's.

Lorna and Alexi had been rolling together since they had been in diapers. They ran train's on guys and even shared dick to get where they need to go in the game. Alexi was the chulita y bonita. The poster child for Latino lust. While Lorna was regarded as bolutuosa. Which was how you referred to a nice looking, voluptuous woman in Spanish. Lorna had full double-D ta-ta's. Her nipples, when erect, looked like chocolate Bon-Bon's. Her stomach was surprisingly flat for her 5'9" 180lb frame.

Lorna had hips and thighs for days and an ass that would put Kim Kardashian to shame. Her face was the roundaway, girl-next-door type of beautiful. With dark brown almond eyes's, thick lips, and a sun kissed milk copper complexion, Lorna was supremely seductive. Not the conventional or perfect seductiveness that Alexi was. But more of the unconventional Amazon, J-LO type of seductive. Her best asset was her complete lack of vanity and because of this doubt regarding her own beauty, Lorna sat next to her girl on the couch desperately wishing she could vanish into the nearest crevice.

'Why am I tripping?' Lorna thought, as she recalled the suggestion her girl had just made and her rection to it. Nothing bad was intended by Lexi's offer to switch partners. Lorna had never allowed a man bigger than 8 inches to fully penetrate her coochie. She would only allow one big dick to fully claim her and he would be her husband. Yet, she saw how long Rell was and hadn't resisted when he'd entered her fully. The feelings she'd received from the sensations his dick gave were beyond the realm of definition.

When reality kicked back in, she wanted to escape the look Rell would give her once his lust was satisfied and his eyes located what she perceived as imperfections. Except Rell hadn't given her a chance to repel him. Instead he locked his arms around her from the rear and tenderly kissed the back of her ear and neck. For the first time ever in her life, sex had touched her on a level that surpassed the merely physical. Lorna needed time to pull her thoughts together. Make sense of what had just been sprung upon her.

'I'm tripping. Damn, I'm tripping!' Lorna thought as she allowed the anger in her eyes to subside for Alexi.

"Why you spazzing? What's wrong?" Alexi asked Lorna, interrupting her girl's thoughts as the guys, now replenished, were nearing the couch ready for round two.

"Nothing! I just..." Lorna's answer was cut short, when Rell's hand tilted her head, allowing his mouth room to tenderly kiss her neck. His other hand gently teased her aching, aroused nipples.

The scene displayed before Alexi was explaining the look's and tension her homegirl was feeling. Lexi realized that for the first time in her life, she was watching Lorna become completely helpless to the touch and charms of a man. *'Damn! My girl done finally met her match,'* Lexi thought, as Shawn led her off the couch and onto the floor.

"I Can't wait to make you cum again," Rell said to Lorna, as he cupped her face in both of his hands. He kissed her full in the mouth. His next move stole Lorna's breath, when he swiftly scooped her into his arms and carried her effortlessly into the adjacent bedroom.

Once he reached the bed, instead of lowering her instantly, he stood there holding her like a baby. He was tonguing her like there was no tomorrow. After what seemed like forever, Rell slowly lowered Lorna to the bed and smoothly slid between her thighs, allowing his throbbing erection to graze against her moist vagina. He held himself above her looking deeply into her eyes.

"I'm sorry," Rell said, his words shattering the silence.

"For what?"

"For making you bleed," he responded, turning his face away from her in shame.

"Bleed? I was bleeding?" Lorna asked, reaching to check herself to see if she was having an unscheduled menstruation.

"Relax. I think I tore something up in... you know," he said, still looking guilty.

"Well, I'm not bleeding now, so it can't be torn too bad," she said, as she began to caress the head of his semi-hard penis.

"You still want to do this?" he asked, as she caresses coaxed a low moan from the back of his throat.

"Yes. Unless... Unless you want to stop." She released his dick and turned to face the rays of moonlight that illuminated the bedroom.

"Hell No!!" he answered, turning her face to meet his once again.

"Truth be told, I don't want this night to end."

"Really," Lorna asked, not trying to mask her hopes for his approval.

"Are you serious?! Your pussy stupid tight. A man like me could fuck around and get sprung off this shit," he answered, as he took his now fully erect dick and rubbed her clit gingerly.

Lorna reached up and pulled his mouth to her's and the two began to deeply tongue each other.

"Oh shit!" Shawn's scream boomed through the bedroom door from the living room, causing Rell and Lorna to break their kiss and burst into laughter.

"Damn! What she doing to my fam?" Rell asked, lightheartedly.

"I don't know," Lorna answered, spreading her legs as wide as she could, then took her hands and dug her nails into his back, as she bit down on one of his nipples.

"Augh! Uhhh!" Rell moaned, as the head of his dick was nudged inch by inch into Lorna's tight pussy. While they began to re-ignite their passion, Shawn was still screaming like a scalded cat.

In the living room, Shawn's back was pent up against the cushioned legs of the couch with his legs side by side and extended straight in front of him. He had agreed to refrain from using his hands or arms in any way unless Alexi told him to. Now he was paying the price for his promise.

Alexi stood with her back facing him, butt naked, straddling his legs. She then lowered, slowly into a full split, letting her pussy hover above his knee's. Shawn swore her pussy lips were talking to him as he watched her, from this position, slide her camel toe closer to his engorged dick. Once her pussy rested snugly against the base of his shaft, Alexi took her hands and gripped each of his ankles.

Slowly, and masterfully, she rose her coochie all the way up the length of Shawn's manhood and upon reaching the head of his dick, she entrapped it within her pussy. Alexi locked her cunt muscles around the head and began to jerk his dick off, using only her pussy. This was enough to make Shawn toes begin to separate and twitch.

Seeing how open she was making him, she lowered her head upon her hands that still lay wrapped around his ankles. She then released her pussy's grip on the head of his dick and begin to glide slowly down, stopping halfway. Now the toes on his left foot were curling and his right foot stayed twitching. Alexi kept her focus and kept tightening her coochie as she slid up his dick, releasing her muscles momentarily, then gliding back down halfway. Her pussy continued to grip and tighten around his dick like a wet fist.

Alexi swayed and rocked her hips, and gyrated her ass while continuing to flex and relax her coochie muscles during the entire experience. Then just as planned, it happened. Her pussy became too slick to maintain a good grip on Shawn's dick. Now she went all the way to the head, then dropped all the way down to his balls. Instantly, she rose halfway off his length, slamming back down once again. This is what caused Shawn to moan out loudly.

As Alexi rose, she would tighten her coochie as tight as she could, then drop down to his balls, milking Shawn for all he was worth. His toe's were now pointed to his chest and spread wide. Throwing herself off his ankles, Alexi leaned all the way back, until her back was resting on his chest. Every inch of his dick was now buried deep inside her.

"Fuck this!" Shawn blurted out. He spun off the floor and pent Alexi's chest to the seat of the couch with his left hand, his right hand pushed her face into the corner crevice of the couch. He managed to move into this new position while remaining buried deep inside her cunt.

"Shawn! Uh! Uh, no… Ahhhh… Oh!" she yelled as Shawn

began to break her ass off real proper.

"Now this! This that good country dick. Straight from the HEAT OF DURHAM. Straight pussy splitting, that's what we do!" Shawn stated as he laid pipe like his life depended on it. Alexi couldn't hold back. Shawn wasn't fucking her pussy. He was stroking her soul and the shit was absolutely mind blowing.

As Shawn turned the table on Alexi, Rell was just starting to set his. Lorna was still biting on his nipples and her nails were still digging into his back. He was ready to lay some long, smooth dick. He desired a chance to enjoy some of the best pussy he'd had in over two years. Since... *Damn. Since Steph,'* Rell thought, as he forced her name and image out of his mind.

But instead of giving Lorna an intense, slow, steady paced fuck, he stayed resting on his knee's hovering above her, trying to get her to concede from her longing to be beast fucked.

"Fuck me!!" Lorna said, through clenched teeth, which painfully continued to pinch down into Rell's nipple. "Fuck   me,   now!!" Lorna softly demanded.

"Fuck this," Rell said, pulling the head of his dick out of her pussy and quickly rolled off the top of her.

"What's wrong? Why you tripping?" Lorna asked, knowing damn well she was the one responsible for the scene flipping.

"Look Ma. There's a time and place for everything and right now I wanna freak you, and turn your ass out. But you want a brother to be on some gorilla shit," Rell replied causing Lorna to chuckle.

"I'm sorry, papi. It's just... I just..." Lorna fumbled to find the words to tell Rell that she was terrified about the emotions he was creating inside her. She knew that beast fucking him would make it hard for her to become emotionally absorbed. She could dismiss the encounter as nothing more than two adults fulfilling their most carnal need. But to allow him to create intimacy and allow him to penetrate the depths of her soul was a request she wasn't quite sure she was capable of handling.

As she lay beside him searching for words to finish her rambling sentence, Rell had laid on his side and stealthily went to work on her clit with his fingers. Before she could remove his hand, he had her clit firmly gripped between his thumb and index fingers. Gently he began to rotate his fingers around her clit. She let out a low sigh and

Rell slid back between her legs. This time he palmed the back of her head with his right hand, allowing his right forearm to hold his weight as he hovered inches from her face. His left hand was now slipping into Lorna's soaked cunt. The first three fingers sought and found her G-spot.

"Fuuuuuck!!" Lorna moaned.

Her words were perceived by Rell as an indicator that he had found the ladies sweet spot. He was partially right. At the moment of her initial moan, her words did far more than indicate what she was feeling. They described her future emotional state.

I'm fucked!' Lorna thought as Rell's fingers sent her eye's rolling to the back of her head.

As the first current of an amazing orgasm overtook her, Rell allowed Lorna's body to tell him when to remove his hand. When her legs closed tightly and she turned slightly on her side, he caught the signs and pulled out his fingers. He gave her a few moments to gather herself, then slid his palms under her shapely butt and held each cheek lightly.

Lowering his face to the opening of her vagina, Rell fully extended his tongue and licked the tips of her pussy lips. Turning and twisting his tongue into a 'U' shape, he inserted it as deeply into her coochie as possible. The feeling of his tongue slipping into her caused Lorna's thighs to twitch. When he began to suck her cream from her pussy using his tongue as an erotic straw, every muscle in Lorna's lower body locked up.

"D-D-Damnnn!! Oh. Ooooh!!" Lorna moaned, as he sucked the juices from her orgasm, which in turn created another.

Rell sucked her pussy until he'd swallowed every last drop of her cream. Lorna lay flat on her back, chest heaving, heart thumping with a head that was spinning wildly. She was drained and all Rell had done was give her some killer head. She watched as he wiped the last of her cream from his chin all the while looking deeply into her eyes.

Lorna lifted up, and with her tongue, licked the last of her cream from his lips. She then slid her tongue into his mouth, allowing them both to enjoy the taste of her cunt juice.

"Now, was that so bad?" he asked with a slight smile. "Nah, you know you liked it. Now come here and throw that pussy back on me, Mami."

Lorna eased back down to the bed and slowly spread her legs. She reached down between them, grabbed his thick meat, and eased it inside her waiting pussy.

"Like that?" Lorna asked, thrusting her hips up ever so slowly, taking in about 3/4 of his dick.

"Yeah, baby. Just…mmm. Just like that," Rell answered as he kept the rhythm the two had become entranced by.

They kept this pace for quite some time, until Lorna's coochie began to froth over, coating Rell's rod with a thick layer of milky white cream. Noticing how lubricated her body was, he figured she was now ready for the remainder of his dick. Pulling every inch, except for his head out of her pussy, Rell held his position above her. He took her legs, one at a time, and pent her knee's to the bed near her shoulders.

Before she could brace for impact, Rell slid into her slowly, with intent. He buried his dick completely inside her pipping hot walls loving the feel of her closing in all around him. His strokes weren't slow or fast. The pace was steady, but the end of each stroke created shudder's for both of them. Each time he pressed into her he felt an unbelievable sensation rush through him. This went on forever, or at least the pleasure of the experience made it seem that way.

Lorna enjoyed two more body rocking orgasms, one leading right into the next. She was well on her way to another when Rell slowly withdrew from her.

"Oh, Papi. No. Don't stop!" Lorna wined in protest longing to reconnect. Rell slid from between her legs, turned Lorna onto her right side, and shifted himself behind her. He grabbed her leg and lifted it high. Angling himself just right to ensure maximum penetration, he slid back inside her. By the third stroke, Lorna's body was responding to Rell's dick like she was his student and he was her teacher. Feeling her body go limp, he grabbed her hand and slid it down between her thighs to touch where their bodies connected. With his other hand, gripped a handful of her hair and tilted her head back as far as it would go.

As this took place, he let his fingers get soaked by the juice's produced at the entry point of her coochie. With his fingers well lubricated, Rell slid his hand up to Lorna's clit and began tenderly stroking it. The position he held her in, allowed her to take him in deeper. She received every sensation more profoundly, but the tender stroking of her clit is what turned her all the way out.

A Whore's Conscience

When she came this time, her pussy seemed to suck like a vacuum as her body convulsed from the joys of the epic climax she was currently lost in. When she felt the pressure of him pressing deep inside her stomach, it caused her entire body to jolt and tense up. Tiny tremors could be felt inside her as she trembled in awe. As she began to mellow back down, it was then that she noticed that Rell was still experiencing the after effects of busting a monster nut. She also realized what the tiny tremors she felt in her stomach was.

'My man was cumin' hard,' she mentally concluded, as the power of her statement hit her suddenly. *'My man? Girl, you gotta pull yourself together,'* Lorna thought as she lay next to Rell, completely unaware of just how deeply he had touched her soul.

Back in the living room, the sexual free for all was nearing its climax. Alexi had finally managed to remove her head from the service of the couch, only to have Shawn reposition her head once more. This time the whole right side of her face was shoved against the armrest of the couch.

"Ahhhh! Oh, shiiiit!!" Alexi moaned, as Shawn continued slinging dick to her coochie doggy-style. "I… I… I'm Cum… Mingggg!! Ahhhh…Oh!!" she yelled loudly as Splash continued to beat her pussy up.

As the last remnants of her orgasm faded, Alexi reached back with her right hand to slow down the onslaught Shawn was orchestrating.

"What?!" Shawn asked in a half bewildered state never breaking stride. "You can't take this dick?"

Without another word spoken, Alexi lifted her knees off the floor. She placed them side by side on the couch, keeping her thighs pressed tightly together. This position made her pussy wrap harder around Shawn's dick. When she started to thrust back with all her might, the table's turned one last time and it was the cause of Shawn's orgasmic explosion. His eyes squeezed tightly and his hands wrapped around her waist with a powerful grip. The way Shawn's legs shook from cumming, Alexi thought he was behind her dancing. Not being able to go another second, they both crashed hard to the floor and Shawn's orgasm caused him to wail out a sound that was much like what Micheal Jackson does when performing.

"Now that's some good pussy!" Shawn acknowledged, as he held her close fighting to regain control of his breathing.

95

Chapter Twenty Two

"I'm telling you, even my mom and Pam be cheating. I just can't never catch they ass," Kiki said as she entered the townhome Ree-Ree and Shawn shared after Steph.

"They got to be doing something, cause they kicked everybody's ass in spades tonight," Steph agreed as she walked towards the back of the house.

"Ree-Ree!! Girl where you at!" Liv shouted.

"She ain't here," Steph replied, as she re-entered the living room.

"She must be upstairs with that bitch," Kiki stated, crossing towards the kitchen hopping on a stool next to the counter.

"We can find out," Steph said, cutting on the plasma T.V. and turning the station to the channel programmed to receive the signals from the hidden transmitters located in Rell's townhome. The transmitters were remotely operated giving the viewer the ability to choose which room they wished to watch. The first hidden camera, located in the living room, was an instant hit. There in the middle of the couch, Andrea was receiving head from a man, neither Steph, Kiki, or Liv could identify.

"That don't look like Ree-Ree," Liv said, stating the obvious.

"And it damn sho ain't Rell!" Kiki said, rising and heading for the front door.

"Kiki!! Hold up!!" Liv and Steph both yelled in unison as they scrambled for the door to keep Kiki from leaving.

"Fuck it. I'll go out the back," Kiki stated, as she quickly made her way out the house and onto the deck.

"What the fuck!" Kiki blurted out as she took off running towards Ree-Ree's unconscious body.

"Oh my God! Ree-Ree!!" Steph yelled. She and Liv squatted down beside Kiki, next to Ree-Ree's motionless body.

"Is she alive?" Liv asked.

"Her chest is moving. Yeah! She's still alive. Let's get her back inside the house," Kiki said, as she and the girls each took hold of Ree-Ree and lifted and toted her back into the living room.

"Steph go get me some towels and rags. Liv go get me some ice and cold water." Kiki gave out the order as she checked Ree-Ree's pulse for a steady heart beat. Kiki was a nurse, and she was damn good at her trade. Keeping Ree-Ree still she began to open her eyelids looking for any signs of response. *What the hell happened?'* Kiki wondered as she looked at the badly swollen left side of Ree-Ree's face.

"Damn!" Liv said, as she handed Kiki a drinking pitcher full of ice and a punch bowl full of cold water.

"Hand me a rag," Kiki ordered, as Steph approached her. Taking the rag and dipping it into the ice cold water, Kiki squeezed the cold water from the rag onto Ree-Ree's face.

"Ree-Ree!!" Kiki yelled, and she repeated the process again. When this got no response from Ree-Ree, Kiki leaned down and smacked her damp face twice.

"Girl is you crazy!" Steph asked, blocking Kiki's hands from hitting Ree-Ree further.

"You gotta better idea?" Kiki asked, as she pressed hard against the swollen side of Ree-Ree's face causing her to moan in pain.

"Ree-Ree!! It's Kiki!! Can you hear me?"

"Uhhhhh." Ree-Ree moaned low in her throat as she opened her eyes struggling to focus on the face's hovering above her.

After Kiki finished treating her and found no signs to indicate Ree-Ree was seriously hurt, the three of them helped her off the floor and guided her to the couch.

"So what happened?" Steph asked, handing Ree-Ree a fresh towel full of ice to hold to her fce.

"Oh my God!! Oh shit!!"

Andrea's moans from the T.V. startled everybody. The living room was empty, so Steph grabbed the remote and clicked the button to view another room. The screen now showed the bathroom. An empty bathroom.

Click.

The guest bedroom now was on display, but it too was empty.

Click.

From where the four girls were sitting, it looked like some guy was fucking her in the ass.

"Yeah, nigga! FUCK THIS ASS!" Andrea howled out to Sergio, unaware that she was being watched and recorded.

"You are recording this shit, right?!" Liv asked turning to face Steph.

"Yep. The moment one of the cameras pick up any serious amount of body heat, they turn on, instantly recording."

"Good! Kiki, come on," Liv said, with death written all over her face as she rose from the couch and attempted to leave.

"Shit! You ain't said nothing." Kiki jumped up ready to help Liv kick some ass.

"No!! You can't!" Ree-Ree yelled out, and tried to rise off the couch.

"Fuck that wait until tomorrow shit. This bitch done put her hands on you and now she up in my brother's crib fucking the next nigga on his bed. Oh, HELL NAH!!" Kiki blacked, moving towards the door and reaching for the knob.

"If you touch her before Rell get's back, then you all but guarantee that Rell and Shawn will spend the next 15 to 20 years in a federal prison," Ree-Ree screamed.

"What?!" Steph, Liv, and Kiki said in unison.

"Turn that shit off. That bitch's yelling giving me a handache," Ree-Ree said, as she patted the couch singlaing for Liv and Kiki to sit back down.

Once the T.V. was cut off, Ree-Ree let the girls in on the last secret concerning her and Shawn's plan.

"It's like this. For about two years now, that bitch been learning how Rell and Shawn move. She knows when and where they head to, how much they usually cop, and where each one stashes there money. Basically, the bitch knows too much."

"How you know she know all this?" Liv asked.

"We don't. But before we risk thinking she don't know, we'd rather remove all doubt and just kill the problem," Ree-Ree further explained.

"You ain't talking about just kicking her ass anymore, are you?" Steph asked, as she began to realize what Ree-Ree's secret was.

"No. Hand me my cell. I gotta let Shawn know what's up."

Although she never actually said the words, everyone knew the eventual fate of Andrea. Because of her knowledge of Rell's business, she was a threat too big to ignore. That fact alone, was enough to have her killed.

'Tomorrow... Revenge Trinidadian style,' Ree-Ree said to herself, as her cell begins to ring up Shawn's.

Chapter Twenty Three

"Naw, put them back down," Lorna told Alexi, who had attempted to pick up their take-out food containers. "Just help me grab the guys food."

"Okay," Alexi said, somewhat puzzled.,

After entering the lobby of the hotel, Lorna with Alexi's aide, conned the night time doorman into delivering the food to the guys for them.

"They may ask you what happened to us, if so, tell the one with the big pretty eyes to look at this," Lorna ordered the doorman, as she took a note she'd written while ordering the food and placed it on top of the food Rell had ordered. "Can you do that for me?" she asked, waving a fifty dollar bill in front of his eyes.

"Oh yes! Big eyed guy... note in food. Gotcha!" The doorman took the money and wished the ladies a good night.

"You know they gonna wanna know why we didn't come back. Hell, I wanna know why myself!" Lexi said sounding upset. She stopped Lorna in the parking lot, turned her around, allowing them both to stand face to face. "Oh, no Mami!" Lexi said sympathetically as she wrapped her arms around her crying friend.

Lorna wept hard and was unable to respond to Alexi. She hoped that just this once she would figure this one out on her own. Alexi unknowingly answered her Lorna's silent plea. She already somewhat had a clue about what was up. She just had no clue about the depth of her girls feelings.

"Let it out Mami. Let it out," Alexi said, seeking to soothe the pain her girl was facing from falling in love.

***

"Yo, they should've been back by now," Splash stated in between puffs as he and Rell smoked a blunt.

"Damn, cuz! She got your ass open, huh?" Rell joked.

"Whatever, cuz. A nigga just hungry."

"I know that's right," Rell agreed.

VREEN! VREEN!

"What's up!?!" Shawn said, answering his cell.

"It's me. Did I call at a bad time?" Ree-Ree asked.

"Nah, so what's the verdict?"

"We gotta clean up for Thanksgiving," Ree-Ree answered, giving the code which would signal that Andrea would have to be killed. With Thanksgiving only a week away, the two small talked about the holiday, to sell the image that they were really speaking about the occasion. With the implementation of Homeland Security policies, one can never be certain when their calls were being monitored. After selling the facade a little more, the two ended the call.

"Ree-Ree?" Rell asked.

"Yeah. She missing a brother. I guess she…"

BAP! BAP! BAP!

The knock at the door cut Shawn's sentence short.

"It's bout time!" Rell said as he opened the door. "What took y'all so long? A yo duke, who you?" Rell asked, shocked to find his food being carried by some scrawny, pale looking white man.

"Are you Mr. Rell?" the hotel doorman asked.

"Yeah, that's me. Why? Who want to know?"

"What's going on?" Shawn asked, approaching the door to investigate.

"Nevermind. Ya eye's bigger than his. Here. This for you," the doorman said, turning and handing him the food with the note inside.

"My what?" Rell stammered, looking at the man strangely.

"The lady put a note in your food for you. Y'all need anything else?" the doorman asked.

"Nah, we good. Thanks," Shawn answered, taking his food from the man, and slamming the door closed. "What it say?" he asked Rell.

"It's personal, cuz. I'll be back." Rell walked into the bedroom and closed the door behind him. Setting his food down on the nightstand next to the bed, he opened the letter and began to read.

Rell,

I'm sorry. I'm so, so, sorry, but I can't handle this. I tried, but I can't. This was just supposed to be about having a good time, but papi, you changed the game. I'm feeling you, Rell. I mean really feeling you. And papi, that scares me. So I chose to bounce. I had to. I need space right now to think. I gotta figure some shit out.

Rell, PLEASE, PLEASE don't be mad at me. But until I can understand this love I have for you, it's best I stay away. Contact Alexi about any business. Her numbers 555-5464. I love you Rell. Please don't doubt this, but I gotta get me right first. I won't risk hurting you. I'd rather die Papi. I will miss you Rell. But I won't be gone for long.

PLEASE don't hate me. PLEASE understand.

> *Tu Quierres Mucho, Papi*
> *Lorna*

'I Don't hate you, Ma. I feel you. More than you know,' Rell thought to himself.

He recalled seeing the look that was on Lorna's face two and a half years ago, though it was on the face of another woman. She took off much like Lorna just did, except she left no note. But the look on her face after they had finished making love was the exact same as Lorna's.

'Damn Steph!' Rell thought, shaking his head. He now realized the real reason why Steph took off and never reached out to him again.

'Thanks Lorna,' Rell mentally stated as he finally understood what needed to be done once he got home.

"Yo, Rell!!!" Shawn yelled, breaking Rell out of his deep thought as he stuck his head through the door.

"Yeah. What's up?"

"I ain't trying to rush you, but as soon as you finish eating, we need to hit the road."

"Why? What's up?"

"Remember the surprise I spoke on as we left home?" Shawn asked.

"Yeah."

"Well, if we wanna get that surprise, our ass got to be on the road in the next hour or so," he said before turning and walking away before Rell could ask another question.

Chapter Twenty Four

"Where they at?" Ree-Ree asked Liv, who was clicking through the screens looking for Andrea and her lover.

"Got 'em! They in the shower... fucking."

"Again!?" Steph asked, somewhat shocked.

"Yep! Like rabbits," Liv replied, cutting the set back off.

"Good! Come on," said Ree-Ree, opening the door and leading everyone to the parked U-Haul. "With everyone doing their part, this shouldn't take long," she said as she opened the back of the U-Haul.

In the back of the U-Haul was five fifty pound bags of quick dry cement. A large five foot spool of plastic and a big bottle of Gorilla Glue. After everyone helped cover the floor with plastic, each girl placed plastic on one of the three walls while Ree-Ree covered the plastic with the Gorilla Glue. Since Liv was the tallest, she was responsible for also coating the roof and the back of the U-Haul. After putting up the second coat of plastic, the ladies loaded the fifty pound bags of cement back into the U-Haul.

"So we gonna kill the bitch with cement?" Kiki half asked, as she and the rest admired their finished work.

"She'll be dead long before the cement touches her ass," Ree-Ree answered, closing the back of the U-Haul. "Come on. I don't know about y'all, but I need a drink," she added as she led the girls back into the Townhome.

***

It was five o'clock in the morning by the time Rell cut off the Camaro's engine in front of a rest stop in Columbus, South Carolina. It had been a long day and the two were extremely tired.

"We just gonna catch a few hours of rest. We'll pull back off before ten," stated Rell, as he reclined the driver seat to its max and closed his eyes.

Shawn was just as tired as Rell, but the idea that he had to be the bearer of bad news as well as the one who would ultimately have to convince Rell to kill Andrea, was beginning to take its effects on his nerves. The closer they got to Durham, the harder his heart pounded.

'Damn, I'll be glad when this shit over with,' Shawn thought as fatigue conquered his anxiety, sending him into a deep slumber.

***

"It's about time you motherfuckers woke up," Steph said as Kiki and Liv entered the kitchen still looking half asleep.

"What y'all cooking?" Liv asked while looking over Ree-Ree shoulder.

"Uh-uh! Girl, go brush yo shit," Ree-Ree snapped, covering her nose with her hand.

"Ree, stop fronting. My shit don't stink," Liv protested, causing everyone to laugh.

"I don't know what you laughing at Kiki. Your shit tart too!" Ree-Ree added, still holding her nose.

"Fuck you bitch!" Kiki said playfully as she and Liv made their way to the bathroom.

"Let me see again," Steph asked Ree-Ree, leaning over to get a good look at her face. "Damn you heal quick," she said, looking at the slight puffiness and small black spot under Ree-Rees left eye.

"The swelling was the worst part. Once I got that down, I knew the rest would heal quickly," Ree-Ree added, flipping the turkey sausage and bacon over in the skillet she was tending.

"Are you scared?" Steph asked, pausing mid stroke as she slowly resumed stirring the grits.

"Of killing her?"

"Yeah."

"I don't know and honestly, I don't care to know. I'm gonna do what I gotta do," Ree-Ree answered while cutting off the burner that

105

cooked the meat.

"Hey! Where the hell is my car?" Kiki asked as she and Liv entered the kitchen refreshed and fully awake.

"I moved it around back last night after y'all went to sleep," Ree-Ree replied as she watched Steph cross to the living room and cut the T.V. on.

"Ummmm!! Oh, yeah!!" Andrea moaned as she rode Sergio's morning wood.

"Damn, does the hoe ever sleep?" Liv asked truly wondering if the woman spent all night screwing.

"If you having doubts, maybe you shouldn't be here," Ree-Ree murmured quietly to Steph.

"Who you talking to?" Kiki asked, mistaking Ree-Ree's comment as being for everybody.

Ree-Ree ignored Kiki's outburst and waited for Steph to answer.

"I'm not having doubts. At least not concerning her ass," answered Steph, cutting the T.V. off again.

"Then what's wrong?" asked Ree-Ree as she pulled out four plates and began loading meat onto them.

"Nothing. I'm just trippin'. I'm nervous I guess. It's nothing." Steph said the lie with a straight face, not trusting her insecurities concerning Rell to be known to anyone. For over two years she'd fiend for Rell and if she was honest with herself, she had wanted him since the first day she'd seen him. But for one reason or another, the two never linked up. That is, until that one fateful night two and a half years ago. *'Allah, please give me one more chance to have him,'* Steph mentally pleaded as she rose to rejoin the other ladies in the kitchen to eat.

***

"Why we stopping back here? Is that Kiki's car?" Rells questions come in rapid succession. The two had made quick time cutting through the rest of South Carolina and reaching home before noon.

"In order to get your surprise, we gotta park back here. Now come on, cuz. A nigga trying to get to bed as soon as possible." Shawn exit the drivers side after popping the trunk.

"Alright cuz. What you gearing up for?" Rell asked, watching Shawn grab one of the .45s from the trunk.

"You gonna need this," Shawn said, handing Rell one of the .45s.

A Whore's Conscience

"What you not telling me Shawn?" Rell asked as he chambered his .45 and gave Shawn a look that said he wasn't in the mood for surprises.

"This is something you gotta see for yourself. Just know that whatever you decide, I got your back," Shawn said, as he shut the trunk and lead Rell towards the back patio of his townhome.

Inside the townhome, the ladies were gearing up as well. All the girls had wrapped their hair into buns and covered them with stocking caps. They then tied bandanas over top of them. They tied up their Timberlands and smeared Vaseline over their faces. As they were doing this, they heard a door slam indicating that someone had entered the townhome. Grabbing her baby .380, Ree-Ree motioned for the girls to be quiet and headed towards the living room to investigate the source of the sound. Before she could step out of the room, the voice that she longed to hear echoed through her ears.

"Baby! Baby where you at?" Shawn yelled, looking for Ree-Ree.

"Shawn!"

"Hey boo!" he replied as he held his baby tight. "What happened to your face?"

"Rell! What's up bro?!" Kiki greeted her brother.

"What the hell y'all bout to get into? Or should I say who?" Rell asked, noticing the way the girls were dressed.

"Come here Rell. You too Shawn," Steph said, pulling an angered Shawn away from his girls bruised face.

Steph clicked on the T.V., but it only showed an empty bedroom. She clicked the remote again and now the screen showed Andrea lounging on the couch sipping coffee while looking at her television.

Steph clicked the remote once more causing the screen to show the bathroom where a guy sat taking a dump in Rell's master bathroom.

"Do you know this guy?" Steph asked.

"What the fuck?! Yeah! That's Netta ex-husband. Uh…Sergio. I think that's the nigga's name," Rell blurted out, cutting his eyes towards Shawn.

"Remember, I got your back," Shawn said as he locked eyes with Rell, then motioned for him to look back at the screen. When Rell turned back to the T.V., he saw the taped footage of Sergio ass fucking his wifey on his bed.

"What the fuck!!" Rell barked out loudly.

"Hold up, Rell. There's more," said Ree-Ree and she tilted her face for him to see her bruises. "She did this to me when I confronted her about all these guys she be fucking," Ree-Ree said, allowing tears to moisten her eyes.

"All these guys!?! You mean more niggas been in my..." his words cut off as anger began to run hot in his veins.

"Rell, be easy fam," Shawn said, gripping Rell's shoulder's trying to calm him a little.

"Move! Let me go, cuz!" Rell said while trying to free himself from Shawn's grip. "Cut that shit off!" Shawn yelled, ordering the image and the sounds of Andrea fucking to be cut off.

"Rell, I need you to listen to me, fam." Shawn was trying to bring Rell from the realm of insanity, back to reality.

"I did right by that bitch, cuz. She needed for nothing. I took care of that bitch and her kid. I told her shit she wasn't supposed to know because I thought I could trust her. She gonna just... How she just gonna fucking play a nigga," Rell vehemently rambled.

"Rell! If we go up there, ain't nobody allowed to live. Do you understand what I'm saying cuz?" Shawn spoke again, seeking to reach an understanding with Rell.

"You ain't got to worry about that. Kiki, Liv...come on!" Rell stated as he shook himself loose from Shawn's grip.

"Rell, hold up!" Shawn yelled, but Rell was already out the front door, with Kiki and Liv following close behind. "Damn! Come on!" Shawn ordered Steph and Ree-Ree, as he took off in pursuit of his boy.

Chapter Twenty Five

"Andrea! Andrea, come on girl!" Sergio yelled out for her as he lay on his back, butt naked, stroking his dick while waiting for another round of sex.

"I'm coming. Give me a minute," Andrea yelled from the bathroom as she kneeled by the toilet wiping her mouth from puking.

Clink!

The front door of the townhome opened and Rell crept in slowly, looking and listening for any signs of where they may be.

'Beware of the snake.'

The words of his grandfather echoed through his mind.

'Kill this bitch,' was his next thought, followed by a low hissing sound. The sink was running full blast as Andrea tried to erase the taste of vomit from her tongue by gargling water.

"Damn girl, what's taking you so long!" Sergio yelled from Rell's bedroom formally announcing his exact location.

'This nigga in my bed! I'mma kill this whore!' Rell mentally concluded as he got ready to bolt through the bedroom door. Suddenly, Kiki grabbed hold of him, stopping his inital forward motion.

"What?!" Rell whispered, agitated.

Kiki didn't answer. She just motions her head to the approaching

Shawn and stepped out of the way.

"Rell, fall back for a minute," Shawn whispered, pulling Rell back towards the front door.

"Fall back?!" Rell asked with angry disbelief.

"The girls got something to do first," Shawn explained.

"Like what?" Rell asked, in a voice a tad louder than a whisper.

"Ree-Ree gonna get Andrea to come out here. Then me and you gonna handle the nigga while they handle that bit... you know," Shawn corrected himself as he further explained out the details of the plan. When Rell bobbed his head, Shawn nodded his to Ree-Ree, signaling for her to set it off.

"Andrea! Andrea! Bitch this shit ain't over with. Come out before I come back there and drag yo ass out!" Ree-Ree yelled, knowing Andrea would take the bait.

"Whum dem Fumk?!" Andrea mumbled around the dick she had just place in her mouth.

"Who's dat?!" Sergio asked as he balled up like some bitch.

"Relax Nigga! It ain't Netta. Just the bitch from downstairs. This won't take long." Andrea threw her gown on and stepped out the bedroom.

Ree-Ree stood directly in front of the door with a can of well shaken pepper spray. On both sides of the door stood Liv and Kiki, ready to pop off. Steph stood by the front door, watching out making sure nobody surprised them. As soon as Andrea opened the door, all hell broke loose.

For a brief second, she saw Ree-Ree's face, then suddenly her eyes were on fire and she couldn't see shit. The moment Andrea threw her hands up to rub her burning eyes, Kiki and Liv were on her. Kiki landed the first blow catching Andrea directly on the right side of her chin. The punch sent Andrea leaning towards Liv, who rocked off two right uppercuts to the lower left side of Andrea's chin.

All the years of training in the gym boxing with Steph's dad had paid off. Andrea threw no punches, and except for one faint cough made by the effects of the pepper spray, she hadn't made a sound. On the floor at their feet, Andrea lay knocked the hell out.

"Come on y'all, help me move this bitch," Ree-Ree said, bending down to pick Andrea up. But Kiki and Liv were in the bedroom, observing their brother's work.

BOOM!

A Whore's Conscience

Rell let one shot off into the mattress Sergio lay upon, allowing his .45 to open up their conversation.

"Oh shit!" Sergio yelled, falling off the bed scared shitless.

"The fuck you think you going nigga?!" Rell barked as he walked up on Sergio. While looking him in the eye, he placed the .45 three inches from his face. Rell could see that Sergio was scared enough to possibly try to go for the gun lying on the nightstand. "I know what you thinking nigga. Can I make it? Can I get to his gun before he pops off another shot? Maybe you can, but look to your right. Can you get to his gun too? Huh, nigga?!" Rell yelled, smacking Sergio across the dome with the .45, robbing him of his last ounce of courage.

"Yo, Rell, lets take him outside. I got the perfect spot set up," Shawn informed Rell, who looked ready to open the nigga up right there.

"You heard the man. Move nigga!" Rell barked, allowing Sergio to walk between him and Shawn. The two of them lead him into the living room where everyone else stood waiting huddled around Andrea's semi-conscious body.

"Please man! Don't kill me!" Sergio begged, trembling from head to toe as both guys kept their .45s aimed firmly on him. "Aww shit!" Andrea moaned, trying to rise off her back.

"Somebody shut that bitch up!" Rell shouted, looking at his sisters who still stood motionless, watching their brother pointing his gun at the frightened, naked man.

"Ahhh!" Andrea moaned even louder as Steph left her post at the door to come snatch her off the floor.

"Bitch! Shut up!" Steph ordered as she caught Andrea by the hair. She lifted her up by her roots and popped the bitch two stiff jabs to the jaw.

"Hold her up. I want that bitch to see this," Rell shouted as he pulled back the hammer on his .45 and pointed it between the eyes of Sergio.

"Rell!" Shawn tried to protest, but was cut off.

The snake was charming Rell. It had him truly hypnotized with its whispering hisses.

"Oww!!" Andrea moaned in pain as Steph threw her into a full Nelson hold.

"Ree, cover the front door," Steph said as she angled Andrea to give her a perfect view of the nigga she had been fucking.

"Kiki, Liv, open her eyes. Make her look at this shit," said Rell. "Get on yo knees nigga," Rell ordered Sergio.

"Please, Rell! Ahh!" Sergio yelled as Rell smacked him with the butt once again.

"Nigga, didn't I tell you to shut the fuck up!" Rell stood over the now squatting Sergio, with the barrel of the .45 stuck to the temple of his head.

"Rell, man! Not here," Shawn pleaded.

"Shut up!" Rell yelled insanely, pushing the barrel harder into Sergio's temple.

Feeling death at his doorstep, Sergio burst into tears. Streams upon streams of tears flowed from his eyes. The man was physically a wreck.

"I can't believe this shit! This nigga up in MY crib, fucking MY pussy, eating MY food and drinking MY beer. This nigga shitted in MY house!"

BOOM! BOOM! BOOM!

Rell squeezed the trigger three times. Each bullet ripping a hole straight through Sergios dome.

"Ah!!" Ree-Ree screamed as Sergio's blood splattered and spewed all over Rell and Shawn.

The snake continued to mesmerize Rell with its charming suggestions. Its whispers influencing Rell to turn and draw on Andrea. He could see Steph's lips moving, but somehow her words were muted. The snake's presence was steadily intoxicating Rell more and more. *Hiiiissss!!*

Andrea was fixing her lips to yell out 'No,' but not before more shots rang out.

BOOM! BOOM! BOOM!

Andrea fell backwards on top of Steph from the force of the bullets that ripped through her chest. Rell walked over and stood over the splayed out Andrea and emptied his clip. Blood was everywhere. He stared down at her in silence watching the blood pool beneath her lifeless body.

That's when he noticed Steph. She lay underneath Andrea and she wasn't moving. Quickly, Rell kicked Andrea off of Steph and kneeled to see if she was okay. He knew from her face that she wasn't. Blood poured abundantly from Steph's left temple. She was dead.

"No!!" Rell screamed insanely.

Shawn smacked the gun in Rell's hand from the temple of Sergio. 'BOOM!'

The gun discharged one round into the ceiling as Shawn bear hugged Rell from the side and began screaming in his ear, hoping to wake Rell out from under the snakes trance.

"Rell! Don't do this! Not here, Rell!"

"I killed her. I killed the woman I love. I killed her Shawn. I killed Steph," Rell sobbed as he crumpled to the floor.

"Steph ain't dead cuz. She's right there," Shawn said, as he motioned to Steph, who still held Andrea in a full Nelson.

"But...I. I shot her and..." Rell stammered around his words as he looked across and saw Sergio balled up, lying in his own piss.

"You shot the ceiling, cuz," Shawn said, pulling his main man back to his feet. "You alright?"

"Yeah! I just need some air," Rell replied as he walked out the living room to his overly spacious patio.

"Come on, girl," Liv said to Kiki and beckoned her to come with her as she followed Rell.

"Nah, I got him. Y'all come grab this bitch," Steph said as she flung Andrea to the ground where the sisters stood. "Just give us a minute," she added as she swiftly made her way out to the patio.

Rell was sitting on the edge of one of his patio stools, rocking back and forth. On the nearby table rested his .45. From where she stood, she could see tears trickling down his face. Steph grabbed a nearby patio stool and slid next to Rell. He continued rocking and chanting to himself.

"Astagh fir-Allah! Astagh fir-Allah! Forgive me Allah." Rell repeated the words incessantly as tears continued to stream from his eyes.

"Rell, talk to me baby," Steph said softly as she grabbed his right arm and began to caress it. Between her gently spoken words and caressing his arm, Steph was able to soothe Rell enough to finally get him to talk.

"It seemed so real. I thought I had really lost you," he said, sobbing out the last few words.

"I'm right here, Rell and I ain't going anywhere," Steph replied while steadily comforting the love of her life.

"I can't keep doing this. I can't keep playing with Allah like this.

I gotta get my shit together." Rell stood and began to pace in front of Steph as he continued to verbalize his thoughts. "My money is stacked. I got everything I could ever want. Well, almost."

He stopped pacing and raised his eyes from the patio floor and looked Stephanie directly in hers. He knows how he feels about Stephanie. His heart had been hers far longer than he cared to admit. Stephanie was down to earth. Down for whatever, classy, silly, attentive, loving, athletic and adventurous. She was a brawler when upset and could put the foulest mouth sailor to shame.

Stephanie, more importantly, was Rell's friend. Always have been. There wasn't a woman alive who could ever own a place in his heart other than Steph. But was her heart as endowed to him as he was to her? Did she love Rell, or was she only in love with his street rep? Maybe all she wanted was her own meal ticket. As reality sunk in, he dismissed this notion as nothing more than his nerves getting the best of him. Steph was no gold digger. *'Shit! She got her own money,'* Rell thought. He continued to stare in her eyes as his mind continued to run through everything he knew about her.

"What's up?" Steph asked, growing somewhat uncomfortable with all the staring.

"Steph, if I quit hustling, would you still want to rock with me?" Rell dropped his gaze to the patio floor as he waited for her response.

"Rell, baby. I love you," Steph said as she rose from her stool, wrapped her arms around him, and hugged him passionately. "Fuck hustlin'. I've been ready for you to pop the clutch on that bullshit anyway."

She stepped back a bit and kissed Rell lovingly. Her kiss was long and long overdue. The kiss said more to Rell's soul than any words he could have hoped for. The kiss informed Rell's heart that his love would be fully returned. But like any love worth having, Stephs love for Rell overwhelmed him, empowering his spirit and gave him a sense of peace. It was a sudden calm, that only the love of a good woman can create during troubled times.

When they broke the kiss, the two of them held each other tightly, allowing the moment to fully sink in. When the reality of the situation taking place in the townhome began to sink back in, Rell was the first to speak.

"What am I going to do with this bitch?" he asked Steph leaning her back just enough to look into her face.

"Do you really have to kill her?" Steph asked, stepping out of Rell's arms.

"She knows too much."

"Can I ask you a favor?" Steph scooped up the .45 and held it in the palm of her hand.

"Steph, if it's about Andrea..."

"What does Money say?" she asked, cutting off his reply.

"About all this?" Rell was trying to stall.

"Rell, you told me a long time ago, that if you ever left the game it would be due to Islam. So I started studying the faith, and unless I'm wrong, you can only kill Andrea if she was your wife or if you got four witnesses to her performing homosexual acts. Am I right or wrong?" Steph asked, playing dumb.

"Fornication is also a sin and she was... you know... fornicating." Rell stumbled through his answer.

"Rell! Don't play with Allah!" Steph warned him.

"So what am I supposed to do, act like some sucker for love and let the bitch live?!" Rell spat with a tone that showed he was becoming upset.

"Actually, yes. If you want to do right by Allah, because you love him, then you must follow his commandments about all things, at all times. That means even now!" Steph said, putting the gun in Rell's hand and stepping back from him.

"So I'm supposed to go in there and just let her walk away? She just goes Scott free?" Rell protested once more.

"Not exactly. She can be flogged. I mean beaten, but after that, you have to let her go," Steph stated, looking in Rell's eyes for a sign that he would agree to obey Allah's word.

"Humph! And I guess you wanna handle the beating part, huh?" Rell allowed himself a little smirk, giving Steph the first sign that she had won this debate.

"Gladly. You take the guy, we take the bitch," Steph said as Rell threw his left arm over her shoulder and led her back into the house.

"Let's get this over with," Rell said as they both entered through the patio door and stepped into the living room. Scanning the living room, Rell saw Shawn still holding Sergio at gunpoint. While Kiki and Liv both had one of Andrea's arms twisted and extended above her head, applying severe pressure.

"Glad to see you looking better. Let's take this downstairs,"

Shawn stated as he motioned for Sergio to get on his feet.

"Nah, Cuz. Change of plans," Rell replied.

"What you mean?" Shawn asked.

"Look, this is how we gonna do it," Rell said, then whispered the plan into Shawn's ear.

"If you say so," Shawn said after hearing the entire plan.

Rell gave his gun to Steph and Shawn gave his to Ree-Ree. If either one of you try to defend yourself, one of these ladies is gone put a hole in your ass."

Rell immediately popped off on Sergio with a vicious hay maker. The sisters took this as their cue and commenced to putting their feet up Andrea's ass. Sergio and Andrea were beaten without mercy. When everyone became too tired to throw another punch, they finally decided to stop the beatings.

"You got one minute to grab yo shit and get out my crib. That goes for you too," Rell said to both Sergio and Andrea, as they both lay in pain, moaning from their injuries.

The two of them looked like they had been dropped into a pit of hot coals. Their bodies tried to move, but the beating they had just endured left them unable to move with any speed or certainty. They just staggered and moaned, falling all over the place.

"Stop! Just Stop!" Rell yelled, growing frustrated at the unsightly commotion.

"Even if they make it out the house, they still ain't in any shape to be driving," Shawn stated, looking at Rell with the 'Now What' expression.

Rell was racking his brains for ideas when his eyes ended up on the door to Alana's room.

"Hmph," Rell grunted as a Kool-aid smile spread across his face.

"What is it baby?" Steph walked up to Rell and stood close to his side.

"Shawn, hand me the cordless." Rell dialed up the only person he could think of who would care enough to pick Andrea and Sergio up.

"Hello?"

"Hey, is this Netta?" Rell asked.

"Yeah boy! You know it's me. What's up? Y'all ready for me to bring Alana back?"

"Nah! Actually, I need you to let your daughter watch Alana, and come here alone."

"Rell, what's going on!?" Netta was a little alarmed.

"I'll let Sergio tell you." Rell knew this would get Netta started.

"Sergio? What's he doing over there?" Netta snapped.

"Come see for yourself." Rell ended the call leaving Netta full of curiosity.

Chapter Twenty Six

'Damn!' Andrea thought, as her day went from bad to worse.

"If you can, please tell me what happened," Detective Young asked as he stood next to Andrea's hospital bed. He had already asked Sergio a bunch of questions, but found him unwilling to cooperate. He doubted Andrea McWater would be any different.

"It happened too fast," she answered in a faded, weak voice. Her comment caused Netta to tense up in her chair.

'Rell promised all hell would break loose if the cops were brought into this. I know this bitch ain't that dumb,' Netta thought as she held her breath, waiting for the outcome of the investigation.

"What happened so fast?" Detective Young questioned.

"I don't know," Andrea lied. She remembered everything, the mace, the punishing blows, the threats, the shame, the fear. She remembered it all.

"Tell me what you do remember." Detective Young was well aware at this point that she wasn't giving anything up.

"One minute I was meeting my friend, the next thing I know, someone sprayed my eyes and then I woke up in here."

Andrea began to weep as she talked, hoping that her tears would help end this pointless interview. Her tears weren't fueled by sorrow, nor self-pity. Her tears were fueled by rage. Andrea wanted revenge.

A Whore's Conscience

'How could I let myself slip so bad?' she silently questioned herself.

"Sir, I'm sorry, but you're going to have to leave," the nurse ordered.

"Alright. I'm sorry I upset you. I'll come by tomorrow when you're feeling a little better." The Detective bowed his head, then made his exit.

'Rell, I don't know how, but somehow, someway, your ass is gonna pay for this nigga,' Andrea thought as her eyelids grew heavy. The nurse was administering Andrea a mild sedative to calm her. 'You gonna pay Rell. You.. you... gonna... um." Those were the last words Andrea mumbled out loud before drifting off into a drug induced slumber.

Chapter Twenty Seven

Ms. Ce-Ce's Grapevine: Part Two
Cause Niggas Still Nosey

Phew! The past few days have been hectic. I got a call from Steph two weeks ago telling me about how she and my son done finally become a couple. She sounded so happy. She told me how everything went down. How everything led up to her and my son hooking up. I knew that bitch Andrea wasn't shit. I told Steph to keep his eyes open because that bitch might try something. That's when I found out Shawn and my son were staying in some upscale hotel until they could locate somewhere else to stay. The two felt it was best to change up their entire lifestyles.

Both were selling their townhome's and leaving the dope game alone, which I personally am happy to know. Best of all, my son was finally going to put his two year degree in business management to good use. After a week of staying in the hotel, my boy and Shawn moved out to a nice suburb in Cary. You're not gonna believe this, but both of their houses are on the same block as mine. I tell you, God is good. God is oh so good.

Oh yeah, I almost forgot. Rell and his girl done got they Muslim on. For those that's a little slow, it means they both became Muslim. I'm glad he finally got his mind right. I ain't crazy about all this Islam stuff, but anything is better than nothing.

Honk! Honk!

Oh shoot! That's my ride. I'm going off to join the others at Shawn and Ree-Ree post engagement party. Ain't that some wild shit. A post engagement party. Boy, I tell you. Black folks will take any occasion and turn it into a party.

***

"Baby, maybe you should go to the doctor," Steph suggested as she rubbed Rell's back while he puked into the toilet for the second time that day.

"Nah, I'm good love. Ain't nothing a little Pepto-Bismol can't handle." Rell stood and went to the sink to rinse out his mouth and then grabbed te mouth wash.

"You said that last week too," she said with concern in her vice.

"Baby, I'm good," Rell replied as he grabbed the Pepto-Bismol and swallowed two spoon fulls. "You ready to go?" he added as he bent to gargle his mouth once more.

"Yeah," Steph said softly. She turned away and shook her head in disbelief at Rell's stubbornness.

***

Down in Georgia, Lorna wasn't faring too well either.

"Mami! You can lie all you want, but I know what's going down. You can front, you can deny. I don't care. It don't change the facts, Mami!" Alexi said as she held a cold rag against the back of Lorna's neck.

"I'm not pregnant. It's just something... It's gotta be something I ate."

Lorna fought to convince Alexi as well as herself of this option. One week after Rell and her were together she'd woke up sick as a dog. During the week that followed, she had experienced two more bouts of nausea and vomiting. Today was the fourth time in two weeks. It didn't take a genius to figure out something was up. After the third incident, Lorna went out and bought a pregnancy test. Three tries later, the results had all come back the same. Positive! Lorna was carrying Rells baby.

"You can keep ignoring me, I don't care. When you ready to tell me the truth, then I'll back off. Until then..."

"Ooo... Oohh... Ooo!!" Lorna began crying uncontrollably.

"I'm sorry, Mami! I only want to help," Alexi said as she held Lorna, trying to soothe her.

121

"What am I going to do? What if he don't want kids," Lorna sobbed beginning to stress.

"Calm down Mami. We'll work this out," Alexi said as she continued to soothe Lorna while thinking of ways to help.

***

During this same time, Andrea was going through transitions of her own. The beat down had caused her to suffer a miscarriage forcing her to become a hermit for nearly four weeks. It took her body that long to fully heal. But the time she spent in seclusion was spent well. Andrea had thought about numerous ways to gain revenge on all her enemies, but couldn't come up with one satisfying way to strike them all. By herself, the task would be damn near impossible, but with a little help, her plans just might work.

Andrea needed people who wouldn't ask many questions when given instructions. People she could manipulate into doing some of her dirty work for her. She knew just where to find them. *'At the strip club,'* she thought as she realized her past experience in this field was about to pave the way for her revenge. 'Once I give them my sob story, the rest is a piece of cake,' Andrea thought as she sat on the floor of her unfurnished, run down one bedroom flat.

Andrea went from sugar to shit dam near overnight. From being on top of her game, to being shitted on by the game. Her fall from grace was a brutal one, leaving her even more heartless than she already was.

'I know where I fucked up. I got too cocky,' Andrea thought as she rose off the floor. She grabbed her car keys and headed for the front door. *'But I can fix this,'* she said as she left her flat to start her quest for the perfect strip club to target.

***

"Gloots?"

"Gloots!" Rell restated, letting Shawn know he heard right. "Glute's like in ass?"

"Yeah! But instead of a 'u' we spell ours with two O's and no E." Rell informed Shawn as the two sat at the counter of the Waffle House in Cary, drinking coffee.

"Cuz, I don't know," Shawn doubted for the umpteenth time. Since leaving the hustle, Shawn had found the square way of life unfulfilling. He missed the rush of living life on the edge. He hated watching his street cred fade away, as word spread across Durham that he and Rell had left the game.

Now Rell on the other hand was taking well to the change in lifestyle. With Rell, the hustle wasn't about fame, it was a means to an end. Shawn and Rell had always disagreed on their reasons for hustling. However heated the conversation got, they always agreed to disagree on the subject.

"Look cuz, the building is already built. The renovations and furnishing of the spot will cost around $170 to $250k, give or take a few thousand. Wachovia and Fidelity bank are already trying to invest in the idea. They know there's money in this restaurant shit."

"If done right," Shawn interjected negatively.

"If done right!? Cuz! We gonna blow Hooters off the motherfucking map. Tell me what man don't want to be in the company of fine women? We gonna have ass of all flavors. Girls with the Jessica Simpson ass, we'll call them colts. Chicks with them Beyonce butts, we'll call them stallions. Then we gone have them Clydedales. You know, asses that look like Blac Chyna's."

"Sound like you running a strip club nigga," Shawn said somewhat bitterly.

"Look fam. I told you about that nigga shit. Call me Rell, brotha, cuz..."

"Yeah, yeah, yeah!" Shawn said, speaking over Rell's protest over the use of the 'N' word.'

"What's up Shawn? You've been cuttin' me off while I'm speaking and coming out you mouth all sideways and shit. Something you wanna put in the air, cuz?"

"Look, I ain't feeling this 'Gloots' thang, but hey, do you playa!" Shawn said as he rose from the table. "We'll get up later." He swiftly made his exit not giving Rell time to utter any kind of response.

'Ever since we stopped hustling bricks, that brother been on some real kiss my ass type shit,' Rell thought to himself as he watched the back of Shawn's shirt as he left.

Chapter Twenty Eight

April 9th
Three and a half months later...

It was Friday night and the place was packed wall to wall. Girls were giving lap dances with two or more fingers stuck in their pussies or ass. Some were standing in dark corners called 'The Gap,' giving out $50 to $100 dollars for a five or ten minute Flip Session. For you slow cats, that means two guys on one girl. This isn't some classy joint. This is your everyday run-of-the-mill, hole in the wall, ranky-dank ass club. The floor was uneven in spots and the roof leaked when it rained. The V.I.P section consisted of two chairs and two hole infested pleather couches that was illuminated by a lamp that sat in the corner of the room emitting a soft blue light.

The spot was called '14k' and their clientele included all age groups. They varied from 14 to 60 plus. The ladies, however, were even more varied. Some were as young as fifteen, which Andrea had even witnessed getting their hustle on. Then of course you have the buss stop hoes. You know, the hood tricks. No car, three or more tattoos, and at least one kid. No man, but always got their legs open type chick. You had some prostitutes come through too.

These normally occupied 'The Gap' getting trains ran on them all night. Then came the worst breed of all, the cute girls who were strung out on crack. They were only there to get high, then bounce. These bitches were every strippers nightmare. Why? Cuz they fucked the price of pussy up. Sucking and fucking for five and ten dollars. Tonight was no different. Andrea and her new acquaintance Keisha, were wiping each other down with baby wipes in the back as they waited for 'Fire-ball' who was the owner, to join them.

"What's the matter, Kiwi?" Keisha asked as she wiped the small of Andrea's back.

"Nothing. Can you go a lil' lower?" Andrea said in response to her stage name.

"Yeah. It's not Travis is it?" Keisha pried further, as her hands wiped close to Andrea's ass.

"Girl, after my last experience, I don't stress over no nigga," she lied, silently hoping Travis would come.

For the past month and a week, Travis had been coming to '14K' to see Andrea a.k.a Kiwi. Each Friday she found that he fit the bill more and more when they interacted. He was exactly what she needed to get back at Rell. Travis was a hustler. He sold everything from cane to heroin, to weed, to pills. Pick your poison and he had it. After three Fridays of half priced services and small talk, Travis finally opened up.

'It must have been my Pinchy and Jumpy act that did it,' she thought as she pondered on how she won his trust. He had tried to cop cheap feels, but she had put the brakes on him immediately. She made it a priority to demanded his respect. She had fed him a sad song that would ensure she gained his pity. You probably heard it yourself once. You know the story.

'I only been with one man. I fell in love and got knocked up. He beat my ass all the time. I finally was able to bounce. Now my bills too high and I ain't got no help. My family ain't shit, so I gotta shake my ass for cash.'

But Andrea gave names and when she called out Rell's, Travis damn near barked her ear off talking his gangsta shit. Apparently, Rell and Travis had beef that went back a little ways. With her new story about how he violated her, the old beef was rekindled with new flames.

"Got my money, ladies?" Fireball asked as he strolled through the back room.

"Here you go." Andrea handed him his cut of her and Keisha's money.

"Damn you wet girl!" Keisha said as she bean rubbing Andrea's coochie, coaxing a moan from the back of her throat.

"I knew you two were fucking," said Fireball while he stood there counting the stack of money all the while cutting his eye to Keisha's hand.

Buzz! Buzz!

Fireball's cell phone began and vibrate in his pocket.

"Look, I hate to go. LORD KNOWS I hate to go, but I gotta take this call," he said after checking the caller I.D. Oh! That nigga you always milkin' is out there," he added as he stepped to the far corner.

Andrea stepped away from Keisha's touch. She slipped into a spare black thong, then walked out to the central room. She scanned the floor for Travis and it didn't take her long to locate him. China was all over him.

"Excuse me!" Andrea said in her best 'bitch puh-lease' voice, even though her presence alone was enough to chase off China, 'the crackhead' from attempting to make Travis her third trick of the night.

"I thought you stood me up," Travis said as he pulled out a fifty dollar bill for Andrea.

"Nah, boo. Not tonight. Tonight, you get your reward," she seductively whined and climbed in his lap backwards and leaned back onto his chest. Holding his knees, she arched her butt firmly against his crotch and then began to move to the beat of the song thumping loudly through the speakers.

Touch me
Tease me
Feel me
And caress me
Hold on tight
And don't let go
Baby I'm about to explode

The song by Case was helping her coax Travis into skeeting all over his True Religion Jeans. The more she grinded, the more he held on for dear life. With her back resting on his chest, she turned her head to whisper into his ear.

"Tonight I'm going to let you have some. That is if you want some."

"Don't play Kiwi," Travis groaned, trying to keep from bussing in her presence.

"I'm not. I'm waiting on you. Mmmm!" she moaned as she pushed a little harder on his erection causing her pussy to consume part of his imprint along with her thong.

That did it! Travis came all over the inside of his jeans.

"Ahhh, shit! Come on! Let's get outta here." Travis damned near ran her over while rushing to the exit.

"Hold up boo. Give me two minutes and I'll meet you out front. I need to holla at Keisha and grab my stuff!"

Andrea was headed to the back door at the same speed Travis was heading to the front. She grabbed her personals from her locker, then wrote some quick instructions on a Post-it. She pulled out her house key and wrapped it up with the note. As she made her way out the club, she passed the note to a gyrating Keisha.

"Hey, you leaving?" Keisha asked while taking the note.

"Yeah, but read that ASAP!" Andrea pointed at the note while making a hurried bee-line to the front door.

Two hours later at the 'Guest Quarters' hotel in Durham, things were beginning to jump off. Andrea had showered, then snacked on some Little Debbie cakes and soda she'd bought for her and Travis. She had pumped the vending machine with quarters earlier that day in anticipation of the current situation.

Travis sat on the bed up against the headboard with his feet crossed, while puffing on a strawberry White Owl. Posted up like a boss in his socks and boxers, Andrea admitted to herself that the nigga was looking pretty good.

"You gonna keep ya socks on?" Andrea stood fully in the nude in front of the bed.

"Yeah, ah nigga feet and toes kinda jacked," Travis replied, causing them both to burst out laughing.

Andrea climbed onto the bed, straddling Travis' thighs as she pushed him onto his back. Leaning down, she took the blunt from him and took two long pulls. Aiming for the ice bucket, she flung the rest of it into the bucket.

Reaching her right hand up and sliding it under Travis' head, she leaned as close as possible, then kissed him deeply. As she did this, she took her left hand, reached between her legs and found Travis' swollen manhood. She then slowly sized him up with a gentle caressing motion. He was at least ten inches from what she was holding. *'Good, he has more than enough to make this work,'* Andrea mused and guided his wood to her kitty. When Travis tried to push in, Andrea sprang up and started running game.

"Uh-uh! Boy, that thing is too big for me!" Andrea whined as she sat balled up by the foot of the bed, trying her best to look scared.

"Girl, stop playing! Ah nigga shit hard as fuck!" Travis said before spinning off his back to face her. He pulled her legs from her chest so he could get her to lay flat on her back. "How you scared of this and you done already had a baby," he asked in question of her sudden fear of his dick.

"Look! You see this? I didn't have a natural birth. I had a cesarean section." She pulled her abdomen tightly in different directions to show him the faint, well healed scar.

"So you ain't fucked, but one nigga huh?" He had his bitch please face on.

"I already told you. Rell was my first and only and he was not as big as you. Maybe only about half and it would still hurt sometime. Ain't no way I can do this Travis." She tensed her body up and made her eyes tear up.

"Baby, don't cry. Look, I ain't gonna hurt you." *'This bitch think she got me fooled.'* "Just let me stick the head in. If it hurts, I'll stop. I promise," he added as he rubbed the head of his dick against her coochie.

"Don't play T."

"I'm not," he said, coaxing her to relax.

Travis spread her thighs eagle style, then easily slid his tip in. *'I knew this bitch was frontin,'* Travis thought as he held his position for a few moments. He moved back slightly as if he was pulling out, but once the very tip was almost free, he rammed his piece all the way in with full force. He began to move in and out rapidly and viciously in her cunt.

Andrea knew the temptation would create this reaction. As he was reaching his climax, she brought tears to her eyes and fought to free herself from under him.

"Aaaah! Owe! Teeee… Uugh! Stooooppp! Ooh! Stop T! Ahhhh!" Andrea moaned, protested, cried and moaned some more. She pushed at his chest as he proceeded to pump harder and faster. She had to allow him to go 'ham' on her pretty little pussy for a little bit. This would help her next step go down all the more smoothly. "Get off me! OFF! STOOP!!" Andrea screamed with all her might.

Her screams finally got through to Travis. He flinched just enough for her to quickly slide backwards out of his grip. Before he could grab her, she shot him a quick elbow jab to the ribs. Andrea took his moment of surprise to hop off the bed and dash into the bathroom faster than a bat out of hell. Once inside, she locked the door, just as Travis grabbed the handle.

"Open the door. Yo Kiwi! Open up," Travis yelled from the other side.

"Aaww. Ooooh!! Damn it, Travis. I told you I was… Oooh!"

Andrea laid the 'anger tears of pain and sorrow' on thick during her theatrics. She reached for the clutch bag she stashed in the room earlier and retrieved a pack of dark cherry Kool-aid. She then poured the entire pack on her coochie. Taking one of the hotels complimentary bottles of shampoo, she emptied half of it into the sink, then filled it back up with water. After she shook it hard a few times, she lay on the floor and proceeded to pour the soapy mixture onto her vagina as well. With her hips angled upwards, she used her index and middle finger to mix the 'pussy potion'.

"Kiwi.?" Travis called to her softly through the door. "Open up. I think the front deskman is at the door." Travis was getting nervous as hell, but he maintained his cool as he attempted to persuade her out of the bathroom.

Leaning forward and letting her pussy muscles relax, Andrea allowed the gooey mixture to run from her vagina and into the toilet. Once satisfied with the amount inside the toilet, she stood and let the rest run down her leg and drip on the floor.

'Now it's time to freak this shit,' she mentally plotted as she opened the door and continued her theatrics. "How could you T? I trusted you. I, oohh!!" Andrea bellowed between fake sobs and tears.

"Aw fuck. I thought you was fa… Damn! I did that?!" Travis asked, turning to find Andrea sitting balled up in a thin puddle of fake blood. She continued to leak fake blood as each sob made her story all the more believable. "Damn! Look, let me run these hotel people off alright? Come on, I may need you to help." Travis handed her a towel and pulled her to her feet.

After convincing the deskman that everything was fine, they sat at the foot of the bed for a discussion.

"I guess all I was to you was just another trick huh?" Andrea asked still producing tears and soft sobs.

"Nah, Ma! But I ain't gonna front. I thought that 'one nigga' shit was a game."

"GAME! GAME?! So I'm shaking my ass in some hole-in-the-wall club cause I gave my virginity to some small dick asshole who beat me? Does that shit sound funny to you? Huh?!" Andrea snapped as she crumpled into Travis' arms and cried.

"Kiwi, I'm sorry. I'm..."

"I thought you were special, T. I thought I could trust you. Why? Tell me why you couldn't be the one?" Andrea sobbed and trembled and boo-hooed.

"You think I'm dumb. All you tryna do is keep me from calling the cops and screaming rape. You don't give a fuck about me," she said while checking the bath towel for fake blood stains for added effect.

"Let me make this right. Come on. Trust me, Kiwi," Travis pleaded softly as he pulled her to her feet.

"No Travis. It's obvious that we don't share the same feelings."

Andrea pulled away from him and made her way to her discarded clothes. As soon as she bent down to pick her pants up, Travis scooped her up into his arms and carried her towards the bathroom.

"Put me down, T," Andrea pretended to protest, kicking and wiggling, trying to free herself from his arms.

"Relax, baby. I'm gonna show you how sorry I really am."

Travis placed her in the tub, ran some water and mixed in some bubble bath liquid. He gently and affectionately began to bathe her. The next two hours were spent with Andrea receiving multiple messages and countless kisses all over her body. No sooner had she relaxed from the soothing attentions of Travis when he pinned her legs wide and did a tongue dive deep into her vagina. He licked and lapped on her coochie tenderly for uncountable minutes until she had to force her legs closed.

"Did I hurt you? I'm sorry. Damn, I keep fucking up."

"Gill, T. I just wanna know something," Andrea interjected, cutting his apologies short.

"What's up?"

"Will it always hurt and bleed when we... you know?" she asked as she put one finger into her coochie, pretending to be looking for blood.

"I think I broke you all the way in, so you shouldn't."

"If I wanted to..." she began, but Travis cut her off.

"I'll be gentle this time, I swear! If it hurts, I'll stop. I'll pull out this time. That's my word."

"I believe you T. But please, go slow," she said, sounding doubtfully.

"Don't worry, Ma. I got you."

Travis pulled her in close and kissed her softly. When he felt her relax, he parted her legs and used his hips to guide his throbbing manhood to her warm pussy. Pushing firmly on the very top of her clit, he caused her to squirm and moisten even more. Feeling like she was ready to take him, he reached down between them and placed his dick at her entrance.

As she clenched the muscles in her vagina as tight as possible, Travis struggled slightly to get his dick in her tunnel. He kept his word and took it slow, all the while she kept running game. By the time they finished, she had Travis thinking he was Mr. Superdick.

Travis had made the fatal mistake of allowing his self control to completely shift into the hands of Andrea. She capitalized on his weakness by using her two strongest trump cards, guilt and infatuation. When these cards are played together properly, not many men can escape their trap. And Andrea had played hers flawlessly. Travis had been bamboozled by a pro. With her goal now achieved, she began scheming on the next phase of her plan for revenge.

***

Vvvreeen! Vvvreeen!

"Hello!?"

"Girl, give me that. What's up?" Shawn said after he snatched the phone out of Ree-Ree's hand.

"Who is this?"

"Who you think it is?" Shawn said roughly.

"This Alexi, I'm looking for Shawn."

"What's up, Mami!" Shawn responded a little too happily,

causing Ree-Ree to elbow him sharply.

"Nothing, Papi. Just wanted to give you the heads up on what's popping."

"Go ahead, I'm listening." Ree-Ree was in Shawn's face trying to get him to give up the callers identity.

"Me and Lorna moved down here last week. We changed locale's, but the game ain't changed," Alexi stated.

"Here? What you mean here?"

"North Cack, baby. We moved to Raleigh last week."

"Say word!"

"No shit? When can I come see you, Papi?" Alexi was dripping sex appeal into the phone.

"Shit! We talking business or..." Shawn posed a half question to keep Ree-Ree guessing.

"Nope! I'm trying to fuck. You wit that, Papi?" Alexi asked, sounding as sexy as possible.

"Hell yeah! Where you at?" Shawn asked as he scribbled down the word 'Business' and showed it to Ree-Ree who caught the hint and backed off.

"Meet me at the IHOP on Capital Blvd."

"Bet! Give me about thirty minutes, alright?!" He hung up before Alexi could reply.

"Business!? What you mean Business!?" Ree-Ree asked as soon as Shawn ended his call.

"When I get back, I'll explain. But right now, I gotta go." Shawn said as he hurriedly grabbed his keys and wallet. He gave Ree-Ree a quick kiss on the lips and then swiftly breezed out the door. "Don't wait up," he yelled as he pulled the door closed behind him.

"What the hell is going on? I thought they were through with the drug game," Ree-Ree said aloud to herself as she dialed up Stephanie on her cell. She's going to get to the bottom of this ASAP.

Chapter Twenty Nine

9:17am the next morning at the McDonalds in Wellon Village.

"Know he didn't," Keisha said from the passenger seat of Andrea's Mercedes Coupe while they were waiting in the drive-thru for their order.

"Yes, he did girl. Then had the nerve to KEEP saying that shit. Girl, I finally shut him up by telling him I loved him too." Andrea's statement and facial expression caused them both to laugh hysterically.

Meanwhile, inside the same Mickey D's...

Ree-Ree and Stephanie were waiting in line to pay for their food.

"That'll be $8.78," the cashier stated as she accepted the ten dollar bill from Stephanie. "Here's your change."

"Thanks. Now for the hundredth time Ree-Ree. I am not lying," Steph said, trying to calm her homegirl.

"I can't believe Shawn would lie, then stay out all night on me without being hurt or damn near dead." She was worried sick about Shawn's absence.

"I don't know what to tell you, but he wasn't with Rell, because he was home all last night." Steph grabbed the food off the counter and reached for some napkins.

Over in Drive-Thru, Andrea's eyes had locked on the two unsuspecting women through the glass. "Excuse me miss, here's an extra twenty dollar bill. I need you to make me two milkshakes as fast as you can. Keep the change if you can do it in less than two minutes," Andrea bribed the drive-thru cashier.

Ree-Ree unknowingly bought Andrea extra time as she stood at the counter fixing her coffee.

"What you need them milkshakes for?" Keisha's curiosity was suddenly peaked.

"I need you to throw one."

"On who?" Keisha sat up in her seat to peer inside the restaurant.

"Remember them bitches I told you about?" Andrea had her eyes glued on them.

"Yeah!"

"I see two of them inside. Hand me my purse," Andrea said, but she never took her eyes off of the two women.

"Mace! I thought we was gonna throw milkshakes on them hoes?" Keisha was slightly confused about what Andrea intended to do.

"Here are your milkshakes and your food. Sorry for the short delay and here's the change."

"Nah, girl. That's yours, " Andrea blurted out, then pulled from the window.

"You think he cheating on me? Or maybe it's the wedding. Maybe..."

"Or maybe you're stressing for nothing," Stephanie said while opening the door that lead to the parking lot. Ree-Ree stepped in stride beside her, still asking questions.

"So I'm tripping right?"

SCREEECH! PLOP! PLOP!

Before the either of them could react to the sound of the squealing tires, Andrea and Keisha doused their ass with the milkshakes.

As they each wiped their faces clean trying to see, Andrea sprayed mace into their eyes, nose, and mouth. As they fought to breathe, Andrea and Keisha started beating their ass ruthlessly. When the manager threatened to call the cops, Andrea and Keisha bounced, laughing and talking shit in the process.

A Whore's Conscience

'Kiwi? Who the fuck is Kiwi?' Steph thought as she struggled to compose herself. "Whoever you are bitch! You better be right with Allah before I catch you," Steph mumbled under her breath before silently promising herself that she WOULD get her back.

***

Back in Raleigh...

"From the way it sounds, we both owe our good fortunes to Rell," Alexi said to Shawn as she chopped an assortment of onions and peppers for their omelette.

"How you figure that? I ain't with this square shit. Personally, I was happier in the game," Shawn said as he stirred chunks of unidentifiable meat.

"Then why'd you stop?"

"Cause Rell punk ass wanted to retire," Shawn stated in a tone that left his words open for interpretation.

"I didn't ask about Rell. I asked about you. Why did you stop hustling?"

***

In the back hallway of the three bedroom home they shared, Lorna stood listening to Shawn whine about the choices Rell had made.

"When Rell left the game, he took all his connects with him," Shawn explained as Alexi dropped the peppers and onions into the skillet with the meat.

"Why he cut you off like that?"

"He said it's the only way to protect his neck. Something about his name being used by whomever he turned on to his plug as a bargaining chip with the cops. Basically, if I wanted to keep my hustle, then I would have to find my own plug," Shawn concluded, as he watched Alexi toss the eggs into the pan.

"What you cooking?" Lorna walked in shooting Shawn a 'Nigga you foul' look.

"What's with you?" Shawn asked, sensing the static in the air between them.

"Don't pay Mami no mind. She just pregnant," Alexi said to Shawn as she lifted the pan to show Lorna the omelettes.

"So when you gonna tell Rell?" Shawn took a seat at the kitchen table.

"No disrespect, but that's none of your biz," Lorna said while pulling a jug of orange juice out of the fridge.

"You know what, that's my cue. I'm out. You got my number. Hit me up later," Shawn said as he checked his pockets for his keys and left.

"Is that how you be talking about me when I'm not around?" Lorna asked, sitting down with her glass of orange juice.

"Oh! You heard that shit too."

"Yeah, and I didn't like it. I didn't like it one bit," Lorna stated, as she cut her eyes towards Alexi briefly before turning away and losing herself in thought.

***

Before Stephanie left the parking lot of McDonalds, she had already contacted Rell by cell and told him what had just jumped off. They agreed to meet at their house and discuss the matter more thoroughly. Rell tried to contact Shawn, who was still M.I.A., and his efforts were futile. Unable to reach him in person, he left two voicemails, and went back to comforting the ladies.

"You sure you don't know Kiwi?" Stephanie asked again.

"Look, love. I don't know no Kiwi, Mango, or any other chick with a fruity name," Rell said as he handed Steph a fresh bag of her favorite fruit, strawberries, and a pack of ice for her bruised temple.

"And you didn't send Shawn off to handle some drug deal?" Ree-Ree asked Rell, looking at him skeptically.

"Ree, you can re-word and re-ask that same question a million more times and my answer gonna be the same. I'm out of the drug game," Rell replied, growing a bit annoyed by the twenty-one questions he was being assaulted with from both sides. Between Steph and Ree-Ree, they were keeping it HOT on his ass.

Shawn received the voicemails from Rell and immediately beelined his way to Rell's spot. He came in through the side door as Ree-Ree was mid-sentence into another question that she decided was worth re-asking.

"And you don't know where he was all last night?" Her question sounded more like an accusation.

"I already told you. You need to be asking your man about that," Rell stated tensely.

"Ask me what!?" Shawn asked as he entered the living room.

"Where the hell have you been, huh!?" Ree-Ree's flying bag of ice was caught by Shawn inches from his face.

"What the fuck? What happened?" Shawn asked when he noticed the knots, bruises and small cuts both girls had.

"You know some bitch named Kiwi?" Steph spits out at Shawn. "Is that who you been laying up with?" Her words caught Shawn off guard and he was stunned speechless.

"Steph chill! I got thi..."

"Nah, fuck that! You been all in my shit over this nigga the whole time and I let you do you. Now when I ask some questions it's hold up? It's chill? You must be trippin!" Steph spazzed on Ree-Ree angrily.

"Cuz, get your girl," Shawn warned Rell as the tension began to mount.

"You serious! Get my girl!? Our girls get jumped and for all I know it because of you."

"Hold up, Nigga! You tryna pin this shit on me?" yelled Shawn.

Rell was hot. "What I tell you about that nigga shit?!" he said as he crossed the room towards Shawn.

Ree-Ree runs in between Shawn and Rell, pushing Shawn towards the door. "Nah, baby. Chill! Come on, let's go."

"This is what happens when you quit the game! Niggas test yo' gangsta. This shit your fault Nigga!" Shawn barked as Ree-Ree pulled him out the side door.

"I got yo nigga!" Rell snapped as he lunged for Shawn, missing him by a couple of inches just as Ree-Ree got the screen door shut.

***

Two hours had passed since the blow up between the four friends had happened. Rell was still visibly heated, but Steph had waited long enough. She and Rell needed to talk.

"Baby, can we talk?" she asked as she moved to sit next to Rell on the couch.

"What's wrong?"

"Do you really think Shawn is the reason we got jumped?" she asked as she lay her head on Rell's shoulder.

"I dunno. I hope not."

"You think he still hustling?" Steph continued to press.

"I can't say. He been acting real strange though. Real slick mouthed and shit."

"I ain't trying to tell you what to do, but I think you need to keep your eyes on Shawn." Steph sat up from his shoulders to look in his face. "I mean it."

"Relax, bay. I got this," Rell said as he thought about how to track down info on Shawn and a bitch named Kiwi.

Chapter Thirty

Three weeks later, Rell had torn through his sources looking for this mystery woman. Finally, he caught a break from a guy who used to cop ounces from him. Kiwi was a stripper at '14K.' Even though he doubted she was the chick he was looking for, he still decided to check the intel out.

It was almost Twelve o'clock when Rell stepped inside the club. The place looked like a death trap and smelled like an outhouse. As he scanned the room, his eyes fell on a huge barrel chested guy who had to be a bouncer. Making his way through the crowd was harder than he thought. He couldn't take a step without some girl propositioning him. None of the chicks knew Kiwi or at least, were not going to admit as much.

"I need your help," were Rell's words to the bouncer after his eyes fell on the C-note that was floating in his face.

"What'chu need?"

"I'm looking for someone. A girl named Kiwi. You know her?"

"Yeah," the bouncer replied flatly cutting his eye from Rell and raising his eyebrows at the bill.

"Is she here?" Rell handed the money over, catching the hint.

"Nah. She stopped working here about two or three weeks ago," the bouncer replied.

"Damn! Do you know anybody that can reach her?" Rell was desperately hoping for more info.

"Nahhhh. No, wait!, Keisha! Keisha might know," he said, remembering Kiwi's homegirl. He pointed to a chestnut brown sister giving an extremely erotic lap dance, midway across the room.

"Good looking," Rell said and moved on his target.

"Now what's a baller like you doing in a place like this?" Keisha asked as she rubbed her tits in his face while she grinded on his lap.

"If I answer your question, will you answer mine?" her John asked as he palmed her ass to stop her from grinding.

But before she could answer, Rell cut in.

"Excuse me! Keisha?! You Keisha right?!"

Before she could brush him off, Rell noticed who she was servicing. Shawn! *What the fuck!* thought Rell as he noticed Shawn giving him the 'Get lost I got this' face.

"Damn! My bad, wrong Keisha," Rell lied, then strolled off to a far corner to wait for Shawn.

Moments later, Shawn nonchalantly strolled over to Rell.

"Look, we heading to the Residence Inn on Highway 55. Follow us over." Shawn spun away on his last word, then walked out before Rell could respond. The two hadn't spoken in three weeks and from the look of things, Shawn was still feeling some type of way.

Rell had let the incident become water on a ducks back, because in his mind, Shawn was still his man's. They'd been through too much to let some foolish argument come between them. At least from Rells point of view.

"Yo, Shawn! Hold up!" Rell yelled, causing Shawn to stop and face him. "Give me a call whenever you find out what she know about Kiwi, Aaight?" Just then Rell spotted Keisha making her way out the club.

"Yeah." Shawn said with a blank face. He then turned to hop into his midnight grey Hummer.

I know this nigga ain't trying to trip,' Rell thought as he hopped in his tar black Escalade and hit the ignition button. "Fuck it! Let him be mad. I ain't kissin' nobody ass." The deep gurgle and powerful growl of Rells' V8 engine mimicked his mood, drowning out his thoughts as he peeled from the parking lot.

***

"Oh shiiiit!" Shawn yelled as Keisha sat on his dick in a hybrid version of the 'reverse cowgirl.'

Leaning forward on her elbows with her knees as support, she butterflied all over Shawns dick. Having received the info he needed from Keisha, on the ride to the room, Shawn decided to enjoy the night and fuck her anyway. His initial plan was to just beast fuck Keisha and get a quick nut, but the girl knew how to work her hips something fierce. She was doing shit with her hips and finessing his dick in ways words could never explain.

By the third time he came, Shawn knew he was in trouble. Between her talk game, her head game, and her pussy popping, Keisha had Shawn fucked up. I mean all the way up! Maybe it was the mounting stress he'd been going through, or maybe it was just nice to be in his own element again.

Whatever the underlying cause was, it most certainly helped Keisha obtain her lifetime goal. *'I got me one!'* Keisha thought as she sat on Shawn's back and massaged him to sleep.

***

"Another dead end, cuz. The Kiwi chick moved back up to New York, somewhere. At least that's what she told Kiesha. On another note, meet me at your booty store around 7:30 tonight. We need to talk." Shawns voicemail answered one question, but left another. It was ten minutes to eight and Shawn was nowhere to be found.

'I'm gonna give him until Eight. Then I'm gone,' Rell said to himself as two ladies roamed into his place. "I'm sorry ladies. We're not open for... Lorna!" As the ladies turned to face Rell, his attempted brushoff was halted when he noticed who stood before him.

"Hey Rell!" Both ladies greeted him simultaneously.

"Sorry I'm late, but I had to swing by their place on the way over." Shawn said, referring to the ladies that stood between him and Rell.

"You guys are an awfully long way from... hold up! There place!" Rell stated, catching on late to what Shawn had said.

"We moved to Raleigh a little over three weeks ago."

"I thought Shawn told you," Lorna replied, turning to face Shawn.

"Not my biz, remember," Shawn said shooting her a 'what, you forgot?' look.

A Whore's Conscience

"Here you go. I got something else to handle," he added as he handed Rell a note and walked off towards the door.

"Yo, I'm getting sick of your shit! What's your fucking problem?" Rell asked, finally becoming Fed up with Shawn.

"You! Nigga! Ever since we...! Yo, Fuck this! I ain't gotta explain shit to you. I'mma do me, you do you." Shawn turned his back on Rell and started to leave. In the blink of an eye, Rell had crossed the ten feet that was separating him from Shawn and scooped him up from behind.

"I told you about that nigga shit!" Rell said as he kicked Shawn in his ass, sliding him across the floor on his chest as he tried to rise.

"Rell, chill! Y'all fam!" Alexi said as she and Lorna each grabbed one of Rell's arms. Shawn got up from the floor and charged at the restrained Rell.

"Back up Shawn!" Lorna said as she turned her back to Alexi. Something had to be done, and fast. "Rell! I'm pregnant with your baby," Lorna said, watching Rell's whole face change from anger to shock. "Alexi, take Shawn outside," she added.

"Fuck that! I'm good! Me and you gonna finish this, cuz!" Shawn barked as he brushed off Alexi and exited the restaurant mumbling angrily.

"Are you for real? How? I mean... Whoa!" Rell said as he sat in one of the neary booths.

"I'm sorry you're finding out like this. It was the only thing I could think of to keep you two from scrapping," Lorna said as she and Alexi sat down across from Rell. Lorna's paper was just as long, it not longer than Rell's, so she wasn't trying to entrap him with some pregnancy story.

"So what we go do?" Rell asked after a long pause.

"That depends on you."

"Look, I'm gonna be in the car. Y'all take your time," Alexi said, sliding out the booth and excusing herself.

"What you mean?" Rell asked once Alexi was out of hearing range.

"Look, Papi! I'm not trying to raise a baby on some broken home shit. You know, one Mami's, no Papi. Nah! Either we gonna raise this child together or I'm gonna find another man to be a dad," Lorna said, vehemently placing all her options on the table.

"What you mean another dad? Ain't no other man raising my

kid!"

"Be easy, Papi. I'm just keeping it gangster. I could leave tomorrow and you could never find me or our baby. Either you gonna honor my situation fully, or I'll find somebody who will," Lorna stated, cutting off Rell's angry command.

"I can't just up and leave my girl. How can you box me in like this?"

"I told you from the start how I felt and I never once ran game. But to be fair, I'll give you time. As a matter of fact, I'll give you one month. That should be more than enough time for you to make a decision. Now come here," Lorna said as she grabbed Rell's left wrist and pulled him around the booth's table. Once he was close enough, Lorna kissed Rell lovingly. "I'll be in touch," she added as she rose and left.

'Fuck!' Rell thought as he wondered what other drama Allah was going to throw at him.

***

That night Rell had planned to go home, get a bite to eat, hold his lady tight and get some sleep. There was no way he could keep Lorna's pregnancy a secret from Stephanie. But until he could consult with Imam Hakim, his Muslim community leader, he wouldn't discuss or decide anything concerning the pregnancy.

However, when he got home, he found the entire house lit by candles and exotically scented incense. He and Steph had ordered various assortments of Liberator position assisting wedges. The wedges were meant to help couples perform and maintain certain sexual positions longer. Today, their order had finally arrived.

Although sex was the furthest thing from Rell's mind, the wedges arrival, the house ambience, and the lingerie Stephanie wore, formed a temptation he couldn't resist. Leopard print spotted her silk bra and matching thong. A black garter belt wrapped her waist, while its straps connected and held her black fishnet stockings in place. Her feet sported six inch heels of the same leopard print.

When Rell entered the bathroom, he saw Steph's reflection in the mirror. Her reflection showed her in the bedroom, bent over the wedge created for the doggy style position. Her right hand was bracing her upper body, while her left fingers stroked her pussy.

'Damn! She pumping that R. Kelly too,' Rell thought as he realized anything less than him fucking tonight would result in an

142

argument.

Two hours, fifteen minutes, and no breaks later, Rell was still laying pipe to Stephanie. Every way a man could lay the dick, Rell, had laid it. He had half stroked it, stirred it like coffee, beast fucked it, and was now currently administering long, deep, slow strokes. Those were Stephs favorite because this was when Rell would get to talking real nice and nasty to her.

"Ahhh! Gawd! Ohhh, baby! Yesssss!!" Steph moaned as she lay on her back, while a smaller wedge lifted her pussy about four inches off the bed. The wedge placed Steph's pussy and pelvis at a height and angle that naturally forced her legs open, thus freeing Rell to focus on her with all his energy.

The way he spoke so tenderly to her and how he was maintaining his rhythm while he was pleasuring her, became too much for Steph to handle. The sensation was overwhelming, and when she moaned from her soul for the fifth time that night signaling another orgasm, they came in unison. His body tensed as he blasted off what felt like ten gallons of sperm into Steph. He had never in his life came like this.

"Ahhh!!" Steph gasped as she felt two simultaneous thumps tap the inside of her stomach. As she dug her nails into his back, he collapsed on her breast, exhausted. The anger, anxiety, lust, and fear Rell had built up inside all rushed from his body. Stephanie had understood and had let him have his way with her.

'I've got to figure out how to keep my baby and my lady,' Rell thought as he lay slumped on top of Steph.

'Allah, let those thumps I felt be what I've longed for,' Stephanie prayed as she allowed her eyes to mist over with tears while she rubbed her mans sweat drenched back.

***

Back in Durham, even more stress was being worked out.

"Yeah motherfucker! You like that?!, Huh? Huh!? Now what's my mother fucking name!?"

"Ugh! Kee...ooh!!"

"I can't hear you! Say it, spell it! Say that shit!" She slowed down the strokes, realizing her pace was too much for her love to handle. "Is that better, baby? Huh?!"

"Yeah!"

"Now say it. Who's your mother fucking wifey, huh!?" She asked as she pumped his dick in ways that would put Vaness Del Rio to shame.

"Yoooou! Oh damn! You! You! You, damnit!" Shawn bellowed and moaned as he lay on his back, hypnotized.

"Nah, nigga! You gonna say my name!" She was quickening the pace once more, milking his manhood with her warm moisture.

"Oh, shit! Fuck it!! Ka... Ka... Keishaaah!!" Shawn screamed like a bitch as Keisha brought the house down with her surfboard hip motions once she heard him submit to calling her name.

Shawn came so hard that he bit his lip drawing blood. Keisha had done things to him that no other chick could, nor would dare.   He had started staying more and more with Keisha and had only slept at home once in the three nights since he had met her. He was quickly losing interest in Ree-Ree. To him, she represented the path that was well worn and now in his past. Keisha was the icon of his future. He just needed more time to push Ree-Ree out of his life as smoothly as possible.

Keisha had laced her web tightly around Shawn, and knew she had him completely open. *Everything going as planned,'* Keisha thought as she sucked and licked every trace of sperm and cunt juice she could off of her lover's dick. 'My peoples ain't gonna believe how open I got this nigga,' Keisha thought as she took Shawn's freshly cleaned, half limp cock and smacked its head against her lips and tongue, coaxing him into another erection.

Chapter Thirty One

Noon the next day...

Steph, Ree-Ree and Ms. Ce-Ce were out enjoying lunch. The three ladies had agreed to meet in Durham and discuss the recent problems that had emerged. The Italian pizzeria was packed, but after a thirty-five minute wait, the ladies found a seat and sent Stephanie off to place their order. Steph had a tan that made her able to easily pass for Sicilian and since she had spent some time in New York, it helped her learn how to pull off the accent.

"With her placing our orders and flirting a little, we'll have our food in about ten or fifteen minutes," Ms. Ce-Ce said, trying to lighten the somber mood Ree-Ree was in.

"Yeah," she said, giving the one emotionless word.

"Shawn still not coming home?" Ms. Ce-Ce asked, sliding out the booth on her side to sit next to Ree-Ree.

"No! He even called off our wedding."

"Girl, hush! Don't start that shit," Ms. Ce-Ce stated watching Ree-Ree's eyes fill with tears.

"Ms. Ce-Ce, it's all I can do. All I got left is my tears. He won't come home. When he do, he won't talk to me. He smell's like alcohol and cheap perfume. And when he looks at me, it's like he's disgusted with me. I don't know what to do."

"Well, for one, stop looking at Shawn like he's the only dick in North Carolina," Ms. Ce-Ce said, not caring how her words were received.

"But..."

"This ain't no debate. I got you by over 20 years. So what the hell you gonna teach me about a man? Huh?" Ms. CeCe said, cutting into Ree-Ree's reply. "Now, I love Shawn. I love him like a son, but if he dumb enough to lose a good girl like you, over some cheap fix out in them streets, then fuck it, and fuck him. It's his loss. Now what you got to do is let him know you mean business. You gotta let him know his ass can hit the door if he ain't gonna get his shit together. But don't talk about it, be about it," Ms. Ce-Ce continued to instruct Ree-Ree.

"How I do that?"

"By giving him an ultimatum and when the times up, do what you gotta do. Whether you gotta leave him, cut him, or go Rambo on his ass, do what you gotta do for you. Fuck the tears! Save them shits for funerals and sad songs. Take control of your nigga, understand? Take control of your shit," Ms. Ce-Ce said with conviction. She then turned Ree-Ree's face to her own. "And when you get control of your shit, stay on top of your shit. Don't let another bitch turn your man's head again. You hear?"

Ree-Ree nodded her head soaking in every word Ms. Ce-Ce had to say.

"Ree-Ree, take these plates. I gotta go back to the rest of our stuff," Steph said, handing some of their order over to Ree-Ree.

"You need some help?" Ms. Ce-Ce offered Steph.

"Nah, I got it," she replied, heading back to the counter.

After Steph left, Ms Ce-Ce continued. "If you really wanna keep Shawn, think about what I said. And if you feel like he worth going all out for, then take care of your shit. But if you feel like it ain't worth the fight, then move on to greener pastures," Ms. Ce-Ce added as Steph placed down the rest of their food. "Now, let's eat!" Ms. Ce-Ce said as Steph handed everyone their drinks.

***

Across town, another meeting of the minds was taking place...

Rell was at the Fayetteville Street Masjid, seeking guidance from Allah and assistance from his Imam.

A Whore's Conscience

"Let me see if I'm hearing this right. You and sister Stephanie are bound by Muta (Muslim equivalent to dating), but Lorna predates your current union. Now you believe this Lorna is now carrying your child. She is threatening to leave with your unborn child if you do not commit to her. Have I stated the facts correctly?" brother Hakim asked as he turned through the pages of his Holy Money.

"Yes," Rell answered.

"You really think this child she is carrying is yours?" Hakim asked, continuing to thumb through his Holy Money.

"Brother Hakim, I know what you're thinking. But truth be told, I'd have more to gain from this than she does."

"Then are you willing to do what Allah commands of you?" Hakim asked as he stopped turning pages and looked Rell square in the eyes.

"Yes, I may not like it, but, yes."

"You're in a union with sister Stephanie. You took an oath with her and Allah. An oath that must be honored at all costs. She is your wife in Islam. Lorna is not. If you shame sister Stephanie, you shame Islam. Lorna isn't Muslim, therefore, we can't sanction her under our faith's rules. However, I shall have two care packages made up regarding this matter. It will contain information that will inform both ladies how to handle the recent developments, according to Islam, should they desire to take this route. As for you, it is to help you form wise decisions as Allah has guided you," brother Hakim informed him.

"But what if she still bounces off with my child?"

"Read Surah 94, Ayat 8, and when you become at peace with that, remember this: NO gift ALLAH has given you, can man deny. And nothing denied by ALLAH, can man give you," Hakim quoted, then stood to embrace Rell.

"Thank you brother," Rell said as he embraced Hakim.

"Dua," brother Hakim said as he began invoking the blessings of ALLAH for brother Rell.

***

Back at the Italian pizzaria, the ladies were leaving the eatery.

"It's good to see you two laughing and smiling," Ms. Ce-Ce said as the ladies left the restaurant and walked the sidewalk of the strip mall of Wellen Village.

'Oh hell no! I know that ain't who I think it is,' Andrea thought as she

stopped in the middle of the parking lane she was in, and watched the ladies entered the Urban World Clothing Store. *Where the fuck they parked at?'* She coasted through the nearby parking lanes searching for anyone of Rell's three cars. She came up on a platinum colored Lexus ES 350 with a vanity plate that read 'STEPHS.'

"Bingo!" Andrea said, as she spotted what could only belong to Steph.

'I got something for your ass.' She parked her car two spots up from the Lexus. With her plan formulated, she hopped out her whip and dashed into the grocery store to make a quick purchase.

"I can't keep lugging around this coat and purse. Give me the keys Steph. I'm going to toss my stuff in the back seat," Ms. Ce-Ce said. She took the keys from Steph and made her way towards the exit of the clothing store.

'Hell yeah!' Andrea mentally screamed as she scanned for the girls on the sidewalk and parking lot, but they were no where in sight. No sooner than she turned her head from the clothing store and proceeded towards the Lexus, Ms. Ce-Ce stepped out.

'I must be tripping, cause this bitch in front of me, looks like Andrea.' Ms. Ce-Ce watched the back of Andrea stroll up to Stephs' Lexus.

"Fuck!" Andrea muffled her curse as she tried to open the gas cover, but couldn't.

"They're called cover locks," Ms. Ce-Ce said, causing Andrea to flinch and turn. Before Andrea could respond properly, Ms. Ce-Ce tossed her jacket over Andrea face to block her vision.

Now Ms. Ce-Ce wasn't no spring chick, but she wasn't no old bird either. She was fourty-four even though she looked to be in her early thirties. When she got crunk though, all hell would break loose.

She scooped Andrea, causing the girls face to hit the pavement first. Ms. Ce-Ce jumped on her back and began hitting Andrea on all sides of her face. "I've been waiting to get my hands on your ass," Ms. Ce-Ce said as she rose from Andrea back and began kicking and stomping the bitch.

"Hey! Hey you!" a male passerby yelled, getting Ms. Ce-Ce's attention. "You know there's a Polic sub-station right over there," the anonyymous man added while pointing toward a building less than sixty yards away.

By the time Ms. Ce-Ce looked back to Andrea, she was up and sprinting to her car. "Bitch! Get back here!" Ms. Ce-Ce yelled.

A Whore's Conscience

"Ma! What's going on?" Steph asked as her and Ree-Ree came up on the scene late.

"Oh, hell nah!" Ree-Ree said as she caught the face of the Blazer's driver. But before she or Steph could pursue, Andrea was bolting out the parking lot, scared to death.

"Bitch! I ever catch you around my son, I'm gonna..."

"I think she got the picture," Steph's words lightened the mood enough to cause all three women to break out into laughter.

***

"So let me get this straight. Andrea was gonna put candy bars in Steph's gas tank? Then mom dukes swole her up?" Shawn asked, enjoying the fact Andrea had gotten beat again.

"Yep," Ree-Ree replied through her cell.

Shawn and Keisha were waiting in the parking lot of the Bojangles on Highway 55 for some nigga named 'T' that keisha wanted to meet Shawn. Shawn had let it slip out that he was looking for someone who could hustle off the kilos he readily had access to. Someone he could take under his wig and possibly make his right hand man.

"You coming home tonight, Shawn? Cause we need to talk," Ree-Ree added while the mood was right.

"If I do, it will be a late night. We'll talk tomorrow," he said treating her almost as if she wasn't a part of his life anymore.

"Alright. I lo..." the sound of the dial tone cut her sentence short. Shawn had hung up on her once again without saying a word.

"Who was that?" Keisha asked from the passenger seat of Shawn's Hummer.

"Don't start. Yo, this 'T' nigga can't tell time or something?" Shawn said, noting the nigga was ten minutes late to their first meeting.

"Chill, baby. I think that's him now," Keisha said, pointing at the Oldsmobile Cutless making it's way towards them.

"Oh, hell nah!" Shawn yelled as he realized who the car belong to.

"What baby?" Water from her water bottle splashes her shirt from the outburst. "What's wrong?" Keisha asked, as Shawn pulled his .45 from under his seat.

"T's real name is Travis. Me and him have been beefing ever since he started getting jazzy with his mouth talkin' like he gangster

149

an shit," Shawn said, taking the safety off the .45 as the Cutless pulled directly in front of the Hummer.

"I'm sorry, baby. I didn't know. I was only trying to help," Keisha apologized.

"If you really wanna help, hop out and tell that nigga ain't nothing popping," Shawn ordered her. Without another word spoken, Keisha hopped out and approached the driver side of Travis' car.

"What's up girl! Everything still on course?" Travis asked as Keisha bent over, placing her face into the car window.

"Everything's going on according to how Kiwi said would happen," Keisha replied.

"Good. I guess ole' girl knew her shit, huh?" Travis stated, sounding more confident than before about their scheme.

"Yep. Kiwi about to get our ass paid, but look I gotta go before this nigga get noid. I'll holla!" Keisha said as she turned and walked away from Travis whip. *This nigga just don't know,'* Keisha thought as she hopped back into the Hummer. When she got in, she gave Shawn a fake smile. *'If only he knew.'* She fell back into her act pretending to be down with Shawn.

***

"Meet me around noon at the restaurant. I really need to see you," Lorna was listening to a voicemail from Rell. It had been a little over a week since Lorna last contacted him in person. She had been longing to see or speak with him since. She wanted to bed Rell, especially. Her coochie was hotter than the pits of Hell for his big dick. But until she got an answer from him regarding their future, dick was a pleasure she refused to indulge in. Unless, of course, it was Rell's. To allow another man to enter her while she was carrying the baby of the man she adored, was a shame Lorna had no intentions of having.

'Okay, Mami! Stand your ground no matter what he says. Stand your ground,' Lorna thought as she exited her Navi and entered the 'GLOOT's restaurant.

"Lorna! I'm glad you made it," Rell stated as he walked up to her and wrapped his arms tightly around her.

'Damn! He looks good, smells good, and Lord knows he feels so damn good,' Lorna thought as she savored the affection she was receiving.

"Have a seat. I've got to go grab your gift from the back," Rell stated, dashing off towards the office before Lorna could question him. Moments later, Rell came towards the table carrying a large gift wrapped box.

"For me?" Lorna asked, standing up next to the booth as Rell placed the gift on the table.

"Now, before you can open this box, there are some things I need to tell you."

"I'm listening," Lorna replied.

"Since I left the game, my entire life's been one humongous transition, but no change has been profound as my choice to become Muslim. In this box is information concerning female and male obligations to one another concerning parenthood. This information isn't from some self-absorbed wannabe guru. All this information is from ALLAH. ALLAH means the true, one and only God in Arabic. Allah has no..."

"Be easy Rell. I ain't slow, Papi. I got a cousin who's Muslim. He used to try to get me to convert all the time," Lorna interjected, explaining to Rell that she knew the basics of ISLAM well enough.

"Then you know that whatever ALLAH commands, I shall do my best to obey."

"Yeah," she replied.

"You said your cousin tried to bring you to ISLAM. Why didn't you?"

"My lifestyle was mad hectic, and if I'm gonna do something, I'm gone do it all the way right or not at all. Understand?" Lorna said, opening the box peeping over the contents.

"Can you respect my faith enough to allow me to do as I'm commanded to do? Or are you gonna make me choose between you and my God?"

"Rell, I would never put you at odds with your faith, but this baby needs both of us and I'm trying to do whatever I gotta do to give our child the family it deserves," Lorna answered as she walked next to Rell.

"I need for you to be sure. So read everything and watch every video that is in this box. Then let me know when you're done. Alright?"

"Yeah, sure."

"I'm not trying to rush you out, but I got the city inspectors coming through shortly. Grab the door for me and I'll carry the box to your whip," he said, scooping the box up and heading towards the front door of the eatery. Rell was doing his best to appear relaxed around Lorna. Unfortunately, not even he was fooling himself about the tension emitting from them, let alone Lorna.

As Rell loaded the box into the back of the Navi, he noticed a variety of baby catalogs. Reality checked him hard.

"Rell, are you alright?" Lorna had caught Rells reaction.

"I'm good. You be safe." Rell tried to dash away during his reply, but Lorna caught him by the elbow and tugged him back.

"Rell, during the next three weeks, it would be nice to have dinner and talk sometime. Unless, maybe, I'm asking too much?"

"Nah, that sounds good to my ears. Call and let me know when. Oh shit! The inspector's are here. I gotta go," Rell said, then turned and dashed away.

Lorna began to chuckle to herself when she realized the look that she had seen on Rell's face when he saw the baby box in the back seat. The look was one of sheer surprise. A look that she once sported. She had hi scared shitless about this baby. And he had her scared shitless concerning love. *I'm gonna have my man,'* Lorna thought as she crunk the Navi and threw it into gear. *'I don't care what it takes,'* she mentally concluded, as she turned out the parking lot and merged into traffic, heading home.

***

Across town on Alston Ave and Highway 55's meeting point, a gift from ALLAH was in the working within a royal blue house, trimmed in powder blue. This was where Keisha went to get her nails done. Kendra lived here with her man Glenn, who was a hustler. His name was solid, but his main problem was he lacked a true drug connect. His street rep was as cold as a cold blooded killer can get. This adversely affected him when suppliers were scouting for good product pushers.

Glenn knew his shit when it came to hustling, and had taught his lady how to conduct her hustles, just as he conducted his. No shorts. No games. No nonsense.

Along with doing nails, Kendra was a natural at freaking braids and cornrows. Today, Keisha had brought Andrea along to get her nails done by Kendra also. Kendra was just putting the finishing touches on Keisha's nails when Glenn entered the crib.

"KENDRA!" Glenn shouted, trying to locate his lady as he closed the front door.

"In the kitchen doing nails baby. What's up?" Kendra said, leaning her head back, allowing Glenn to steal a quick kiss.

"What's up Keishaaaa!" Glenn slurred her name playfully off his tongue.

"Just leting your girl hook me up as usual."

"Hey baby. We got any three inch T-bones left?"

He opened the deep freezer which was right next to where the girls were sitting.

"I'm not sure. Check the two back corners of the freezer. Come on Andrea," Kendra stated as she released Keisha's left hand and motioned for her and Andrea to switch chairs.

"What the Fuck!?" Glenn said, because someone had bumped him, causing him to bang his head against a box of rock hard frozen okra's.

"Sorry" Andrea offered an indifferent apology. She turned her attention back to Keisha and asked her to repeat her question.

"I said, how did you know Shawn wouldn't work with Travis?"

'Shawn? Nah. They can't be talking about Rell main man,' Glenn thought as he faked his continuing search for the steaks. He was really ear hustling on the low.

"Any beef Rell got, Shawn got. That's how I knew he wouldn't go for it," Andrea answered as Kendra began stripping her nails. "I still can't believe Rell quit the game, leaving Shawn out there like that," Andrea added as Kendra started examining her cuticles.

"Baby, which corners did you say to look in again?" Glenn allowed the freezer to block his right hand from view. When she looked over, Glenn gave her their code for milking info out of people. Kendra nodded her head to show she caught the signal. She proceeded to milk both, Andrea and Keisha for all they knew, without them even knowing.

"Let me guess. Rell and Shawn are a couple of ballers y'all met while stripping," Kendra said, as she grabbed the fingernail file and went to work on Andreas nails.

"They definitely ballers, but not that type of ballin'. They pump keys real heavy," Andrea answered.

"So when and how we gone do this? I'm ready to get paid, gurl!" Keisha asked, pausing between sentences to blow on her nails.

"We gotta figure out where them niggas at. Then, me and 'T'

gone need the right moment to do our thang."

"T? I know you ain't talkin about Travis from the South side!?" Kendra interjected, making her disgust towards Travis known to both women. Having heard enough, Glenn rose up from being bent inside the freezer.

"Fuck them T-Bones. I'm tired of looking. How's three inch sirloin sound?" Glenn asked Kendra, who nodded once more to show Glenn she was fine with his decision. Placing four steaks in the sink to thaw, Glenn walked out the kitchen and into the master bedroom.

'I can't believe this shit. These hoes trying to set Rell and Shawn up.' Glenn hopped on his cellular phone and dialed up Rell's Aunt Kay asap. Kay copped weed from Glenn on the regular, so if anyone could get the warning out to Rell and Shawn, it would be Kay. Glenn had never hung with nor dealt with Rell or Shawn personally, but when Glenns cousin, Stacey died, Rell went to a great deal to show her family mad love and respect. And for that alone, Glenn wasn't going to let Rell or Shawn get laid on. Not while he could do something about it.

"Hello?" Kay answered her phone trying to sound like a white girl.

"Hey! It's Glenn."

"I know nigga. What's up? You got some fire over there for me?"

"Hold that thought. I need you to do something for me." Kay noticed how serious Glenns tone was.

"What is it?"

"I need you to contact Rell or Shawn, or anybody that can reach them, and let them know niggaz is trying to hit them up. If they need more information, give them my number."

"Who trying to get at my nephew?"

"Now what did I just say? Have them ring me up if they need more info, alright?"

Kay caught Glenn's drift and didn't press any further. She immediately hung up so she could get on her grind and track Rell or Shawn down to pass the warning on.

***

Meanwhile, back in the kitchen, Kendra was still busy milking Andrea and Keisha like a pregnant cow. While hooking up their nails

154

and listening to every detail. As they blabbed on and on, Kendra realized that loose lips can and will sink ships. The more Andrea and Keisha talked, their ship sunk lower and lower.

'*That's right girls. Keep talking,*' Kendra thought as she realized how Glenn would profit off of the intel she was catching.

Chapter Thirty Two

"Excuse me, gentlemen!" Rell yelled out to the inspectors over the sound of the renovators drills and hammers. His cell had buzzed continuously for the past ten minutes. Calls had come from his Aunt Kay, his mom, and even Shawn. When Shawn called the third time, Rell's curiosity got the best of him. After excusing himself from the inspectors and checking each voicemail, Rell dialed up Shawn.

"Yo! Don't say shit. Just stay put and keep your ass inside the restaurant. Me and mom dukes on our way over."

CLICK!

"What the hell is going on? Hello!? Hell!?" Rell was speaking to himself because Shawn had hung up after he spoke his last word.

***

It took them a little over twenty minutes to reach GLOOTS. After another ten minutes or so, Rell was fully debriefed.

"So why they feel comfortable enough to say all this around you and your girl?" Rell asked Glenn, who had been brought along by Shawn to break the news.

"Very few people know that I'm from Durham. Most people think me and my lady from the backwoods somewhere. No one thinks we know much about the who's who in Durham. We play dumb. They slip and me and my girl capitalize," said Glenn as he looked from Rell to Shawn.

"So how much we owe you for this heads up?" Shawn asked in a mocking tone.

"Be easy Shawn. It ain't like that with him." Rell stepped in before Glenn could respond.

"Whatever!" Shawn said in an 'if you say so' tone of voice.

Feeling the tension brewing, Ms. Ce-Ce stepped in. "Glenn would you give us some privacy." She took hold of both Shawn and Rell's neck's and guided them away from earshot of Glenn.

"I thought you two could work this out. I guess I was wrong," she added, once she made them face each other.

"Ain't nothing to work out," Shawn said, defiantly.

"Alright. I guess its hoe-card time," Ms. Ce-Ce started with Shawn by cupping his face in her hands. Looking him squarely in the face, Ms. Ce-Ce pulled his hoe-card.

"Shawn, all your life, you and my son been ripping and running, but you were always Robin. Never Batman. Eventually that side-kick shit gets played out and a man needs to test the waters. He needs to find out if he can stand on his own, and by you staying in the game, this is your own way of testing the waters. But this Boss of Boss's son of mine won't let you spread your wings. He can't accept the fact that you don't need him anymore and your too scared to be a man and respectfully tell him what's going on with you. The two of you been like two bitches actin dumb as hell whenever the other one is around."

Shawn tried to protest, but Ms. Ce-Ce covered his mouth to let him know that she had the floor for now.

Ms. Ce-Ce turned to look upon her son. "Ma, don't..."

"Boy shut up! Your selfish pride about to get you and Shawn killed. While you mad over Shawn wanting to become Cheif, Andrea or Kiwi, whatever the hoe calling herself, is out there doing her best to put y'all asses in the ground. Baby, I love you, but you wrong on how you are handling Shawn. Give him what he needs to stay in the game, and remain on top. It's his turn to drive. Stop throwing up roadblocks and give him the green light."

"Now, back to you." Ms. Ce-Ce turned back to Shawn. "Stop thinking you too good to take advice. Remember, for over ten years, Rell guided you through the game, and not ONCE did you see a jail cell. Listening to him won't make you weak, it will only make you stronger. And heres some more advice...be careful of who you shit on. Be mindful of where you rest your head. And remember, what you give is what you get. Now! I'm gone shut up and let you two hoes do whatever it is that hoes do."

Her wisdom dispersed, two cents applied, her job was done for now. She headed off towards Glenn.

With her points well made, the guys fumbled around with their apologies and squashed the bullshit.

"So how should we handle this?" Shawn asked as he and Rell watch Ms. Ce-Ce sniff out Glenn suspiciously.

"Me, you, and Glenn should be able to pull this off," Rell replied.

"Hold up, cuz. You trust him like that?"

"It ain't about trust. It's about lust. Glenn would love to be on a team of go getters. You can give him the chance to see real money." Rell was eyeing his mom and Glenn, who seemed to be into some type of funny business at that very moment.

"I need more connects in order to pull that off. Right now all I have is Alexi," Shawn informed Rell.

"I'll take care of that. Just don't endanger me or my family, and do Glenn as I did you. And Shawn, just cause I'm out the game don't mean I ain't gonna watch your back and ride for you when necessary." Rell dapped his main man on that note.

"I know, man. So you think this Glenn cat gone merk a nigga to be down?" Shawn was still doubting Glenn's gangsta.

"Never underestimate greed, Cuz. Never." Rell and Shawn made their way over to Ms. Ce-Ce and Glenn. It was time to make the Master Plan.

***

Back in Cary, at Rell and Stephanie's home, Ree-Ree and Steph were looking at the third tape on Islamic duties of a believer.

"I'm no rocket scientist, but I think Rell trying to tell you something." Ree-Ree glanced from the T.V. to Steph.

"Like what?" Steph held her breath, wondering if Ree-Ree would unravel her suspicions.

"From what I can tell, you about to be a mommy."

"Whatever," Steph said, trying to play it off.

"You think I'm playing, but I'm serious. Rell trying to tell you he wants some kids." Ree-Ree placed a pillow under her shirt to make her belly look big. They both started laughing when Ree-Ree began to waddle around the room.

VREEN! VREEN! VREEN!

"Hello! Yeah. Right Now? Alright. Um hum." Ree-Ree hung up after Shawn finished instructing her.

"Who was that?" Steph asked being nosey.

"Shawn. Look, I gotta go home and handle some stuff. I'll call you later." Ree-Ree was grabbing all her stuff at one time, then she dashed out the front door.

***

"Shawn! Shawn?!" Ree-Ree yelled once she entered their home and secured the front door. Shawn had asked her to hurry home when he had called earlier. His voice had her worried that something was wrong.

"Back here!" Shawn's voice echoed from down the hall. As Ree-Ree made her way down the hallway towards the master bedroom, she caught the faint sound of running water. It sounded like the tubs faucet was running, but Shawn hates baths. He never took them in fact.

"Shawn, I don't feel like playing games. Where are.. AHG!!" Ree-Ree screamed and jumped when Shawn grabbed her shoulders from behind, scaring her damn near to death.

"It's me, love. Calm down, it's just me," Shawn said with a chuckle. He appeared amused by the way he had caught his shorty off guard.

"Fuck you, Shawn!" Ree-Ree was fuming as she hit him with a two piece on the arm.

"I'm sorry. I wasn't trying to scare you, honest." Shawn was struggling to keep his laughter in during his apology.

"We need to talk Shawn, all jokes aside."

"I know, but can I say something First? Please?"

Shawn took her by the hand and lead her to the master bath. He bent over to cut the water off and when he turned back to face her, Ree-Ree's facial expression told him everything her mouth wanted to say. However, she was speechless. Her eyes were glowing with submission to his will. The tub was full of warm bath oils and bubble bath. He had bought them to use on Kiesha, but Ree-Ree need not know that. Right now, Shawn had something else on his mind to give

Kiesha, and it involved his ratchet.

On top of the bath water, petals from various flowers were adrift. Roses, violets and sunflowers floated around giving off an intoxicating aroma. In the sink was a bottle of deep six body oil, warming in hot water.

"I know this ain't much, but it's a start. Ree-Ree, I'm sorry, baby. Please, please forgive me for treating you so fucked up," he said dropping to one knee to do his begging.

"Why the sudden change, Shawn? That bitch you were fuckin catch you in a lie? Or, let me guess, you got tired of her like you got tired of me?" Ree-Ree lashed out verbally.

"No! It was nothing like that. I had a long talk with mom dukes and I realized I was hurting the only woman I ever loved. The only woman I ever want to love. And I realized that my recent actions were going to cause me to lose the only thing I have worth living for. I'm sorry Ree. I'm so, so sorry for the way I've been shitting on you. And I'm... I."

Shawn's words got stuck in his throat and his eyes began to mist over. He hanged his head to hide his tears from Ree. The pain his soul felt was caused by the look of shame and hurt written all over Ree-Ree's face. His lust for the game and that life style that accompanies it, had placed him in one helluva corner.

"Shawn. Lord knows I love you, but you did much more than just shit on me and I'm not sure what I should do about us. Should I just say Fuck it and leave? Or are we worth saving?" Ree-Ree's voice began to crack.

'Pull your shit together. Swallow the pain nigga. Swallow!! Don't do this! Come on nigga, fight! Oh fuck!!' Shawn fought mentally to subdue his emotions, but failed. Tears of fear poured from his eyes. *'How could I be so dumb?'* Shawn thought as his first sobs escaped his throat.

"Shawn! Baby, I'm not trying to be cold." She stooped down next to him and pulled his face up to look him in the eye. "But if you ever disrespect me again or shame my name again, I'm gone. I'm for real Shawn."

The tears continued to flow as Shawn tried to pull his face from her hands so he could hang his head and hide his tears. The stronger he fought to free himself, the stronger she held on.

There was no doubt that Shawn's apology was sincere, because Ree had only seen him cry once before. It was when he found out that his parents had died in a plane crash. Except for his two estranged brothers, Ree is all Shawn had. To watch him cry was killing her inside, but the ultimatum had to be given. He had to understand, love or no love. After this, there would be no more second chances.

"And lastly, I'm giving you two years tops and not a single day more to be done with that drug game shit. Right now, you're hooked on that shit. But when the day comes, you gonna have to choose, us or the streets. Do you understand that?" The ultimatum in its entirety had been played.

Shawn nodded his head in agreement, then pulled her close. The moment that they were in each others arms, they both started crying, allowing all the hidden pains and love to flow forth from the deepest parts of their being.

***

At the Apple-Bees on Kildaire Farm Rd. in Cary...

Rell was busy creating the bait for a carefully laid out plan. If set right, Andrea would never know it was a trap. After an agreement with Shawn, it was concluded that Shawn's spot would be the stage. Rell had called up Netta and arranged to meet her for drinks at the Apple-Bee's. The two hadn't talked since the day she had to pick Sergio and Andrea up and transport them to the hospital. A day that set so much in motion.

"Sorry I'm late. How have you and Alana been?" Rell asked as he strolled up to a stool at the bar next to Netta.

Netta's jeans were so tight that they appeared to be painted on her skin. Her short sleeve top had a silky look and seemed to fit her upper body like a glove. She was working an Anita Baker style short cut like she was the first to ever do it.

"Good. Money is a little tight, but we good," she said and took a sip of her mixed drink with the air of a bad bitch.

"The last time we talked, I told you to contact me if that... If your sister left you and Alana hanging," Rell said, pretending to still be angry.

"I hate the idea of asking you for anything. Alana is my responsibility now. Lord knows, her hot in the ass momma could care less."

Netta's lips were moving, but her eyes and mind were on Rell. He was GQ, head to toe. She sucked her bottom lip halfway in and gave it a little bite. A teaser.

"Netta, don't start. I'm trying to be a man of God." Rell had a smooth smile on his face when he said this to her.

Netta responded to his game with a genuine laugh and some suggestive innuendo's. "Boy, please. We both know you can't handle all this," she joked as she put both hands on the stool in between her legs, arched her butt, and began grinding the seat like she was riding pipe. "But seriously, what did you call me out here for?" she asked, once they had stopped laughing.

"Next week is my restaurants grand opening and I was wondering if you would allow Alana to come?" Rell was sliding a piece of paper to her as he was talking.

"What's this?" Netta couldn't decipher the words and numbers written on the paper without explanation.

"That's the address and directions to Shawn's house. Make sure Andrea gives an okay to this and let me know before Sunday." Rell gave the blonde bartender a twenty to cover Netta's drink and tip.

"I just told you, Alana is my responsibility. Andrea is never home. She done dug her claws into some nickel and dime ass hustler. Every other blue moon, she'll come through and remind Alana what her mama looks like," Netta said, a bit flippantly.

"Bad blood is an understatement for what exists between me and your sister, so just humor me and this one Netta. Let me know her answer, BEFORE, Sunday," he reiterated, glancing at his watch.

"Alright. Now, on to a better subject." Nettta wanted to play.

"Sorry love, but I gotta see a lady about a cat." Rell rose off the stool ready to exit.

"I thought the saying was, see a man about a dog?" Netta joked with Rell and he paused midstep.

"It is, but I don't get down like that." Rell gave her a devilish smile and waved bye to her as he dashed out the door.

"Boy, you a fool!" Netta laughed, none the wiser that she had just been manipulated into sending her own sister into a death trap.

***

VREEN-VREEN-VREEN!

"Why ain't she answering her phone?" Stephanie redialed Ree-Ree's number for the fourth time.

VREEN-VREEN-VREEN!

When the call was answered, Stephanie heard the phone being

fumbled around on the other end. Then she noticed a Jahiem song pumping in the background.

Ain't nothing stopping me from getting back tight with you
Go ahead and flip, you got the right to

"Hello?"

CLANK!

Ree-Ree and Shawn bust into laughter.

"Hello!?" Ree-Ree was trying to maintain her composure.

"Hey girl. I was calling to make sure you were alright, but from what I hear, you doing just fine," Steph said enthusiastically.

"Yeah, I am now. But look, let me call you back."

"Uh-uh! Don't call me back, I'll talk to you tomorrow." Steph ended the call without any further conversation.

VREEN! VREEN!

"Didn't I just tell you we'd talk tomorrow?" Steph said too soon.

"Um, no, but I'm calling to speak with Rell. Is he in?"

"Huh?! Who is this?" All Stephanie could tell was the chick had a latina accent and she was checking for her man.

"I'm sorry. My name is Lorna. Is Rell home?"

"Who are you? Why are you calling my man?" Steph was pissed but the woman's calm demanor was fucking with her patience.

"Lor-na! And me and Rell have a little history. I was calling about our future."

"You got something you wanna say? Then say it, cause you starting to piss me off!"

"I'm sorry. We shouldn't be having this discussion. I didn't call to upset you. Just let Rell know I called please," Lorna calmly and politely stated.

"I ain't telling Rell SHIT! YOU NEED TO... HELLO! HE-LLO?!" Stephanie looked at the phone disbelievingly. She was shocked and mad as a bull. "I know this BITCH didn't just hang up on me!" Steph went to look at the caller I.D., but the number was restricted. There was no way for Steph to trace Lorna's call.

SLAM!

"Steph! Where you at? I brought dinner!" Rell yelled when he entered the house from the back door. When he got to the kitchen, he immediately sat the food on the island, then got to work. He grabbed the glasses, forks and plates to set the table. While Rell was putting ice in the glasses, Steph walked in unnoticed.

"Who is Lorna and why is she calling our house?" Steph stood at the entry to the kitchen, arms folded, eyes on Rell.

"Why? What's up?" Rell's stomach was churning on the low, but he kept his demeanor cool, calm and collected. *Why the hell did Lorna call so soon. What did she say? SHIT!'* Rell was brainstorming the situation and hoping to find a solution fast.

"Don't try to play me like I'm slow Rell. Now...who...the Fuck...is LORNA!!?" Steph yelled, glaring at Rell with a look that could kill.

"Alright! If you must know. Lorna was supposed to notify me when she got through with her Islamic studies. She is supposed to sit down with me and you and discuss with us what her studies revealed," Rell answered truthfully, just not fully.

"Why she got to sit down with us?"

"Baby, you got Brother Hakim's number. Call him. He's the one that set all this up. Ask him why. Maybe he'll tell you something he didn't tell me." Rell was pouring Pepsi into the cups of ice as he spoke trying his damndest to keep calm.

There was a thirty seconds pause, but it seemed to stretch halfway into the evening. Until Rell knew how Lorna was going to approach his offer, he saw no need to inform Steph about her pregnancy.

"Well, I'm guessing that she's done since she called HERE asking for you," Steph said, looking at Rell with her eyes narrowed down to slits. She didn't move a muscle. She only moved her eyes from left to right following Rell around the table as he spooned beef fried rice out of the Chinese box onto the dinner plates.

"We can call her tomorrow, but tonight, right now, if you quit trippin, I'd like to go half on a baby." Rell smiled coyly as he handed her a glass of Pepsi that was fizzing and foaming at the top. When she took the glass, he moved in close, placed his hands on her waist, and kissed her neck and behind her ear.

"I ain't trippin. I'm just not going for no bullshit. You my man now, so you need to make sure all yo lil hoochies understand that," Steph said seriously, but with a pouty baby face look.

"Fuck this! Come on!" Rell said, moving to the bedroom, with Stephanie in tow.

"Rell! Stop playing, boy!" Stephanie was squirming in his arms as he quickly scooped her up in his arms. Relllll! Our food gonna get cold," Steph said, trying to wiggle free.

"That's what microwaves are for," Rell said not falling for her antics.

"But I..."

"I know, you need to be fucked." Rell tossed her onto the bed and started stripping her clothes off. That night he punished that pussy, but in a good way.

***

VREEN! VREEN!

"Hello?" Netta answered groggily. The call interrupted her late afternoon nap.

"I know you ain't in the bed at no 9:38 pm!" Andrea was a little too turned up.

"Oh! So you finally decided to call back. Damn, I'm glad me or Alana wasn't hurt."

"Girl, whatever! What's going on?" Andrea asked.

"I was calling to let you know I'm going to drop Alana off at Rell's friend Shawn house next Friday. That's when Rell is having his grand opening party and he wants Alana to be there. Unless you object, I'm gonna take her." Netta unwittingly just delivered Rell's bait.

"Don't take my child no two or three hours away from home." Now Andrea was fishing for a location or an address.

"I'm not. It's not far from Raleigh."

"Girl, where you trying to take my child?" Andrea decided to be direct, beating around the bush wasn't getting it.

"The nigga stay in Cary somewhere, damn! Do you want the address too!?" Netta was being sarcastic.

"Only if you don't mind." Andrea had a pen and paper ready before Netta even got up to get the info Rell left her.

With Shawn's address in hand, Andrea let Netta return to her nap. She got Kiesha on the phone ASAP. *This hoe ain't gonna believe what just fell in my lap.'* Andrea's mind was working overtime. She could smell it in the air and it was strong. It was making her mouth water. Revenge was brewing and it smelled oh so sweet.

***

Back in Raleigh, a different set of sister's were having an

164

intervention of sorts.

"Say what you wanna say, Lorna, but that shit you pulled was foul. Rell is good people. You don't do familia like that." Alexi was giving Lorna an earful for the stunt she pulled by calling Rell's house.

"All I did was place a call to a friend. It's not my fault his girl rude as shit. I was polite and calm with her the entire time." Lorna was acting coy, and this behavior spurred Alexi's contempt.

"Whatever Mami! You got jokes! I'm trying to help you see what you about to fuck up." Alexi threw a throw pillow at her sister for effect.

"Aye, Mami! No need for violence! I'm listening."

"You and I both know that Rell is as solid as they come. So what gave you the right to play with his life like that?" Alexi went to sit next to Lorna on the couch.

"I just..."

"You just what? I'll tell you what! You broke your word. What happened to that month you gave Rell? Huh? All day long we have been watching tapes on Islamic rules regarding y'all situation. So now that you see your options are not to your liking, you go and change the rules." Alexi was waiting to see if her wisdom hit her sisters heart. Yet her stubbornness continued to justify her actions.

"You buggin' Ma. All I did was call to see how he was doing." Lorna knew it was a lie and regret showed on her face.

"Bullshit!" Alexi began to speak softly. "I'm boricua too. You trying to cause drama in that man's house. Lorna that's his home."

"So what if I am! If she can't hold on to her man, she don't need him," Lorna challenged Alexi's reasoning.

"Fuck it! I'm through trying to reason with you. You think you're going to win Rell with games? Them games gonna leave you looking stupid. Real stupid Ma!" Done with the subject, Alexi rose from the couch and departed to her room.

Lorna sat on the couch fuming because she knew her sister was right and she was dead wrong. She hated to admit it, but it was true. Plain and simple, she had sought to infuriate Rell's woman in hopes of putting a wedge between the two. Truth be told, she wasn't too fond of her other options. According to Islam, Rell could ask her to become his woman while keeping his current lady, as long as both women agree to Muta. Or, he could ask for custody of the child, to raise under his own roof, an option Lorna wasn't even going to entertain.

If she could trust her intuition, then Rell was going to ask her to be his second lady, in two weeks. She would have to share. She was not sure if living a lifestyle of polygamy was something she could come to terms with. Picking up the phone, she dialed Rell's home line again. She had no clue how she was going to respond to his forthcoming proposal, but she knew what had to be done to insure she had two more weeks to decide.

'Hi! Sorry, we're not home to answer your call. So please leave your name and number.' Rell's answering machine took the call.

'Good, this should be easier,' Lorna thought, as she left a message that would set order to the chaos she caused.

Chapter Thirty Three

Ms. Ce-Ce's Grapevine
Cause Nigga's Never Learn…

"Lord, this Ce-Ce talking to you. Lord, Jesus, I feel like… Oh Lord, grant me peace. Better yet, grant me forgiveness cause I'm about to body this hoe. All these years I've been waiting for my son to bless me with a grandbaby, and now that he about to give me two, I should be rejoicing. But no! Ms. Hoe Almighty wants to play gangsta. She wanna make plans to hurt my boy. Not happening! Trust and Believe! It ain't going down like that.

"Where the fuck is Ralph? I called him hours ago. He should have been called me back. I tell you, when you want shit done right, you gotta do it yourself, and that's exactly what I'm gonna do. First, I gotta take Stephanie to her OBGYN appointment. Then I gotta call this Lorna girl and talk some sense into her silly ass. But, before I rest my eyes tonight, I'm gonna figure out how to take care of this bitch Andrea, for good. Mark my words, all this bullshit about to cease. Hallelujah."

***

One week and five days later…
The day before Gloot's Grand Opening, and two days before his

deadline with Lorna, Rell found himself succumbing to the stress his life was placing on him. Today is the last day of the hiring process before the grand opening. He had brought Shawn, Glenn and even ol' Uncle Ralph to help with the selection of ladies who would service his future customers. He had even invited Lorna out to the festivities.

"You loving this ain't you?" Lorna asked while cutting her eyes at Rell, who was eyeballing a well endowed young lady as she strutted her stuff.

"Umm hmm. Now bend over and touch ya toes," Rell instructed.

"Excuse me!?" she protested. "Oh hell Nah!"

"Yeah, you right! You excused!" Shawn yelled with no remorse.

The five of them sat behind a huge table laced with buffalo wings, popcorn shrimp, and an assortment of other finger foods. Ladies were lined along every inch of the inside and outside walls. Every girl with an ass worth noticing, was here today.

"Oh hell yeah! What's your name little mama?" Glenn asked a Lisa Raye look-a-like with an ass like Ms. Cat on steroids. She had pranced up to the front of the table of judges like she knew she had the job yesterday, but she came today just to let everybody else know.

"Girl, you! You something special." Uncle Ralph was shaking his head in sheer awe of the chick's beauty and swag. Yeah, shorty was like that.

"Look, how many more of these girls we gotta interview?" Lorna had seen more than enough skin for the day and she was growing bored with all the antics.

"I'm sorry. I called you out here for two reasons and watching all this wasn't one of them." Rell waved across the room with one hand, for emphasis. He then paused, focused his mind, and then turned to face Lorna.

"I sure as hell hope not," Lorna smiled and playfully rolled her eyes. Her personality was humane, humble and so tamed that it turned Rell on. He deftly shifted in his seat so his erection could extend freely down his leg.

"I'm not going to beat around the bush, so here it goes. I would like you to join me in Muta. I truly believe it is the best option all around," Rell said making his decision known.

"I sort of knew this was coming. How does Stephanie feel about this?" Lorna put the question in the air while she reached for another buffalo wing.

"Until I have your answer, I see no need to tell her just yet."

"I hope you don't expect an answer right now," Lorna protested.

"Nah, but when my deadline is up, so is yours." Rell grabbed the buffalo wing Lorna was reaching for and began feeding it to her.

"You trying to seduce me, Papi?" she batted her eyes innocently before taking a bite of the boneless wing.

"Nope. I'm just trying to love you." Rell watched the mother of his unborn child, in all her beauty, devour the buffalo wing as if nobody was watching.

Rell words weren't the most romantic. They weren't even all that fly, but the look in his eye and the passion in his voice, caused a shiver to tingle up her spine from top to bottom. Nothing compared to hearing a man saying that he loves you, especially when you knew they truly meant it. This moment caused Lorna to have an epiphany. A divine intervention. Rell was literally, one in a million, and she would not pass the opportunity to become one with him.

"Time out! I'm getting a little moist down below," she said smiling. "I thought you had something else to tell me?"

"Oh yeah! First, you gotta promise me you won't flip," Rell said, trying to soften the blow he was about to deliver.

"I'll make no promises, but I agree to try, " she responded honestly and up front.

"Tomorrow, during the grand opening, I have to dip off to handle some beef with Shawn and Glenn. I can't be talked out of this because it's either them or us." He reached for a spicy wing this time. This was his offering to Lorna, to see if she is willing to take the heat.

Lorna spoke first. "I don't like it, but I'm not going to trip. I've seen you in action and that's how I know you're ready for whatever. Plus, I know you wouldn't dare leave our little bambina with no Padre." Lorna leaned towards the wing, but her face moved pass the wing and her nose met his. She lifted her eyes and then her soft, full lips met Rells lips in a kiss of passion.

"Go Carmen! It's ya birthday! The girl Shawn was cheering on was milk chocolate brown with a perfect bubble of a butt sitting on her backside.

"Uh uh! Oh hell nah!! This ain't no strip joint. A brother turned his head for one minute and y'all got my prospects pussy poppin'. I tell ya boy. Niggas never change." Rell's sudden outburst coupled with the look of shock on the young woman's face caused everyone at the table to laugh until their sides cramped.

***

After receiving the call from her OBGYN concerning the results of her pregnancy test, Steph called Ms. Ce-Ce over to her and Rell's spot to discuss the news over coffee.

"The gynecologist isn't 100% certain, but by the time I have my visit in three weeks, he should be able to confirm his notion." Steph was beaming with pride and expectation.

"Twins?! Wow!" Ms. Ce-Ce paused to sip her coffee.

"I can't wait to tell Rell when he get's home." Steph was ready for the next phase of their relationship.

"Wait until tomorrow after the grand opening," Ms. Ce-Ce suggested.

"Why?" Steph was curious about what her mother-in-law was thinking.

"If you tell him tonight the boy won't be any good for tomorrow's event. Lord knows he's already stressed to his limits with his business, Shawn, and that crazy bi... Oh! Nevermind." Ms. Ce-Ce caught herself before she spilled the beans.

"Ma, don't play. What crazy bitch you talking about? What's going on with Rell? Is he in trouble?"

"That's for Rell to say."

"It's that crazy ass Andrea isn't it?"

"Look, I have to go see a man about a dog. If you need something, ANYTHING, just give me a call." Ms. Ce-Ce was on a mission now. She had to make sure she handled her end of business. She grabbed her purse and keys, and hit the door.

***

"It's about damn time!"

Andrea was obviously pissed off. She had been on the stakeout with Kiesha in the parking lot of 'Gloots' for two and a half hours before Rell finally came out. Luckily, the parking lot was still full because of all the interviews. He had left Shawn and Glenn in charge of recruiting females for the last six openings. Rell and his Uncle Ralph were headed to enjoy a late lunch with Steph and Ree-Ree.

"Don't let him see you tailing him," Andrea instructed Kiesha, as she climbed into the back and lay flat across the seat.

"He won't, trust me." Kiesha crunk up the dark green Explorer, and exited a few seconds behind Rell.

Rell had thrown Andrea a curve ball. The address that she got from Netta was bogus. She had staked out the place with Travis for two days, and the only people she saw was a couple in their forties enter and leave the place. Either Rell had played her through her sister or her sister had shot her the shit. Whichever it was, it left her with only one option, she had to track down Rell or Shawn on her own. The ride wasn't a long one. Rell lived five minutes or so from his restaurant. Despite the long stakeout, both girls were pleased at how easy the mission was.

"You know why we're being followed, by any chance?" Uncle Ralph had his head held straight ahead, but his eyes were on the side view mirror.

"Yeah, I saw the jeep. It's on schedule." Rell was not surprised Andrea had found him and followed him damn near to his driveway. He pulled up next to Steph's big body LEX and killed the engine.

He and Ralph hopped out the truck in unison. "Care to humor me nephew?" Ralph's blood was pumping. He was feeling giddy.

They were both inside before Rell spoke. "Nothing, Unk. Just know that everything is going as it should."

Steph and Ree-Ree appeared in the hallway to the foyer. The girls were all smiles and giggles.

"You just don't know how right you are nephew," Ralph said this under his breath to himself.

"Ralph, you gotta see this. Follow me, if you will." Rell lead his uncle up an oak wood staircase to the Master Suite. They walked into a spacious closet, one the size of a small bedroom, and he opened a five foot safe that was standing in the back corner. When he opened the steel door, they were immediately blinded by the reflection of sunlight bouncing off of sixteen pieces of chrome hardware. Rell had strategically placed the safe diagonal from the sunroof, specifically for this effect.

"Daaaaamn! Now this MY type of party!" His eyes glowed as he admired all the toys and accessories. Being a vet and having served in Nam, Ralph was a human live wire with a short fuse. Even though he had been Honorably discharged from the Marines more than five years ago, that special-ops shit was his second nature now. He was only enthusiastic about a few things. His money. His country. His beer. These are the few things he loved. When it comes to family, well, let's just say he intends to go AWOL. It didn't matter if you were his mom, sister, brother, nephew, or a third cousin twice removed. If you were connected to his family tree, then you were family. And nobody fucks with his family. Nobody.

"These work?" Ralph was speaking of the aluminum silencer he was fingering. It was one of ten Rell had fitted for each handgun he owned.

Rell pulled out his Heckler & Koch special.

"Yep, brand new and custom fit for each gun. I have two due in three weeks for the sniper rifles. They take a lil more engineering than the rest."

"What would you say if I asked to borrow these?" Ralph held up a .357 Smith & Wesson with the matching silencer."

"I'd say you would be pleased to know that it comes with two speed loads and Dum-Dum Head Ammo. Excellent choice." Rell used a British professional accent that both men found hilarious. They looked like lunatics surrounded by shiny hardware. Ralph definitely was.

***

"And you sure he didn't see y'all?"

Travis, Kiesha, and Andrea were sitting in his living room, rollin' and smokin'.

"Nope!" Kiesha took two tokes, then passed the blunt back to Travis. "I was extra careful. Plus, he don't know me. As far as he knows I..." Keisha began coughing and wheezing. Cough...cough! Wheeze, cough! "What The fuck y'all staring at!?"

"You bitch! You was talking and just damn near died!" Andrea snapped at Kiesha frowning. She knew the bitch was high, but fuck it.

"Oh yeeeeeah," she said and laughed. "I wuz, um yeah. We was invizdibul." Kiesha squinted her eyes, cutting them left to right. When she turned her head and met Andrea's open gaze, they stare at each other in silence without moving a muscle for about ten seconds.

"Bwaaaahahahaaah!" They both fell out laughing.

Travis was stiff and paranoid. All business. The girls bantering was making him think they weren't taking him or the situation seriously.

"Look, yo." Kiesha dropped her smile and tried to sober up a bit so she could calm Travis down. "If he did happen to see me, he wouldn't have recognized me. As far as he would be concerned, I was visiting somebody in the neighborhood."

"I don't know. It all just sounds too easy if you ask me."

'Damn! This nigga acting like a bitch. If we didn't need his muscle, I'd tell Kiesha to Nod this nigga right now. I can't wait until this shit over. Come this time tomorrow Rell, Shawn, Travis, and whoever else I see as a problem, I'm gone make sure they walking with God before the sun rises.'

Andrea left her thoughts alone for the time being. She caught Kiesha's eye and gave her a *'Come on girl. It's time to go to work,'* look, and gave a quick nod in Travis direction. They both stood up in unison and walked over to stop in front of him. Slowly they began to strip down to their panties and bra.

"Yo, what's the deal?" Kiesha took the blunt front him and laid it in the ash tray. Andrea walked up behind him and started massaging his shoulders and chest while she licked and kissed his neck, ears, and back.

"You think he ready?" Kiesha asked Andrea, as she pulled his knees apart, backed into his lap, and softly grinded on his pelvis until he was at full attention.

"Hell yeah I'm ready!" Travis held his throbbing erection in his hand. He was harder than a five cent jaw breaker.

"Ready for the BOTH of us?"

Andrea pulled Travis' head back until it was facing the ceiling. Covering his eyes, she nodded her head to Kiesha who took the cue. As Andrea tongued Travis down from the back of the couch, Kiesha moved his hand from his dick. With no hands, she forced his wood past her lips and stretch her throat as she slowly took every inch of him in her mouth.

"Damn!"

Both, Travis and Andrea gasped at the sight of Keisha damn near getting his balls to go down too.

Andrea stood Travis up and then took to her her knees behind him as Kiesha continued her deep throat trick. Spreading his butt checks apart, Andrea blew lightly into his Anus.

"Whoa! Hold up!" He tried to protest, but before he could reach back to stop her, Andrea had already stuck her tongue deep into his asshole. "Oh fuck!!" Travis moaned as his knees buckled momentarily from the combined pleasure he was experiencing.

'Humph! Just like a lil' bitch!' Andrea thought. She and Kiesha would be keeping Travis busy for the rest of the night, that way he

wouldn't be able to cast anymore doubt on the situation.

***

Back at Ms. Ce-Ce's house, a dark green Explorer was the subject of conversation.

"You sure it wasn't black?" Ms. Ce-Ce asked Ralph as he sipped coffee at the kitchen counter.

"Yep! Me and Rell both saw it. It was a dark green Ford Explorer. About an 04 or 05. Seems Rell was expecting it. He said it was about time they showed up or something to that effect."

Ms. Ce-Ce walked over to the counter and stood next to Ralph.

"I don't know what he's up to and honestly, I do not care. Ralph, don't let nobody hurt my boy. Do what you do. Understand?" Her eyes began to water a bit.

"Don't you do that. Don't you dare start crying. Uncle Ralph got this. Now, make me a few snacks. It's gonna be a long night." Ralph's gaze lowered just a bit, then he zoned out.

***

Now at the same time, just down the street, plans of a similar nature were underway.

"You sure you down with this?" Rell gave Glenn one last chance to back out.

"I'm bred for this shit here. If they don't hoot, I'm gonna shoot. Straight like that!" The Hennessy Glenn was sipping was fueling his fire and he loved it.

"You sure they gonna show up here?" Shawn was a little skeptical. He wasn't sure that Andrea had the brains to track Rell's spot without fucking up.

"They followed me home from the restaurant the other day. So she got my location. She'll be back." Rell saw Shawn slowly accepting his logic. "If they knew YOUR location, they wouldn't have risked following me."

That's all Shawn really needed to be sure of. "Aight. Well, I'm off! I'm gonna follow the ladies to the hotel. You ah... You sure you don't want me to swing back through?" Shawn raised up to leave, slightly concerned about the fact that Andrea knew where his best man lay his head.

"Nah. I'll be straight. Plus, I got gunner Glenn watching my back." Rell chuckled at himself.

"Oh! That's cute! Real Cute!" Glenn said aggressively throwing up a middle finger at Shawn and one at Rell.

They all dapped fist and slapped backs as Shawn left. Shawn wasn't totally sold on Glenn. He knew Rell could be naive at times. You should never underestimate your enemy, especially during war.

***

Down at Shawn's crib, Ree-Ree was trying to calm Steph down.

"I don't understand why we gotta stay at a hotel! And why is it that every time I ask a question, the answer is always, don't worry, it's under control?" Steph was pacing the floor being theatrical. She was upset, but more so because she was worried and nobody would let her help.

"You new to this, so I understand your frustration. Hell, I was the same way early on," Ree-Ree said, trying to be patient with Steph.

"But they could at least tell us why we gotta leave. All this cloak and dagger shit getting on my nerves." Steph's pacing came to a stop in the living room when a set of headlights crossed over the windows.

"Look at it this way, we have comfortable lives that our men have provided for us. There are certain measures that must be taken to protect our lives and all of this," Ree-Ree expanded her arms to signify their blessings of a nice house in an upscale neighborhood with multiple luxury cars, money, clothes and jewelry.

"If we needed to know something, they would tell us. Rell and Shawn have always kept me safe and provided for me. I've learned to trust them and do whatever they ask of me, because sometimes, the less you know, the better you can rest."

Ree-Ree's innuendos hit home. She squeezed Steph's shoulder as she walked past her to open the door for Shawn. "You just have to trust them." Ree drove her point home as she opened the door for Shawn.

"Y'all ready to go?" Shawn asked as he stepped in. He glanced inquiringly at both ladies with one eyebrow up and one down, as he instantaneously picked up on the tension.

Ree-Ree was the first to respond. She had her arms folded, looking directly at Stephanie. "I am. What about you Steph?"

"Yeah," Steph answered solemnly. She knew Ree-Ree was right, but she still wasn't feeling this shit all the way. But she knew the outcome of beating a dead horse, so she rolled with the flow.

***

It was ten minutes before twelve when Andrea pulled back up to the yard directly across from Rell's home. She had left Kiesha passed out on top of Travis. They both fell asleep shortly after they ended their two hour threesome. Now she sat across from Rell's crib scanning the street for any signs of life. Once she felt comfortable that she was alone on the street, she hopped out the dark green jeep and crouched low with a pair of razor sharp wire cutters by her side. Swiftly, she crossed the street into Rell's driveway.

***

"Hey boy! Get up! It's almost ten minutes to twelve." Ms. Ce-Ce was standing over Ralph, who was napping his ass off in her suede oversized Lay-Z-Boy. A beautiful all white recliner she'd got from Rell as a housewarming gift.

"I'm up!" Now he was. "I appreciate the wake up call. I'm gonna use the bathroom real quick like, then I'm gone." By the time Ralph was on his feet, he was in 'Go-Mode.'

***

Rell had leased a brand new Cadillac Escalade earlier in the year around tax time. Ya know, to keep the government off his ass. It was a blacked out beauty. He kept the factory twenty-one inch wheels and tires on it since they were big enough to stunt in. Plus, the dealership advised against changing them because of the warranty, and he didn't want to be too flashy with this one. It made the statement just the way it was. This truck is a successful businessman's vehicle, with all the bells and whistles.

None of that was on Andrea's mind as she slid halfway under the Escalade. Rell's truck was safe once she realized he probably wouldn't be driving the Caddy to the grand event tomorrow. Nah. Rell's time to shine would be tomorrow and nothing shined harder than his 745. That mother fucker was immaculate.

Its long body was painted Matte Azzure with white tinted windows and twenty-two inch white Asanti wheels and low-pro tires. The inside had white oak wood grain trim with all white leather seats. Sky blue stitching lines the inside setting that shit off. If the Escalade was his 'Night,' then his Biemmer was his 'Sunday.'

'Gotcha.' Andrea slid under the BMW with the stealth of cat woman and immediately went to work. She had the brake lines cut and four King Sized Milkyways jammed down the gas tank in less than ninety seconds. *That caramel should definitely do the trick if the breakes*

don't.'

Andrea was smiling as she ambled back to her jeep. As soon as she reached the drivers door, the front door swung open a few houses up the street. "Shit! I don't need to be seen out here." She panicked a little, but quickly hopped in and starts the jeep without delay.

"What the hell?" Ralph said aloud. He noticed the parking lights come on when he stepped outside, and by the time he locked the door and turned to face the street, the jeep cranked up then speeds off down the street with the headlights off.

Even though it was too dark to be dead sure, Ralph was still confident that the vehicle he just saw, was the same one from earlier.

"Yep! This was gonna be a long night" Ralph mumbled as he threw his knapsack over his shoulder and climbed the ladder in the back of the house.

***

Later that Morning...

It was a little past 10am when Rell hopped into his Bimmer and pulled out. He didn't notice the brake fluid that stained the drive way. "Ya Refoon-Na Nemata ALLAHEE Thooma," Rell chanted as he recited the Muslim Ayats. The six disc collection each had a spot in his six disc changer. Lucky for him, the volume was moderately low for him to hear the repeated 'Ping' sound from the car. Next, he noticed his brake light flashing.

Rell got all his vehicles serviced at the dealership every four months and the Biemmer had about three more months to go, so he assumed it was nothing. He mashed the brake just in case, and the Biemmer stopped on a dime.

"Must be technical. I'll have it checked out later on."

VREEN! VREEN!

"Hello?"

"Hey baby!" Steph was extra chipper after sleeping on Ree-Ree's words last night. "Just checking up on my hubby wubby."

Rell smiled. He felt like a fourteen year old falling in love for the first time all over again. "I'm good," he said smiling widely. "I'm on my way to pick Alana up. You good?"

"Yeah, I'm fine, but I'll be even better when we all meet up at the restaurant." Steph continued to keep Rell company until Ree-Ree invited her downstairs for breakfast.

Rell's luck seemed to be out in full force as he had caught the last two miles without a red light. He felt great this morning. He turned the volume back on for his Ayats while the cool morning air breezed through the car. The clouds were thick, and the sun shined bright through the open sunroof. He was cruising like a champ down Maynard Blvd. at about fifty mph.

Unfortunately for Rell, the driver of an ugly red Chevy Malibu coming from the opposite direction, waited until Rell was damn near at the intersection to try to make his turn by gunning it. With proper anti-lock brakes, the situation would've been easily avoided.

"This dumbass asshole! SHIT!" Rell pressed the brakes gently to slow down and let the Malibu pass, but the pedal slid all the way back to the floor board without resistance. He quickly grabs the Emergency brake and yanks it up. The tires scream as the Biemmer fishtailed. If he was going about 25 to 30 mph, maybe he could've made a complete stop. However, the momentum sent the car flying into the intersection. While he was able to straighten the 745 out, he couldn't avoid the Malibu. The front passenger side of Rell's car slammed into the back passenger side of the Malibu between the tire and the trunk.

CRA-BOOM!

Both cars spun in the middle of the intersection as if they were dancing. Oncoming traffic was slow to react. One car avoided the mess by making a quick right turn in Rells previous lane, but the next car was surprised when his view opened up. The mid-sized pickup swerved from the Malibu, but hit the Bimmer dead between the front and back doors on the passenger side. The pickup truck applied the brakes a split second before impact, but the force of the impact sent the BMW spinning like a coin across the intersection where all the chaos came to a rest. Rell and his sky blue BMW were mangled. Except for the license plate, little else was recognizable about the car.

VREEN! VREEN!

Rell's cell phone rang loud in the silence of the moment.

It was his mother, Ms. Ce-Ce. Her intuition had kicked in and she felt gloom come over her as she thought about her only son. Something was wrong with her boy. *Rell baby, answer the phone.*' She hung up when his voicemail came on, then immediately redialed his number.

Chapter Thirty Four

Back in Rells neighborhood, things were beginning to take shape.

Ralph had been on Ms. Ce-Ce roof under a dark tarp since midnight. He had watched all movement on the suburban street all morning without breaking. The mailman had been observed moving house to house. Neighbors had been watched heading off to work. Ralph had even witnessed his nephew leave to set up his grand opening event. And now he was watching a dark green Explorer creep past Rells house.

'Three marks. This gonna be too easy!' Ralph silently concluded as he watched the jeep turn around and park in the cul-de-sac. *'Yep, too easy.'* He was in motion humming as he climbed down the ladder off the roof.

"Remember, if you see anyone pull up..."

"I got it. Call your cell and let it ring twice. Hang up, then creep up to the house." Kiesha cut Andrea off from repeating the protocol for the umph-teenth time.

"Alright, let's go." Andrea motioned for Travis to hop out and follow her.

As the duo made their way down the street to Rell's spot, Ralph had scaled the ladder and was scampering across the backyards of the houses that were parallel to Andrea and Travis' position across the way.

"Eliminate their best option of escape, then stalk the flustered marks." Ralph recited a mental note to himself.

Ralph stopped behind a house with a dark green jeep idling in the front by the curb. He allowed the two marks in the jogging outfits to head to their destination undisturbed. Crouching low, Ralph swiftly ran from the side of the house to the back driver side of the Explorer. Squatting behind the SUV, he lowered his knapsack from his back and pulled out the .357. The silencer was screwed on tight and fully loaded. In one swift motion, he sprung to his feet and in two long strides, he was at the drivers window. His sudden appearance left Kiesha startled stiff.

"Oh shit!" Kiesha was frozen in shock.

Ralph grinned ear to ear at her. "Good bye."

Before his words even registered, he fired one silenced bullet that speared through the girl's skull, went diagonally through the roof of the jeep and lodged into the trunk of a nearby tree. Kiesha lay slumped over the wheel. Another casualty of greed. All a part of this game called life.

After moving her body over into the passenger foot well of the Explorer, he doubled back for his knapsack. *'And then there was two.'* Ralph broke in to a stealthy sprint to his nephew's house.

When he crept past Rell's home, he spotted the two 'joggers' standing on the side of the home. Slipping past them undetected, he posted up behind the Escalade and eavesdropped.

"Look, no ones around. I got this. You go handle the power box," Andrea ordered Travis into action as she scouted the back of the house.

Ralph could've taken them easily at this point, but he would allow them to enter the home to better control the situation.

After Andrea felt that everything was clear, she rounded the corner only to hear a loud popping noise that sent her into a nose dive into the grass. Ralph almost laughed out loud at the 'Dumb & Dumber' antics of the two. But knew it was best to hold his peace.

"Shit! Fuck!" Travis cursed as electrical sparks shot out at him from the power box.

"Shh! Come on." Andrea got up and dusts herself off. She looked around, then casually walked to the backyard again. When Travis caught up with her at the back door, she took a small rock and cracked part of the small glass window in the back door.

***

"It's time to rock!" Glenn heard the glass break and immediately hopped off the couch and entered the hallway from the den. He put his back against the wall and slid down the hallway into position.

Ralph also heard the glass break. He counted to fifteen, then came around the side of the house where the two had already gone inside. His .357 was at his side ready when he moved in behind them.

"Follow me. The safe should be in the master bedroom. He's not going to keep his money or his guns out of reach." Andrea and Travis were about to head to the stairs in the front of the house, but before they could move in that direction, the sound of a hammer being cocked caused them to freeze in their tracks.

"Don't move." Ralph placed the tip of the silencer to the back of Travis noggin. More from fear than choice, Andrea decided to try her luck by sprinting off down the hallway.

"SHIT!" Ralph used his thumb and index finger on the pressure points on the back of Travis' neck to render him temporarily unconscious.

Andrea cut through the kitchen and weaved her way towards the living room in an attempt to make it to the front door. Ralph had just breached the living room when Andrea spotted the front door and took off full speed.

"Uh-uh," Glenn barked as he caught Andrea by the neck of her sweatshirt and yanked her to the floor. Before she could rebound, Glenn had his 9 mili pressed against her forehead.

"Glenn! What the fuck!?" Andrea didn't see that coming.

Before he could respond, his eyes caught movement. Glenn had just enough time to snatch Andrea up on her feet. He was using her as a hostage and a human shield from the guy pointing a revolver in his direction.

"Put the gun down or your bitch gone feel it," Glenn ordered.

"You must be with my nephew's detail. Hmph! Cute!" Ralph was talking to Glenn, but his gun was trained on Andrea.

"I don't know what you talking bout." Glenn hid his head directly behind Andreas'.

"Look son. I'm Rell's uncle. I've been sent to handle this mess," Ralph said, trying to reason with Glenn.

"That sounds good, but who's to say you ain't lying?" Glenn was unsure of what to make of all of this.

"Son. If I wasn't who I say I am, you'd be dead. You see this .357? From this distance, it has enough power to go through both y'all heads, and half way through the wall behind you before it ever stops. Now stop wasting time and help me handle these two." Ralph lowered his gun slightly.

"If you really Rell's uncle, then let me hear the hoot call."

"Hoot call!? Boy, we ain't hunting no quail. Look, take this and call whoever you need to." Ralph tossed his cell over to Glenn. "Whenever you get your answer, I'll be out back in my nephew's shed handling her friend." Ralph pointed behind him to Travis still crumpled on the floor.

***

"Move! Move! Move! He's not breathing and he's lost a lot of blood," a fireman informed the medics after having to cut Rell out of his Biemmer.

The Local News crews were all out and 'reporting live' on the scene.

"This is Amanda Lamb, reporting live from Cary. I'm here at the scene of a horrific traffic accident that took place at the intersection of Harrison and Maynard Blvd. Police, Paramedics, and Firemen are on the scene, providing assistance with the injured. Oh! Okay, this just in. One of the victims that has been listed in critical condition at Wake Medical, has been identified as Dorrell Medlin. A resident of..."

"Oh shit! Mami! Mami! Come Here!" Alexi shouted over the T.V. to get Lorna's attention.

"What's up!!?" Lorna called back, casually strolling up the hallway to the living room.

"Listen." Alexi pointed to the screen.

"Once again, the injured have been transported to Wake Medical and the young man in critical condition, a Dorrell Medlin, has been... Wait, correction, Dorrell Medlin has been re-routed to Duke Hospital. Stay tuned for more."

"No, Papi! Noooo!" Lorna broke down. Tears flooded her eyes.

"Mami, calm down. We gotta get to Duke Hospital, so come on. Pull it together. Rell needs you!" Alexi grabbed the keys and ushered Lorna out the door.

***

A Whore's Conscience

When Glenn escorted Andrea out to the shed, his face was way beyond somber. The sight of Ralph wrapping up Travis' lifeless body wasn't the reason for Glenn's lowly demeanor. Between making the call and going to the shed, something had happened.

"Who or what pissed in your Tang, son?" Ralph asked as he paused from his chore at hand long enough to examine Glenn's facial expression.

"We've got a problem mister." Glenn pushed Andrea into the ground.

"Call me Shadow. Now what done gone and got you all in a funk?" Ralph put his head back down to resume his task of wrapping Travis in the carpet.

"I talked to Shawn, who confirmed who you were. But you got a call after I hung up." Glenn said, beating around the bush.

"Boy, I ain't getting no younger. Say what ya' gotta say, then get over here and help me with this body," Ralph ordered, growing agitated with Glenn.

"Rell's been hurt. Hurt bad."

"You Bitch!" Ralph sneered as he pumped two shells into Andrea's tail bone.

"Aaaah! Ooooh SHIT!!" Andrea screamed as the bullets burned holes into her flesh.

The speed and precision of Ralph's assault left Glenn shocked and in awe. He had only seen killers of Ralph's caliber in the movies and on sitcoms and shit. But live action up close and personal! The rush was intoxicating. By the time Glenn snapped back to reality, Ralph was shattering Andrea's right wrist. "Oweee! Oh please, stop. Noooo!!" she moaned and wailed in pain.

"My nephew better not die," Ralph stated as he stomped on her freshly broken wrist.

"Fuck all y'all! I hope that nigga die slow!" Andrea realized she wouldn't be spared, so she mentally snapped.

"If my nephew dies, then so does your daughter," Ralph informed her as he placed the end of the silencer to her temple.

"So! I don't give a fuck! I got my payback. Ha Ha Ha Haaaa!" she ranted, then went hysterical.

"BITCH!" Glenn aimed his 9 milli at her.

"No!" Ralph sprang to his feet to halt Glenn.

"Man, why not? This bitch don't even care about her own

daughter. Where's yo fucking conscience?" Glenn yelled down at her.

"A conscience?" she said losing her grip on reality all together. "Fuck a conscience. And Fuck you! Fuck him! Fuck that fucking kid! And you can Fuck Rell with a sick dick, BITCH!" Andrea screamed out like a song.

"Come on, Unk. Let me cancel this bitch!" Glenn begged, looking down at her in disgust.

"No, son. I've got plans for her. Bring me that knapsack from over there," Ralph said as he flipped Andrea onto her stomach. "Um. Nah." He flipped her back over on her backside.

"I don't care. Do what you do. You can't make me fear death. Not Now! And I hope Rell is Dead! Aaaaha hahahaaa!" Andrea yelled, breaking down.

Most people see their life pass before their eyes and become remorseful, becoming full of doubts and full of fear of the unknown. Andrea was none of these things. Her entire life had been led in the sole pursuit of one thing. Not fame. Not fortune. Not Riches. Not love. Only revenge. She had lived her entire life in pursuit of revenge. The breaking point for her came when she finally realized that Karma was a Bitch! All the revenge she had dished out, was now full circle.

"Here you go." Glenn handed Ralph the knapsack.

"Go grab me a glass of water and hurry!" Ralph roughly began to treat Andrea's wounds. She was bleeding on the goddamn floor.

"Oowe! What the hell are you doing!?" Andrea screamed at Ralph, who pulled out a vial of powdery substance. She looked deranged as she watched Ralph shake the vial to loosen up the powder.

"Here." Glenn said, handing him the water.

"Goood. Goood. Right on time." Ralph pulled out a syringe and place it on the table. He then poured an ounce or two of water into the vial and shook it until the mixture was liquified. "This right here gone take the fight out of you."

"What type of C.I.A. shit you on, Unk?" Glenn was loving every second of watching him work.

"I believe this to be the equivalent of what you young guns call 'that boy'."

With one hand firmly around her wrist, he used his other hand with surgical precision and pumped the contents of the syringe into an exposed vein in Andrea's forearm. The effects were pretty much instant. Her eyes glossed over and her entire body went limp.

"What's the plan for her?" Glenn was patient, but he wanted this bitch dead as soon as possible.

"Be easy son. In the Service, we have a way of killing a man without actually killing him. You follow me?" Ralph was smirking and holding up a second vial.

"Aight." Glenn smirked and nodded his head. "I'll watch and learn."

Thirty minutes later, Andrea lay on her back, still as a statue. Her eye's were on the roof of the shed, motionless.

"Is she dead?" Glenn asked as he helped Ralph roll her up in a rug. This was his chance to get some details.

"Nope! But she gonna wish she was," Ralph said as they made quick and efficient work of wrapping her up.

'So much for that,' Glenn said under his breath. Twenty minutes later, Ralph pulled the Explorer around to Rell's driveway. Since Rell kept his Camero in the garage, Ralph was able to back all the way in. He had a short walk to the shed where he and Glenn loaded the 'rugs' into the back of the jeep.

"You see that black and chrome Chevy Tahoe over in Ms. Ce-Ce yard?" When Glenn nodded he tossed him the keys. "Here. Get in and follow me."

Glenn followed Ralph to a small town called Friendship. A bunk town in the middle of nowhere. They came to a stop at a moderate metal gate in front of roughly two acres of land. After Ralph unlocks the gate, Glenn followed the Explorer for about three hundred yards up the winding dirt, gravel path. They stop midway in a wooded area where he had a big dumpster sitting in a thirty by thirty clearing. It was a long, topless metal container he used to burn his trash, leaves, or whatever else he decided to throw in a set fire to.

"You ready to roll, son?"

With their combined strength, it only took about ninety seconds to load Kiesha and Travis into the container and set fire to them. They would burn for another ten minutes and Ralph would dispose the bones later.

"Let's do it," Glenn responded.

Glenn's connections included a 'higher up' at LKO scrap yard. A middle aged white boy in management that loved his powder cocaine. The Explorer would be picked up and completely scrapped in the next ninety minutes with no records.

With those ends being tied, they both hopped into the Tahoe and headed back towards the entrance.

"What we doing about that?" Glenn asked, referring to Andrea, who was still wrapped up in the open trunk of the Tahoe.

"Holly Hill Psychiatric. We'll unwrap her and leave her by the doorstep. They'll assume she's an addict and commit her. By the time they finish pumping her with anti-psychotics, she'll be looney for real. If she ever comes to, her brain will be burnt out. That's why I went ahead and treated her at Rell's with my little cocktail. Plus, I took the bullets off her tail bone, stitched her up, and wrapped her wrist. They'll assume she had already been to the hospital."

Glenn just nodded his head. With this info from Ralph, he was confident that their end was air tight. There was silence for the rest of the trip now that they could focus on Rell's situation.

Chapter Thirty Five

Duke Medical

"Bitch!, You got some nerve coming down here like you belong here!" Steph was irrational and on the verge of an episode. She rushed at Lorna as fast and as hard as possible, making a big scene on the third floor ICU lobby.

Ms. Ce-Ce collided with Steph from the blindside and they crash into a wall. "Steph! Girl chill! Lorna and Rell were before you," she said, trying to reason with her.

The waiting area was filled with Rell's family and friends. Each and every eye was on the live drama unfolding just a few feet away.

"Kiki! Liv! Hold her!" Shawn ordered the sister's to help Rell's mom restrain and clam Steph, while he shielded a very angry Lorna from joining the fiasco.

"Move Shawn! I'm tired of trying to be nice. Move!" Lorna was ready to scrap, but Shawn wouldn't budge.

"Steph. I hate to be the one to tell you like this..."

"No, Shawn!" Lorna quickly covered his mouth before he could reveal her secret. "Rell wanted to wait until I gave him my answer about us, especially before he told her." Lorna whispers that last part to Shawn.

"So what you gonna do?" Shawn's patience with all this was gone and he didn't hide how annoyed he was with the two women bickering while his best friend was down the hall fighting for his life.

"I was going to say yes to me and him…and her," said Lorna quietly.

"Bitch! What you say about me!?" Steph was at it again. She was trying her hardest to break free of the three women restraining her. Her hair and eyes were wild. She looked like a rabid animal causing a damn scene.

Bro. Hakim stepped off the elevator and heard the melee before he saw it. He walked straight down the hallway at a slow deliberate pace, reciting Ayats and invoking peace. "Excuse me, sister Stephanie. I know this is not you cursing and acting like the devil manifest!" Bro. Hakim used the bass in his vocal chords instead of yelling. The deep vibration of sound shifts all eyes to him, then to Stephanie.

"Brother IMAM! I'm not... I'm. It's…"

"Relax sister. I'm not here to judge. I'm here to help guide you and, I guess your sister Lorna?" He motioned for Lorna to come closer, and she responded swiftly and obediantly. "Do you still wish to take your shahada?" Lorna nodded her head.

"What's going on Brother Hakim!?" Stephanie shrugged the women off her and walked over to her IMAM. She was distorted by too many emotions and too little information.

"Sister Lorna called me last night and told me she was ready to cross over into Islam. Are you going to deny her this right, Sister Stephanie?"

Stephanie submitted through compliance. Seeing this, Brother Hakim had each woman stand in a single file line facing him. Lorna was in front and Stephanie was directly behind her. Looking Steph directly in her eyes, he began.

"In Islam, all previous things and all previous conflicts with your fellow believer are forgiven. No Muslim is allowed to draw the blood or wrongfully lash out in violence and assault another Muslim. All ill intentions are forbidden to be acted upon. Ever! Do you ladies understand this?"

Both women nodded their heads.

"Sister Lorna, know that once you take your Shada, there is no breaking this oath. There is no going back to life as you once knew it.

The curse of ALLAH shall be upon you if you violate this covenant. Are you certain that you need to take the Shada?" Brother Hakim asked one last time.

"Yes, I'm sure."

"Sister Stephanie. Are you willing to deny this woman Islam?"

"No Brother IMAM."

"Then come join hands with us if you truly mean what you say." Brother Hakim extended his right hand to Steph. She looked at his hand, she envisioned herself walking over and grasping it, but not one muscle in her body moved. "Come on sister, you can overcome Shayton. You can do this. Think of Brother Rell. He is waiting on us." Brother Hakims' words were cutting through her walls of hate and rage.

Tears streamed down Steph's eyes as she spoke. "ALLAH knows how I feel about her, but she's my sister now. How..." Steph closed her eyes briefly as more tears ran freely showing the turmoil she was going through. "How can I do what ALLAH commands? Do what you ask of me?" Steph was having a spiritual battle with her lower self.

"All you have to do sister is honor your Shahada by helping another take her own. Come and stand with your heavenly father. The one and only GOD. Come back to righteousness." Brother Hakim was steadfast in his guidance.

Steph took two steps forward and dropped to her knees. Pulling Lorna down with him, Brother Hakim began to speak quietly to both women. Steph was crying at first, but Brother Hakims' words and his message soothed her to calmness. After about five or six minutes, Stephanie was in good enough condition to assist him with Lorna's Shahada.

"Never let anyone or anything come between you and your sister. You are bound by your faith." He place Lorna's hand in Stephanie's hand, then watched the two hug and cry.

"The easy part is done. Now the hard part begins," Brother Hakim said as he realized, the only one who could solve the hard part of this dilemma was ALLAH.

***

Rell had taken one hell of a beating from the accident. The doctors had to place him into a drug induced coma in order to treat all his injuries. During the many hours of multiple surgeries, his heart was subjected to the defibrillator seven times. His recovery was a steep uphill battle for the medical teams that fought to save his life. After finally resetting the last of many broken bones and stopping his hemorrhaging, the surgeon's medical battle was won.

His condition was still listed as critical, but stable. Rell would be extremely weak from the blood loss, surgery, medications, and the physical damage of the wreck. He would make it, if all else goes well.

The head surgeon walked into the waiting area with a confident stride and a pleased look on his face.

Ms. Ce-Ce was given the courtesy of addressing the doctor.

"How's my son, doctor?" She was visibily weathered from worry.

"Well, his damages were extensive, but his body held up through the surgeries. His broken bones will mend and his organs and such will regenerate. To my surprise, he didn't show and signs of whiplash, but until he wakes, we can't be 100% on any neurological abnormalities. Otherwise, he is stable. But the induced coma can be tricky too."

He paused, but Ms. Ce-Ce stood firm and didn't interrupt, so he continued. "Because his body needs to rest, heal and regenerate on its own schedule, it would be highly hazardous to use chemicals to bring him out of the coma right now. His body would likely go into shock from the extensive bodily injuries coupled with him being conscious to feel the pain. We can't even estimate how long he will need to rest. He could come out a few moments from now or a few years from now. But either way, he will get our best care. Here is my card. My office and cell are on there."

"Can I see him?" Ms. Ce-Ce asked in a weak voice. She was fighting hard to keep her composure.

The Resident Surgeon had seen the deep look of worry and desperation a thousand times and it still felt like the first time, every time. "Yes. He's in room 412."

Ms. Ce-Ce thanked him, then picked up a quick paced as she walked down the hallway to her son's room. Steph, who was standing closest to Ms. Ce-Ce and the doctor, was the first to break out after her down the hallway. Lorna, Ree-Ree, Shawn, Ralph, and the sister's Kiki and Liv, all noticed Steph's sudden movement at the same time. They all got up and dashed down the hallway at the same time.

A young red headed nurse was pulling a cart out of Rell's room when they arrived. She was backing out with her head down. As she picked up a clipboard and started writing, Ms. Ce-Ce slipped between her into the room. Before she could react, she saw the whole entourage coming like a wild herd of wild bulls. "No-no-no-no! The patient can't see all of you at once. The doctor's orders were no visitors at this time!" she said forcefully, despite how flustered she was.

Steph wasn't gonna let this skinny little heifer stop her from seeing her man and apparently Lorna felt the same way, because they both sucked their teeth and at the same time said, "Bitch, please!" They both powered pushed past the helpless nurse into the room.

The little redhead rebounded quickly and used the cart to barricade the doorway blocking everyone else. "I can explain the three woman damnit, but not the whole bunch of y'all." The little nurse reasoned, hoping the mob would concede.

"There is no need to give this young lady a hard time," said Brothe Hakim. "We all need not crowd the room right now anyway. Let's give his ladies some alone time with him. Come on everyone. We can convene in the lounge." Wise words from a wise man brought peace and understanding.

Only Ralph trailed behind. He had a message for the nurse. "Can you do me a favor gorgeous?"

"Sure!" Her cheeks turn rosy red from blushing.

"You tell that young man's mother in there that her brother has some business to attend to, but I'll be back in a jiffy." Uncle Ralph winked and slipped away towards the elevators.

***

Rell looked terrible. He was cold to the touch and his skin was ghostly pale. The sight of him brought all three women to tears. Ms. Ce-Ce held his right hand as Steph was on the other side of the bed with his left hand in hers. Lorna had her hands and face, splayed across his abdomen. She cried tears on his stomach when she thought about their baby.

"I can't do this alone, Rell. I can't raise this bambina alone, Papi!" Lorna wept loudly.

Being well versed in Spanish, Steph's body tensed, then went numb when she processed what Lorna had said. "Bambina? You... your pregnant!?" Steph said, her tears drying up immediately. She took her time turning her head from Rell, to glare at Lorna.

"Steph! Their baby happened before you and Rell even got together. She can't…"

"I got this Ms. Ce-Ce," Lorna said meeting Stephanie's glare.

"Rell asked me to look over some Islamic videos a while back and gave me Brother Hakims' contact info. He asked me to join him in Muta to keep our child from being born illegitimately." Lorna regained her composure to deal with Steph.

"He didn't tell me nothing. He should have told me," Steph said, getting angrier with each passing moment.

"Until I gave him my answer about Muta, he felt telling you would be pointless."

"Pointless! What you mean by POINTLESS?! I'm his wife!" Steph spewed.

"If I said no to his request, then I was going to leave. I was gonna disappear without a trace so he wouldn't be able to track me or the baby." Lorna was trying to get her anger to subside by being honest and humble.

"And now?" Steph asked cynically.

"I'm gonna stay. If he pulls through…"

She was cut short by Ms. Ce-Ce who had a headache from the constant bickering, mainly because of Steph's attitude.

"Enough you two! Enough! Rell needs our love and attention right now, not y'all feelings. Y'all causing all this negative energy up in here." She was mean mugging Steph as if to say *'Yeah. I'm talking about You!'* "We need to be asking God…"

All three women jumped and gasped in shock as none of them noticed Brother Hakim standing at the foot of the bed with his arms folded across his chest. His thumbs and index fingers met forming a pyramid. He was humming very low staring without blinking out the window on the right side of Rell's bed. The three women watched in silence as he held his position for three solid minutes. Steph knew he was facing the eastern hemisphere reciting a mantra.

Brother Hakim walked over to where Rell's mother was and gently took his hand from her and laid it across his mid-section. He did the same with the hand that Steph held. He then set Rell's arms in a pyramid position the same way he was holding his. The IMAM bent over Rell from the left side, placed his right palm over Rell's heart and pushed down suddenly holding it. He put his mouth near his right ear.

A Whore's Conscience

"Insha ALLAH." Brother Hakim stood erect, spun on the balls of his feet and headed directly to the door without breaking stride or making eye contact. All three women watched the ritual with eyebrows raised.

As soon as he stepped out into the hallway, Steph spoke.

"What the heck wa…"

SLAM!

Lorna jumped, but was just as startled as Steph and Ms. Ce-Ce when Brother Hakim unexpectedly and suddenly, slammed the door extremely hard.

Lorna was disturbed by what she just witnessed. "What in the world is… Oh My God! Dios Mios! Rell!!"

"Uuugggh!" Rell mumbled faintly. The slam of the door had caused him to come to.

All three women rejoiced and ran to his side.

"Rell! Rell! Baby, it's mom! I'm right here, baby." Tears of joy stained Ms. Ce-Ce's face as she kissed his cheeks, his forehead and then went into silent prayer.

Rell fluttered his eyes, trying to clear his mind and figure out what was what. Between the pain, the medication and the coma, he was still pretty much out of it.

"Rell, baby! It's Steph. I'm right here." She wept tears of joy, because his waking up killed all her mounting anger.

"Rell? Can you hear me baby?" Ms. Ce-Ce whispered inches from his ear. He grunted again slightly to her question. "Lorna is here too. Her and Steph done talked. Steph is aware of the situation and don't you worry, son. She's not mad at you. She understands. Tell him Steph." She was eyeballing Steph hard, manipulating the situation to her liking.

"I'm not mad. Rell. I understand." Steph cut her eyes at Ms. Ce-Ce to show her disapproval of being coerced into telling a half truth.

Squeezing her hand as hard as he could, Rell managed to get Steph's attention from his mom. Once she saw his face coated with fresh tear trails, the last of the barriers shielding her heart, crumbled. There was no way she could hate Rell. Deep down, she had known she was missing the main message of the Islamic tapes he had her watch. Now, she had clarity about the whole situation and everything made sense.

This was by far not an ideal situation. However, she had to admit she'd seen situations far worse than sharing a man. Hell, most women shared a man whether they knew it or not. What was it that Brother Hakim had told her after she'd helped him give Lorna her Shahada? Steph was deep in thought as she leaned over and helped Lorna dry Rell's face. Oh yeah!'

'There's your plan. Then there is our Father GOD ALLAH's plan. Which one do you think is gonna happen?'

Steph allowed the reality of this statement to grant her a measure of peace. This moment of peace was amplified as Ms. Ce-Ce sang a soulful rendition of *'His Eye Is On The Sparrow'* for her baby boy and his two beautiful wives.

I sing because I'm happy
I sing because I'm free
His eye is on the Sparro
And I know He watches over me

COMING SOON

BOSS

Caught Up In The Hustle!

COVER REVEAL
COMING SOON!

U. E. Wynn

SEND MONEY ORDER/CHECK TO:	WYNN PUBLICATIONS P.O. Box 40411 2777 Brentwood RD. Raleigh, NC 27604		
NAME			
ADDRESS			
CITY			
STATE	ZIP		
EMAIL			

BOOK TITLE	PRICE EACH	QUANTITY	TOTAL
BEHIND THE MASK	12.00		
FALSE	12.00		
MY BROTHERS KEEPER PT 1	12.00		
MY BROTHERS KEEPER PT 2	12.00		
A WHORE'S CONSCIENCE	12.00		

THANK YOU FOR YOUR BUSINESS

TOTAL	
SHIPPING & HANDLING	6.00
FINAL TOTAL	

www.ingramcontent.com/pod-product-compliance
Lightning Source LLC
Chambersburg PA
CBHW051510170626
46811CB00002B/735